SET CHANGE

A Nina Bannister Mystery

by

T'Gracie Reese and Joe Reese

For information, email **Cozy Cat Press**, cozycatpress@aol.com or visit our website at: www.cozycatpress.com

COZY CAT
P R E S S

ISBN: 978-1-939816-17-7
Printed in the United States of America

Cover design by Laura Redmond
http:lauradawnsky.info

1 2 3 4 5 6 7 8 9 10

To Nancy Britton: Who spent long hours
editing the manuscript and teaching the Reeses
about punctuation

PART ONE: UNDERPINNINGS

CHAPTER 1: THE JOY OF WORKING

Saturday morning in Bay St. Lucy.

A day like fresh cream!

Nina Bannister emerged from a tangle of dreams which, an instant or so ago had seemed so real, so alternatively aggravating and pleasurable, and which a second or so later would evaporate like bubbles on the incoming tide—and, dedicating a breath or so to pure anticipation, opened her eyes.

Doing so was hardly necessary, because on this luscious morning of June 1, with the sliding door open out upon the deck, the freshest of breezes sifting in just strong enough to rustle the curtains, the incomparable smell of salt air permeating the room, sight was the least important of all senses, and the only one which—given that one was allowed to call memory a sense which it of course was—could be completely done away with.

Still, she utilized it.

It showed her a barely lightening ocean sky, bejeweled by one single morning star glittering precisely 3 inches—which translated to a hundred million or so miles in astronomical terms, she assumed—above the horizon.

It also showed her Furl, orange, white, and comatose, sleeping/vegetating on the northwest corner of her bed, the animal's motley flank rising, falling, rising, falling, in precise and natural coordination with the incoming and outgoing sea swells.

"Furl," she growled.

Furl did not move.

No matter.

If she chose to sleep with the sliding door open, this was what she could expect.

At least Furl had not padded across the bed, as he was sometimes wont to do in the predawn hours, to stand rigid with his nose a millimeter from hers, not saying but implying, "All right: what now?"

Boom. Wham. The gates of her conscious mind exploded open and a thousand chores rushed in disguised as thoughts.

Sort them out, sort them out!

For it was Saturday, the day for DOING DOING DOING and getting thousands of errands accomplished, errands which could never have been done at any other time than summer, gorgeous summer, summer of Big Muscle Activity!

So what was to be done, and when?

She tightened the Ninaball that was her body into an even more compact half circle, and made a schedule for the morning.

First, of course, was coffee, that went without saying.

Then came feeding Furl and rushing the beast out onto the deck, where he could shake himself one or two times, circle the wooden platform, rub up against several of the deck railings, and then go back to sleep.

There was undoubtedly a newspaper lying at the base of the stairs leading down to the oyster shell and white gravel driveway that encircled her Vespa. She would make her way down, still robe-clad, holding tight to the rail and expecting the whole thing to collapse at every step—

—which it would not—

—and then return to the kitchen, where there would be toast, marmalade—

—what a delicious word, MARMALADE!

—one was almost tempted to ignore the sticky gooey substance and simply eat the word itself.

—and coffee.

Coffee with cream.

The newspaper.

Yes, this morning would be the morning when the newspaper truly surprised her: Democrats and Republicans agreeing, no horrible acts of violence in strange countries where she had never been, no horrible acts of violence in places where she had been, all married couples spending the night together without mutilating each other, and the local high school, for the betterment of all concerned, vowing to give up football and fire all the coaches.

Of course the newspaper would probably not say such things, but there was always hope.

These procedures had become known to her over time as The Expelling of The Furl, The Making of the Coffee, The Getting of the Newspaper, The Eating of the Toast, The Reading of the Newspaper, The Shaking of the Head, The Saying 'My My My,' and The Recycling of the Newspaper.

Forty minutes or so for all of that.

The sun would be rising behind the never to be extinguished lights of an offshore oil rig; the waves would be swelling-deflating and sobbing and grating and growling, and gradually ever so gradually revealing more beach, more dark shining hard-packed sand, and more infinitesimal creatures stranded until the return of the night tide.

Then to the true errands!

She had to wash the plate glass window that opened out onto the deck. For weeks now she had been bothered by the salt film that always clouded it ever so gradually. She could see through it of course, but it was as though through unwashed glasses. Vinegar, old newspapers, working clothes, hard labor, twenty minutes of good solid scrubbing.

It would be like looking out into a new world.

All right then, that errand done!

Washing!

There were at least two loads of washing, one light and one dark, that begged to be done. But that was routine. This was Summer Saturday! So this was a day to wash the sheets. All of the sheets, especially these into which she had balled herself sowbuglike for the last two weeks, these sheets, which, while not exactly disreputable, had lost the crisp clean feel that made newly washed sheets so adorable to crawl into.

All right, so that was to be done, and then—

What then what then?

Oh this was wonderful fun!

The barbeque grill, which sat under her beach house, and upon which, three evenings last week, she had charcoal broiled fresh fish filets brought to her by Penelope Broussard, once Penelope Royale, and still at least in Nina's mind Penelope Royale, except, impossibly, but seemingly happily, married.

To Tom Broussard of all people.

How could that be?

Oh well.

But, yes, the grill needed a good thorough cleansing. She hosed it down every evening after cooking on it of course, but—why not make it shine like new!

And then—

The refrigerator.

Yes, the refrigerator! She should clean out the refrigerator!

She had been admonishing herself for months about the small clear plastic containers lying hidden toward the back of the center rack. Containers with spaghetti like substances in them, or with strange purple fluids, or exotic mixtures of nuts and salads and—yes, go ahead and admit it—soft cheeses with smells that, even months ago, had been somewhat questionable.

Eating leftovers was commendable, of course, but the line between leftovers and refuse was so blurry—

So of course, then, the refrigerator went on the list.

This was the kind of thing, though, that Frank always loved. The hours at his law office making home life difficult, he savored those mornings when he could roll up his sleeves, prod her out of bed and exclaim, "Come on, Darling, we're burning daylight!"

So it was perhaps, partially in his honor, this reverence for Saturday morning chores.

And what more was there?

What jobs would you have seen, Frank?

Filling the Vespa's tank with gasoline. It was almost on empty now, and she shuddered at the thought of running out of gas along the mile-long stretch between her ocean side shack and Margot Gavin's shop, Elementals: From the Sea and the Earth, where she spent most afternoons helping out.

Of course there were, scattered along that mile strip, fifteen shops whose owners were close friends and where she could pop in to have a cup of coffee—

—and of course walking the distance between her place and Margot's (ten miles an hour if she strode briskly) would have been faster than driving her Vespa at the speeds she was used to (eight miles an hour, not daring to leave second gear)—

—but still there was the principle of the thing.

One did not run out of gas in a community like Bay St. Lucy.

It showed a lack of taste and breeding.

So, gas up the Vespa.

It would be an expense of course.

Gasoline had become so expensive.

Of course the problem was eased some by the fact that the Vespa's tank held only five gallons.

So, yes, she could do that, too!

So where was she? Furl out, coffee, newspaper, breakfast, get dressed, windows, washing, refrigerator, barbeque grill, Vespa gas…

What a morning!

WHAT A MORNING!

"Ok, Furl," she shouted, propping herself on an elbow: "Let's get at it!"

Furl lifted his head three inches, turned slightly toward her and said, "arrrggg," which meant, in cat, "Leave me alone."

"Huh." She watched him as he resumed his previous position, blended into the blanket, and re-entered hibernation.

"Stupid cat," she muttered.

Then she glanced at the side of her bed, where her pile of mysteries lay, comfortingly, two feet away.

"P.D. James."

With an immense effort, she reached over, took the book, opened it, and read:

"Adam Dalgliesh looked into the room. He saw…"

…upon reading which, she shut the book, put it back on the nightstand, hunched tighter into a ball, pulled the covers over her, closed her eyes, and went back to sleep.

CHAPTER 2: THE MOTHER SUPERIOR

She finally did awake a little before noon, made herself a groggy breakfast not realizing exactly what it was while making it nor what it had been after eating it, Furled and Unfurled, and then, realizing exactly what was to happen in the night ahead, descended the stairs and unlocked the Vespa.

"Poor Margot," she whispered to the handlebars, just before she grabbed onto them.

Poor Margot indeed. For tonight was the night that her best friend in Bay St. Lucy—and in the world for that matter—was to make her theatrical debut.

The St. Lucy Community Theater's Summer Production of—

—no, she still could not think of it without having to suppress a laugh.

And Margot playing the role of—

—no, same thing. Even worse, when one thought of it.

Best not to think of it. The whole thing was too incomprehensible.

Brrrrrrup!

She started the Vespa, backed it out of the driveway, noted the perilously low reading on the gas gauge, and then, offering a silent prayer to The Gods of Fuel Efficiency, puttered out onto Bayside Avenue, heading west toward the center of town and Margot's shop.

Brrrrrrup.

Brrrrrup.

What was she up to now? Eight miles per hour, now topping ten.

Slow it down a bit; no need to overdo.

"Hi Nina!"

"Hey!"

A wave to Ann Colton, proprietor of Clay Creatures.

"Don't go too fast!"

"Won't."

"See you tonight? The big show?"

"Wouldn't miss it!"

Was she being serious about the speed?

Hard to tell with Ann.

"Good morning, Nina!"

Maggie Davis of Maggie May's Dress Emporium.

"Hey, Maggie!"

"Lovely day isn't it?"

"Sure is!"

Brrrrup. Brrrup.

How is the gas doing?

So far so good.

Now she was making her way through the heart of the little business district that sustained and defined Bay St. Lucy.

Expressions by Claire.

The Blue Crab Gifts Gallery.

The Social Chair.

Let's Make Up Gifts.

"Hi Nina!"

"Come over some time, Nina!"

"Nice day, isn't it?

"Isn't this wonderful weather?"

And she would of course reply to all of these greetings, allowing herself a slight head turn to the right or left depending on the street side location of the particular shop owner offering the completely meaningless and simultaneously wonderfully touching inanity of the moment.

"Great day, huh?"

"Certainly is, certainly is!"

How she loved Bay St. Lucy!

Although, she mused, as Margot's shop came into view, the day itself was not as superb as it had been five hours ago. Or would have been, had she chosen to utilize it.

No, it had grown quite warm. Summer in the South.

She was beginning to perspire and might almost have been forced to pull off the side of the street and stop to wipe her glasses, had she been more than a quarter of a mile from her destination.

As it was, though, she made it through.

She had not run out of gas or off the road.

She slowed the Vespa.

Brrrrrup.

Brrup.

Then she parked in Margot's lot—a few cars here, good for Margot.

She let the engine idle.

Brrup.

And slow…

Brp

And die.

Rp.

Engine off.

"Well. Made it."

Giving silent thanks to those travel deities who had once again protected her, she dismounted, took off her helmet, stowed it safely away in the compartment behind the seat, locked her back wheel to the metal bike rack, and walked up the stairs leading to the shop.

Beside the door, just beneath the mail box, was an aluminum cylinder, some six inches long and perhaps an inch in diameter. Since Margot, away buying something or attending something or simply doing nothing at all, often depended on Nina to run the shop afternoons, she frequently left written instructions concerning certain things that should be done. Take delivery of a shipment of pottery; expect Ms. Danielson to pick up a hanging fern sometime between three and four; pay two bills lying beside the cash register—

—such things as those.

Nina peered into the tube, upon which Margot had flamboyantly and quite artistically spray painted, "Bannister Canister," and found nothing.

That was, she mused upon opening the door, hardly surprising, since Margot herself was in the shop.

There were also two customers browsing. Neither of them seemed to bother Margot, who, holding a newspaper in front of her and moving it closer and farther from her face, seemed delighted to have an excuse to fold it and put it aside.

"Nina!"

"Morning, Margot!"

"So you've finished the big morning of chores!"

"Sure have."

"You must be exhausted!"

"Well—"

"Come on…let's go out to the garden. I made lemonade."

"Excellent."

She followed Margot, waving cheerfully to the dark haired teen aged girl who was now working mornings at the cash register.

"Have a seat."

"Thanks."

"It's cooler out here now. I've got the big fan going."

"I see. Oh, I love the breeze!"

"Want a big glass or a smaller one?"

"Big. I'm thirsty."

She seated herself in the black metallic chair, scraped it over the floor to the table, rocked back and forth a time or two, and peered into thick and hanging vines.

"Here. Taste."

She did so, but only after pressing the lemonade glass against her cheek and sighing:

"Ooooh, nice and cool."

"Yes, I thought it would be a good day for lemonade."

"You were right."

"Getting hotter out there?"

"Yes it is."

"But I'll bet the morning was wonderful."

"Yep."

Margot folded herself as much as was possible into, around, beneath, and on top of, the overmatched glass top table, sipped from her own glass, and continued:

"So did you get your windows cleaned?"

"Yes."

"Washing done?"

"All done."

"Grill cleaned?"

"Sure."

"Now, what else was it you told me you were going to do? Oh, the refrigerator! Got that cleaned out?"

"Did it."

"Tough job, huh?"

"Well, you've got to do it sometime."

Margot nodded and drank:

"That's certainly true."

The two women were silent for a time, while the rattling of the huge, storklike fan that stood two feet behind them mixed with the soft murmur of conversation going on inside the shop.

"You slept the whole morning, didn't you?"

Nina nodded.

"Sure did. Just got up."

"Me too."

Margot reached into the vast thing that lay on the floor beside her, resembling the mouth of a cavern more than the top of a purse. Then, taking out her lighter and a box of small cigars, she said softly:

"Isn't that a wonderful thing to do?"

"Luscious," answered Nina.

"So when are you going to get the windows cleaned?"

"What windows?"

"That's the spirit."

Margot lit the cigar in the grand and theatrical manner expected from the Ex-Chicago Art Museum director, and blew a tunnel of grey smoke into the turbulent air currents roiling out from the fan. Modern art formed itself in various non colors that eddied and swirled and expanded out into the unsuspecting air above them, ultimately hovering menacingly a foot or so beneath the glass ceiling.

"Are you nervous?" asked Nina.

Margot looked wonderingly at her.

"Am I what?"

"Nervous. Are you nervous?"

"Why should I be nervous?"

"Tonight, Margot. Tonight."

"Why should it be any different from any other night?"

The tinkly little bell that separated garden from curiosity shop—for what better name was there for the thing that Margot had put together in the fifteen months following her move from Chicago?—this bell tinkled, the door opened, and the dark haired young girl asked:

"Ms. Gavin?"

"Yes, dear?"

"How much is the seascape by Ramoula Peters?"

"The larger one or the smaller?"

"I believe the lady is interested in the larger."

"That's one hundred and fifty, Sandra."

"All right. Thanks."

Door closing.

Girl disappearing.

More smoke blown into the cloud hovering like the remains of an erupting volcano just inside the greenhouse roof.

"Margot, this is your big night."

"It's no different from any other night."

"But it is: it's *opening* night!"

"Well. That's so, I suppose. But all plays have opening nights."

"But—"

She hesitated. There was, as she thought about it, not a great deal for her to say.

If Margot was implacable, then she was implacable.

But Nina herself was as nervous as Furl in the vicinity of a big dog on the beach.

And, perhaps as a result of this nervousness, she found herself regressing in time, the lemonade carrying her back three months—was that all it had been, three months?—to a similar afternoon on March 1. What had she done that morning?

Oh—right—she had slept in.

Have to watch that in the future.

Oh well.

How grand retirement was! No more high school English classes to teach!

But at any rate, she had possessed, on that March 1 morning, even more reason to sleep in than she had possessed today.

A shivery, cold wind had been blowing in from Cape Hatteras. The beach, she could remember, was a zone of desolation and the sullen clouds were the same color as the water.

She and Margot had been drinking coffee then; lemonade would have been unthinkable.

The conversation had probably begun with some retelling of the bizarre and still at that time—nor at this time, when one thought about it—not quite completely understood events concerning the Robinson mansion. But then it had lulled, allowing Margot to light a cigar—she had just begun to smoke cigars at that time, and Nina was trying to decide if such a thing might be cause to dissolve their friendship— light the cigar, put it carefully in an onyx ashtray that Nina could quite clearly remember sitting on the table as though made by nicotine loving Mayans for just such an occasion, just such a gift shop, just such a howling wind outside—and say:

"I'm going to be in a play."

There was, Nina could remember, absolutely nothing intelligent to say to that. And so she had replied:

"What?"

"I'm going to be in a play."

Then the conversation had rolled along going downhill with the same necessity as a stone rolling downhill and the same pointless, though vaguely disturbing, outcome possibilities.

"You're going to *what*?"

"The community theater. I'm going to be in their next play. The summer production. It will open in June."

"But why?"

"Alana Delafosse asked me."

"But why?"

"How should I know? Perhaps she took pity on me."

"*I* take pity on you! Why would you want to do this?"

"Oh, why does one ever want to do anything?"

"Money, sex—"

"Well, I have money and as for the other—"

"All right all right—so we'll just leave it that there is no comprehensible reason that you would want to be in a play that the community theater is doing. That's a lost cause. But at least tell me what the play is."

The Sound of Music.

The Sound of Music?

"Is it becoming hard to hear in this garden. Is the fountain too loud? The wind too gusty outside?"

"No, but—I'm just so confused."

"Why shouldn't I be in *The Sound of Music*?"

"Oh Margot there are so many reasons—"

"Name one."

"One? That limits me too much."

"You're being silly."

"But –can you act?"

"Of course I can act."

"When have you ever acted?"

"What do you think a Chicago Art Museum Director does? What do you think all such people do? If it weren't for acting there would be no management positions at all. And look at me now: I'm here in Bay St. Lucy, population two thousand. If I weren't acting every second, if I ever allowed my real 'self' to appear in public—why they'd put me in jail. And with good reason."

"All right, we'll leave that."

"And so we should."

"But, singing?"

"What about singing?"

"You have to do it. If you're going to be in *The Sound of Music*, you have to *make* the sound of music. You have to sing."

"So?"

"Can you?"

"Can I what?"

"Now you're just being difficult. Can you sing?"

"Oh I don't know!"

"You don't know?"

"How should I know?"

"Well, wouldn't you *want* to know before you agreed to be in a musical?"

"I think that would take the fun away."

"What part does Alana want you to play?"

"Mother Superior."

"What?"

"Mother Superior. She's the head of the convent. She's the one—"

"I know who she is."

"Then why do you seem so astonished?"

Nina, even now, could remember the feeling, often associated with bad comedies or good tragedies, of not knowing whether to laugh or cry.

She could remember looking across the table and seeing a woman six feet tall, shrouded in cigar smoke, her cragged face a testament to decades spent in a life that must have been a mixture between political activism, bohemian ecstasy, drug induced stupor, and desperate hand to hand conflict—seeing this woman and saying softly:

"We're all going to be excommunicated. I'm Methodist—and I'm going to be excommunicated."

"Why ever?"

"For allowing this."

"Allowing what?"

"Margot—you're the least Mother Superior-like human being I've ever seen!"

"Nonsense. I may be a bit short on the mother part but I'm long on superior; the two qualities will balance themselves out."

"But the song—"

"Alana did mention there was a song. Only one song though."

"Yes, it's only one song. But Margot, it's a *big* song! It's a really, really *big* song!"

"Something, I believe she said, about climbing a mountain."

"A mountain? Margot, you're going to have to sing…"

And then a customer had come, and Margot had gone away, leaving Nina to ponder the sorry state of a Catholic Church that would allow Margot Gavin to don a nun's habit, even in a theatrical production, and not issue a Papal Interdict.

But the three months had gone by, and no words of outrage or chastisement had come from Rome, and rehearsals had, apparently, chugged along their merry way— and tonight Margot Gavin was to present herself to the community of Bay St. Lucy as a singing nun.

"My God," Nina found herself whispering, to no one in particular, especially not Margot.

"What did you just say?"

"I said, 'How did the dress rehearsal go?'"

"I was splendid."

"How about the rest of the cast?"

"Oh I never notice them."

"Never notice what anybody else is doing. Is that one of your principles of acting?"

"It's one of my principles of life. But no. I will admit, I do notice them from time to time. And they're exceptionally good; they really are."

"How's Macy Peterson as Maria?"

"Macy? Oh, dear; she's a godsend. A true godsend. Those marvelous blue eyes, and that look of complete and unabashed innocence. Why the woman makes Julie Andrews look like a French whore."

"So she's doing well."

"Of course, she's doing well. And John Giusti is a superb Captain von Trapp…"

"He would have to be," Nina said, nodding. "If he could manage to achieve the status of Furl's permanent veterinarian…and anyway, John has always been one of my favorite people in Bay St. Lucy."

"He was your student once, I suppose."

"They all were. But none were as good as John. Solid as a rock. Popular, great athlete, wonderful mind. I'm sure he's great in the play."

"He is."

"All right, and I'm sure you are too, Margot. But just the same, I'll be keeping my fingers crossed for you."

"You'll be there tonight?"

"Of course. Front row. Got my ticket a month ago when they went on sale. I did wonder why you're opening on Saturday night and not Friday night."

"Mrs. Throckmorton, I believe, had a Friday engagement that she could not break. And since she's our pianist—and thus our entire orchestra—well—"

"I understand. Ok, then, Margot, I'm glad you're not nervous. But I have to tell you, I am."

"Clearly you're not a trooper, darling."

"No. No trooper."

Margot stubbed out her cigar, shook her head, and said:

"No, Nina, you're not a trooper at all. 'No Guts Nina,' that's what the town calls you now. Of course, last Christmas, you did unmask a cold blooded murderer and save poor Macy's life. The truth is she'd be locked away in a mental institution for murdering Eve Ivory last Christmas if you hadn't showed yourself to be a bit of a trooper. Enough of a trooper, by the way, to save the town."

"Well—"

"By the way, did you know someone in town is writing a book about the whole thing?"

Nina looked the way she felt: astonished.

"Who would do that?"

Margot shrugged:

"A writer, who, like all writers, is desperate and poor."

"But who would publish it?"

"Some company that publishes books about cats, I heard."

"But there are no cats involved in the Robinson affair!"

"I know, but people always want to buy books about cats. At any rate the book—I believe it is to be called *Sea Change*—will be out soon and will be stocked in every gift shop and curiosity nook in town; you'll be even more a heroine than you have been for the last five months."

"Just what I need. Why in heaven's name is it being called *Sea Change*? The sea doesn't have anything to do with what happened in the Robinson mansion."

"How should I know?"

"The lunatic, the lover, and the poet," Nina sighed, "are of imagination all compact."

"You are, you know, going to have to give up the habit of quoting like that. You're not in a classroom, you know."

"I tolerate your cigars, you tolerate my Shakespeare. Looking back on the whole mess, though, and what they all thought Macy had done—and what everybody wanted to do to Eve Ivory—when I think of all that—there were times when it seemed pretty hopeless."

"Hope is here, Nina."

"It is now. We have the money; Alana Delafosse has made the Auberge des Arts a reality. What was the Robinson mansion has become an art gallery, new theater space, cultural center—and the school will be ready for the fall. Yes, hope might be here now, but—"

"No, Nina. I mean, really: Hope is here. In the shop."

"What?"

Nina became aware that Margot was rising, gesturing, and smiling at a diminutive figure entering the garden.

"Hello, Hope!"

"Hello, ladies!"

Nina turned in the chair, then smiled and greeted the new arrival: Hope Reddington.

This lady had been often referred to around Bay St. Lucy as The Hope Diamond. It was a comparison not precisely accurate, for although Hope the human was slightly smaller than the jewel of the same name, she was much brighter, and she possessed many more facets from which a startling kind of radiance seemed always to be emanating. She was harder, too, or at least she would have had to be, given certain things that had happened in her past. They were not disreputable things, not Homer Baron Robinson murderings or *Supermarket Weekly* gossipings. No, Hope Reddington's griefs had been entirely of the mundane kind that make them less interesting to talk about and far more difficult to endure. Her husband, Marshall Reddington, owner of the town's leading—and for a time only—pharmacy, stricken with a cruel form of cancer and forced to wither in their stately home until mercifully delivered to the grave. Her daughter and son-in law, quite happily married, killed in a freak automobile accident. And her granddaughter Helen, not of Troy but of Bay St. Lucy, stricken by three insidious diseases: the first, beauty, the second, talent, and the third (the only one of the three to prove invariably incurable and unfalteringly fatal), success.

But if Hope did not quite spring eternal then she at least bubbled forth in a dogged mortality, coming as near to timeless as humanity, in its white-tight-ringlet haired, stooped, caned, hearing aided, ninety-genarian but who cares and damn the next century anyway form—could manage.

"Hello, Ladies!"

To which both Nina and Margot replied in chorus:

"Hello, Hope!"

It seemed an entirely appropriate thing to say.

"How delightful to see you! Is that lemonade?"

"It is," answered Margot.

"May I have some?"

"No, Hope. I don't think we're going to let you have any lemonade today."

"Oh, dear. I was so looking forward to it—"

"Well perhaps another time, when we're in a better mood."

"Perhaps if I come over and beg?"

"You could try."

"I believe I shall; it looks so inviting. Just wait for me: I don't move too quickly."

Hope began making her way across the garden. She was, Nina remembered while watching her approach, always looking up and out from under something. This was not hard in Margot's shop, because there was always something or other—a painting, a vase, an ashtray, a pot, a bouquet, a spray, an engraving—to be looking up and out from.

But Hope simply lived life looking up and out from under something, even if nothing was there.

It was, Nina speculated, the end result of being eleven inches tall, or, if not quite that short, at least a height diminutive enough to make her the only Bay St. Lucyan (over the age of seven) to be shorter than Nina herself.

"Now that I'm here, it looks even better!"

"Well, since you've come all this way, we may relent."

"Oh goody!"

She looked up and out from under nothing at Nina (beaming as she did so) and then looked up and out from under nothing at Margot.

Then she folded her bat-like hands in front of her, knelt at Margot's feet, looked up in supplication and asked:

"Will you bless me, Holy Mother?"

Margot, missing not a beat, placed her own hand on Hope's superbly tailored white white WHITE! jacket, and intoned:

"Go and sin no more, my child."

I am, Nina found herself thinking, going to be sick.

But Hope, not moving, shaking her head and staring down at the floor, merely whispered:

"I am too old to sin, Mother Superior."

"One is never too old to sin. Sin is one of the gifts that God always offers us."

Then Hope twisted her neck so that she was, once again, in the position of looking up and out from under something—the burden of sin, Nina surmised—and said quietly but with intense glee:

"Thank you! Thank you! And bless you for that!"

"It was nothing, my dear."

"Both of you," said Nina, as Hope began the painful and lengthy process of rising, "are going to be struck by a bolt of lightning. And I will be too although none of this is my fault and it isn't fair."

"Oh don't be silly," said Margot, helping Hope as much as she could without breaking off one of the woman's arms. "She's just trying to help me get into character."

"Of course I am," said Hope, who had now arrived at half-erectness and was pausing to catch her breath before continuing the ascension. "And I think Margot is going to make a wonderful Mother Superior. I'm *so excited* about tonight! Aren't you, Nina?"

"Nina," Margot interrupted, "is skeptical."

"Why are you skeptical, Nina?"

"Well, the truth is, I've never really thought of Margot as a nun."

"Then I assure you, she's going to prove you wrong tonight."

"Ms. Reddington?"

The girl appeared again in the doorway.

"Ms. Reddington?"

"Yes?"

"Would you like me to wrap your painting?"

Hope beamed at her:

"No it isn't necessary, darling. But would you bring it out here, please? Let us look at it in the better light!"

There was no better light, Nina thought to herself, because of the volcanic cigar haze blocking the skylight; but still Ramoula Peters' seascape radiated a light of its own—how could great painters do that, she wondered; how could they create light with paint?—and the water in the picture seemed to move and glow and respond in perfect keeping with the full moon, which now was shining in the middle of Margot's garden.

"So you were the one who bought this!" said Margot.

Hope took it in her hands, held it up for a second, worshipped it quietly, and then set it against one of the chairs.

"I fell in love with it when I first saw it in your shop a week or so ago. But I had no occasion to buy it. Now I do."

"An occasion?" asked Margot.

"Oh yes. One always needs an occasion. Look. Look at the lines that I've written here!"

She produced a card, on which she had written several lines of poetry in the superb handwriting of people who went to school sometime around the turn of the century and learned Latin, and true mathematics—and handwriting.

Margot read the line aloud:

"I love the soft collision here of harbor and shore, the subtle haunting briny quality that all small towns have when they are situated by the sea." William Styron.

"That's beautiful," said Nina.

"Isn't it?"

"What is the occasion, Hope?"

Hope Reddington looked at her, then stepped back toward the splattering fountain—then put both palms before her mouth.

Then she let the palms drop, and, as though she was a puppet whose hands were attached by invisible strings to the corners of her mouth—which of course raised as the hands now dropped—said:

"Oh I can't tell you that!"

She then placed herself squarely between Margot and Nina, encircled each of their waists with a birdlike arm, gazed upward first at one and then at the other, and kindled a smile that radiated like a small fire, burning purely white and emitting its own heat, as though a star precisely one foot in diameter—the size of Hope's face—had gleefully exploded.

Then she whispered:

"It's a secret!"

Then she swept the painting up and held it against her.

She kissed the card—

—and she turned and tottered out of the shop.

CHAPTER 3: PERFORMANCE!

There is a magic about community theaters.

There is a force which breeds, even in the smallest of settlements, one person who is absolutely perfect for the part.

A village in central Texas, population eight hundred.

Somehow God will provide a hardware store owner, or a mail delivery man, or an attorney or a dog catcher or a whatever—because behind the footlights it matters not in the least—one person who is more like The King of Siam than Yul Brynner.

A 'ville' of some kind. Smithville or Jonesville or Johnsonville or Oilville or Cowville or whatever.

A 'ville' hidden away in the foothills of the Ozarks, two hours drive away from Little Rock

The Forces of Theatricality will combine to throw up, emit, disgorge, make happen some way—a huge South Seas Woman to sing "Happy Talk" from South Pacific and bring down the house.

One of Nina's favorite sayings—she was never sure what culture it had come from, but suffice to say one of those groupings of people less civilized than we and thus infinitely more wise—was the proverb that "A child remains a boy until a man is needed."

In the world of community theater that proverb read:

"An insurance agent remains an insurance agent until Stanley Kowalski is needed."

And in truth, only three years ago—no one could forget it—Marvin Harper, State Farm Insurance agent for little Bay St. Lucy, prim, church-going, father of four, model husband, a bit bookish, somewhat timid except in matters of fender repairs and deductibles—

—this man had transformed much as a werewolf does in the spell of the full moon, into Marlon Brando, had hurled himself upon the stage floor, held his hands open to the floodlights above him, noticed that there was nobody up there except a stage hand or two, ignored that fact, and bellowed:

"Ellen! Ellen! Ellen!"

The audience had been transfixed.

Nor did it detract even in the least from that unforgettable moment when someone was gauche enough to mention, in the anteroom after the performance, over coffee and cheesecake, that the name may have been wrong.

What, the reply had been, is in a name?

Even Shakespeare knew that much!

And if Marvin Harper saw in those floodlights a woman named Ellen and not a woman named Stella, that was his own business.

(He must have seen her there quite clearly, since he shouted out to her in precisely the same manner in the Saturday night performance, the Sunday matinee performance, and the Monday night finale).

Then it was all over, of course.

And, the werewolf-moon having gone down, he returned to being an insurance agent.

Six months later the equally nondescript manager of The Piggly Wiggly became Curly, and Ida Sue Miller morphed herself into Ado Annie.

It was incredible.

And it kept happening.

The only problem with the whole thing was that it kept happening in such an obscure way. Millions might have been enthralled by seeing the citizens of one small community such as Bay St. Lucy outdo the combined efforts of Broadway and Hollywood, except that millions could not fit into the Bay St. Lucy Community Theater Playhouse.

Fifty three could.

The problem was not helped by the fact that certain seats were taken in advance, and could not be offered up for public consumption.

The Mayor, for example, had to be there.

The town council had, if not to be there in their entirety, at least to be represented.

Same with the school board.

"Wouldn't miss it for the world!"

"Couldn't keep me away!"

And whether these sentiments were entirely honest and heart felt, they at least had to be expressed, and they had to be expressed by people who were in fact there tonight, right now, sitting in seat five, row nine, knees held tight and almost up against chest, program held just as tight up to face, cell phones off please, all preliminary chatting and coffee drinking in the anteroom, done, because the time approached precisely seven o'clock, and...

...Mrs. Gertrude Throckmorton arrived.

Mrs. Throckmorton, oblivious to a trickle of applause, made her way through the teenagers standing in the back of the theater, the parents in the middle of the theater, and the town elders in the front of the theater. She adjusted her glasses, patted the bun behind her hair, put her meager body through a few light calisthenics, then turned and faced the piano.

She glared at it as though she hated it.

Nina, no more than eight feet away from her and feeling dangerously exposed in her first row seat, held her breath while the woman threw herself onto the piano bench, threw open the music, threw her shoulders back, and threw her head forward so that her eyes were no more than six inches from the sheet music, which began to glow yellow in a small sphere of light emitted by the piano light.

Then she attacked the music.

BOMBOMBOMBOMBOMBOMBOM—

And there they all came, realized a delighted Nina, closing her eyes and settling back into the three or four inch space that was all she had room to settle back into.

There they all came, cascading and serenading and melting one into another and climaxing and softening and loudening and harmonizing and soloing and intertwining like

Rogers and Hammerstein ropes being twirled into Austria and Alpine Mountain Air!

There they all were, taking Nina back years into the day her father and mother—how old had she been then, ten?—had taken her to Jackson, to the old and huge and red velveted Majestic Theater.

Where she, sitting in the second balcony, had seen Maria gambol out into her mountain meadow.

There they all were again, brought forth into the tiny rarified space of Theater Bay St. Lucy by the fingers of Mrs. Throckmorton, out of a frightened piano that seemed to shiver to the point of collapsing as she drove it like an engineer drives a freight train.

There they all were, the great melodies of *The Sound of Music.*

And then, after a breathless pause during which the audience was too shocked and awed even to applaud the fact that Mrs. Throckmorton had in three minutes and twenty seconds played what seemed a hundred and fifty songs—Macy Peterson was on the stage.

Except she was not on the stage.

She was in that mountain meadow.

And Margot had been exactly right.

She was Maria von Trapp.

She inhaled…

…complete silence for only a moment…

…and it all came flooding back into Nina's mind:

Macy's statement.

The letter opener.

Eve Ivory, dead in the bedroom.

And Macy the Perfect, Macy the Sweet Young Teacher, crying to Nina, who'd been the only one to believe her:

"I didn't kill her! I'm not insane!"

Another moment; another pause, and then Macy pouring out her heart in another way, and carrying the town away:

Singing about hills being alive.

It was absolutely enchanting of course.

And it just got better.

It got better when Margot Gavin stepped onto the stage and proved, of course, that Alana, who for years had directed The Bay St. Lucy Community Theater just as she directed all things artistic in the town—that Alana's eye had been perfect and that, improbable as it seemed, the little town that had produced the for all time definitive Stanley Kowalski had now produced the for all time definitive Mother Superior.

Nina *sensed* this from the time Margot, ramrod straight, stern, crag-faced and habit-enshrouded, called Macy toward her, and put her palms on Macy's shoulders.

She *knew* it though when, upon hearing Margot say that Maria was going to have to leave the abbey…

…an entire crowd of fifty four people sighed as one: "Ohhhhhhhhhhhhhhhhhhhhhhhhhh."

My God she's good, Nina said to herself.

They were all good, of course. Good were Alicia Matthews, age six, Thomas Peterson, age eight, Susan Thompson, age nine, Nancy Espinoza, age eleven, Robert Dowd, age thirteen, Dan Slocum, age fifteen, and Ramona Howe, age sixteen but "Going on Seventeen" and "On the Brink"—every one of whom Nina knew, because, although through with teaching forever, she still had the career educator's habit of seeing every human being in the town at age four and saying mentally, "I'd love to have that one in my classroom," or "Uh, oh."

Good also was Alana Delafosse as a director who, working with a fifteen foot square stage and a one foot high platform, had told Macy to sit with her legs crossed, fake strumming a guitar which she had no idea how to play, while Mrs. Throckmorton, eyes glued into the corresponding eyes of every child on stage, softly ever so softly insinuated the chords as they were the comings and goings of the sea itself:

Bum Bum Bum Bum

Bum Bum Bum Bum

And Marcy, who actually was going to teach these children in the classroom and was already teaching two of them, quietly, encouragingly:

…singing about deer…

…female deer…

...sewing, running...

First the children were hesitant, and then they were whispering, then louder, louder still, and finally standing while belting it out at the audience.

Then they were marching in circles and then they were bisecting the circles and marching rearwards and forwards again and over and under one another and sitting and standing and doing both at the same time and all the while smiling broader and broader and more and more joyously while the audience, hypnotized, began to clap, and stomp, and sing along, which of course no one could stop doing while the ever-moving line of total and absolute cuteness which was the sailor-suited Von Trapp children aka Children of Bay St. Lucy Our Children Will You Look at Them UP THERE?—

—until this model of absolute rightness stopped stock still; the children gazed in wonder at their new Mother Macy who slapped a palm down on the top of her head, sang a superb R over Q minor, the highest and clearest note ever allowed in the universe...

...gasped for air, bowed...

And the house dissolved in delirious applause.

The children stood, as though electrified.

Macy was RADIOACTIVEGIRL, her grin alone powering the cities of the Mississippi Coast.

Quiet was restored five minutes later.

But that was the way the play went, one triumph after another, culminating in the great scene at The Salzburg Festival, which even the real Salzburg Festival had never done quite so well.

At final curtain the applause lasted unabated for a full five minutes.

It was only stopped by the entrance of the play's director, Alana Delafosse.

"My dearest Laaaaydeeez and Gennnntlmen, thank you thank you thank you sssooooo much for coming!"

It would have been worth the price of admission—ten dollars for a front row seat, except nothing at all for Nina, who of course received her ticket free, as she received just about everything free these days, as a small show of gratitude from the town for saving it and making its continued existence possible—worth the price of admission, free or ten dollars or whatever it might have been, simply to see the theatrical spectacle that was Alana Delafosse, just being herself.

Applause applause applause.

Large spray of roses now being handed to Alana by the mayor, Alana kissing the mayor first on one cheek then on the other, the roses being handed to one of the stagehands, Alana, her splendid caramel creole skin shining in the footlights and her Cruella de Ville outfit glowing a red so bright that it seemed ready to burst into flame—Alana, preparing to make an announcement.

Alana, so the stories went, had been born on The Upper West Side in New York City, to a Creole mother and a Senegalese father, who happened to be the United Nations ambassador for his country. She had been educated at the finest private schools until, while still a teenager, she had run off to Paris with her lover, a Russian émigré. This man had been killed in a duel—allegedly fought over her—and she had been whisked away by forces unknown to Moscow, where she'd learned fluent Russian and been trained as a Soviet Special Forces Agent, or, more simply, spy. She had disappeared from sight for a while, but rumor had it that she herself had become an assassin, killing several high ranking generals while working to support revolutionary forces in Chile.

The fact that none of these stories were true held no importance. When juxtaposed to actual reality (Alana had been born and raised in a small trailer home four miles from New Iberia, Louisiana, and had never been west of St. Charles, or north of Lafayette, or south of New Orleans, or east of—well, where she was right now)—when juxtaposed against this abysmally boring and completely incomprehensible (because how could anyone raised in such circumstances have become ALANA?)—reality, the Tolstoy novel that passed as her past simply had to be preferred.

And so that was the background everyone envisioned and savored every time Alana held forth.

Which she was preparing to do now.

"It both deliiights meee—"

(Alana had great fun with, and a deep love of, long vowels, which she seemed never to want to let go of. They became her children from the moment they entered her mouth, and she did not want to allow them out into the world, where who knows what would become of them.)

"—and it greeeeeeeves meeee, to remiiiiiind uuuuuuuuuu, that this will be the last performance, in the hallowed spaaaaaaace, that is the Bay St. Lucy Community Theater Auditorium."

General sigh.

"But as you all knooooooooo, better things are in store for us! The Auberge des Arts is a Reee-ality!"

Applause.

"What had beeeen for so many years the Robinson Mansion…"

(Alana did not much respect words that contained only short vowel sounds, and so she got through them as quickly as possible).

"—has become, as we had dreeeeeeeeeeemed—)

Finally! A word (dream) whose ethereal meaning was commensurate with its vowel potentiality!

"—the cultural center of our community!"

More applause.

"The mansion has afforded us space for two theaters, a black box, and a larger venue, seating one hundred and fifty spectators."

Ooooohs and aaaaahs.

(There might have been a problem getting one hundred and fifty Bay St. Lucyans to go to the theater on any Friday night, especially given the fact that, that hurdle having been jumped, there would have been no one left to go on Saturday or Sunday—

—but that was something for down the road.

Now it was time to celebrate.)

"And so, as you know, the Arts Council of Bay St. Lucy has sent invitations to all of you, to attend a Special Champagne Lunch to be held tomorrow at one p.m. on the grounds of The Auberge. At that time I will have a special announcement to make concerning the inaugural performance of our new space."

Cheers.

Clapping.

Alana making a show of modesty, which was about like a Bengal tiger blending into a set of army-green curtains.

It took a few more shows of flamboyancy to get Alana off the stage, and in these moments, Nina did in fact remember receiving her invitation—which came special delivery, and had contained a handwritten supplication on the bottom of the elegant card the words: "Please come, Nina! You will be our guest of honor!"

She also remembered a dull sense of dread.

Champagne in the afternoon.

Who drank champagne in the afternoon?

And why should she want to be in their company, whoever they were?

Oh well—she could go home at two and sleep the rest of the afternoon.

And so she left the theater, happy in the hope that neither she nor Bay St. Lucy had more to fear in the coming months than a surfeit of champagne.

It would take several weeks for her to learn how wrong she was.

CHAPTER 4: JOYS AND CONCERNS

On Sunday mornings Nina attended worship services at The Second United Methodist Church at the corner of Jackson and Parry streets. There was not a First United Methodist Church. There probably had been one, but something had happened to it, and no one much cared to talk about the matter now.

There was a newer Methodist church on the outskirts of Bay St Lucy, but she had never been tempted to attend, probably for that very reason: namely, that it was newer. Newer was not good in terms of religion. Newer did not promise the same dark burnished oaken pews that she and Frank had sat in for so many years—so many in fact that although Sandra McCallister sat regularly on her right hand now, the spot to her left was, as a matter of courtesy, always left open.

Just as was the spot immediately to the right of Sandra, the place where her husband Tom used to sit.

No matter if there were a space or two left vacant. The congregation had dwindled, was dwindling slightly through the years, and there was no need, as there had been for Christmas and Easter services two decades ago, to bring in folding chairs and place them in the outer aisles.

Indeed, there were some Sundays—the summer ones among them—when the early arriving Nina even wondered if she would be the only parishioner in the congregation.

This never happened of course.

The Barkleys, Benjamen and Darleen, always arrived early too, sometimes even before the minister.

Then came dribs and drabs, as Frank would have put it.

Mudge—Mudge had a last name, but it seemed so prosaic, whatever it was—Mudge, past ninety now, wobbling in and down the stairs that led into the sanctuary from the downtown-side door, helped along as she always was by one or two of the other ladies of the church who took turns giving her a ride.

The Miller family, all three pre-school children between them, all three stuffed there in the pew and being molested every second or so by first their father, then their mother, who saw Sunday mornings as the opportunity to show first hand to the children what the true wages of sin actually were, these being naturally the human condition of being imprisoned in an eight foot space on a gorgeous seaside summer morning and forced to sit in constant, motionless, silent prayer.

"Be quiet!"

"Sit still!"

"Stop that!"

"But he—"

"I don't want to hear it!"

"But she—"

"No!"

Why not, Nina wondered, just bring them on time? Why bring them early?

She did not say 'Why bring them at all?' even to herself, for she knew that would have been blasphemous.

Of course you had to bring them.

"Get out from under that pew!"

"But I—"

"Get out from there!"

Or, maybe not.

At least they were three pews in front of Nina, except that once the children actually got under the pews and became mobile, they might turn up anywhere.

Jana Darnell, seventy three now—her birthday had been announced from the pulpit last week, so Jana's age was fresh in Nina's mind—radiant and beautiful as she must have been at seventeen, with the same sparkle in her eyes and the same straight bearing and the same immaculate and striking red scarf.

Leana Douglas; Florence Robinson; Earl and Nora Springer—

—dribs and drabs, dribs and drabs—

After a time the piano began to play, Nina rejoicing that it was, this morning, as it usually was: one of the old ones.

"Blessed Assurance."

Da da da deee deee…

As the blue robed choir filtered in and the pulpit crew—which she always enjoyed calling them, although they probably would not have appreciated it—prepared to do their respective duties, announcement reading, scripture lesson, song leading, etc.—she prepared herself mentally for the first stages of the service.

Be prayerful, listen carefully, check your wallet to be sure there's something to put in the collection plate, and try not to laugh at anything when you were the only one laughing.

There would be other things to laugh at later on, of course, but they were rigidly controlled episodes of group laughter, and it was just as bad to remain silent within them as it was to guffaw outside of them.

"Good morning!"

From a beaming Reverend Daniels.

"Good morning!"

From a Summer Sparse but Always Eager in the Will of the Lord congregation.

And now—begin.

She listened carefully to the announcements, especially the one she knew without having to hear it, the one pointing out that this Sunday, First Sunday, was Fellowship Sunday, which meant Potluck Lunch.

There were several 'ships' that had to be dealt with in church life, two of the most important being 'Fellowship,' and 'Stewardship.'

Stewardship meant giving more money than you were used to giving.

Fellowship meant eating.

It was much more popular.

And Nina had, as she always did, prepared for it.

Tucked away on a vast drain board down below in the equally vast kitchen—for people in 1902 when the red brick church building was erected knew the importance of eating—sat her big bowl of tuna salad. It was surrounded by countless other bowls, all of them single cells in the vast and complex creature that was fellowship.

Almost invariably Nina brought chicken salad to such events.

Every now and then deviled eggs.

But today—perhaps it was the summer gaiety that had descended on Bay St. Lucy with the luscious warmth and the new faces and the stands along the beach and the corn dog smells—whatever it was, it brought to her a sense of madcap revelry of Lord of Misrule, of Do the Unthinkable—

—and so she had made tuna salad and *not* chicken salad.

So there!

The announcements plodded along. She listened earnestly to them until they reached the phase that she had begun to dread terribly, and through which she knew that she must force herself to daydream about other things, any other things.

This phase was The Joys and Concerns.

She had, in years past, never really minded Joys and Concerns.

But that was a time of a younger congregation, when there had been approximately as many of the one as of the other.

Time had gone on, and the balance had shifted mournfully to the concerns.

Well, that was all right.

If one had no concerns, then of what use was a church anyway?

The problem was that the older women of the congregation had begun to enjoy the thing too much.

They no longer simply said:

"Marge Riddlemeyer's brother has gone into the hospital for surgery."

No, they had learned to become much more specific about the matter, even much more clinical.

And they spoke more slowly, enjoying the dramatic pauses surrounding various organs and symptoms.

"As you know—Harold Witherspoon—was diagnosed—last month—"

Nods from everyone in the congregation, who were all listening to this broadcast as though it were an episode of *The Guiding Light*.

"—with heptomal non-recurring empheriarsis, which began producing malignant tumors on the anterior lobe of both his pineal gland and his lower distending femoral artery."

Pause, for a second, then collective:

"Ooooooooo."

Nina had ceased to be certain whether the low collective moan was a sincere expression or grief or a show of respect for the anatomical knowledge of the speaker.

Another hand in the air; and another, and another:

"I just felt I—had to tell everyone—"

Thousand one, thousand two—

"That Herschell Massey's friend Richard—"

Thousand one, thousand two—

"Has had—a recurrence—of the lymphomatic—cytosis—which seems to have invaded—the non-distillary embolic membranous and subcutaneous—"

"Who," Nina whispered to Sandra, "is she even talking about?"

"Herschell's friend Richard who lives up in Oregon."

"Sandra we don't even *know* this man!"

"That doesn't mean we can't pray for him."

"How can you pray for somebody you don't even know? Why don't we just pray for everybody in the world?"

"Well, we should do that too!"

But it wasn't any good. She couldn't do it. The symptoms, at least those she could understand, sounded too awful. Besides, every time she heard a disease described so graphically she began to think she had it herself. Pancreatic cancer. That was incurable and killed you in two weeks.

Her pancreas began to hurt.

Which side was it on?

No. She had to think of something else.

So she did. She thought of the performance last night. What a fantastic job they had all done! And Margot, wonderful Margot, bringing down the house—which found itself brought down several times, a fitting 'adieu' for the old theater—with her "Climb Every Mountain." Who knew she could sing like that?

And as for the finale, the last scene—

She found her eyes to the far side of the congregation.

There sat John Giusti.

"Good job, John," she found herself whispering.

Like always. In John we trust.

John had been playing Captain von Trapp for his whole life, when one thought of it.

Quiet, unassuming, brilliant, athletic—John had been the only football player in Bay St. Lucy's history to get a Division One scholarship—

—and single.

Always something sad about that.

"AND NOW FOR JOYS!"

Thank heaven, thought Nina,

"I have a joy!"

She turned.

And there, her head barely high enough to be seen over the back of the pew, stood Hope Reddington.

She was farther in the back of the church than usual, and Nina had not even noticed her entrance.

"Stand up!" exhorted Reverend Daniels.

This was a joke of course, since Hope already was standing.

She shook her fist at him a couple of times in mock outrage.

A collective laugh.

Finally it died down and the reverend asked:

"What is your joy, Hope?"

Silence for a second.

And then, was Hope looking directly at Nina?

Perhaps. On the other hand the smile was of such a nature as to make everyone in the building think it directed only at him or her.

"What is your joy?"

"My great joy," replied Hope, "is that my granddaughter—my beloved granddaughter Helen—is coming home."

There was a sermon after that but nobody listened to it. They were all thinking of Hope's announcement and the lovely time they were going to have gossiping about it while eating the potluck lunch.

This happened at precisely twelve thirty, when the doors to the basement dining hall were opened and the congregation swarmed in.

There were 53 Methodist women and they had cooked and brought with them 237 bowls or platters of food.

Which they now tore into while talking only a little about the previous evening's community theater performance and much more about the history of the Reddington family.

"Wasn't Alana Delafosse simply wicked as The Baroness?"

"Oh I hated her!"

"It was so funny how the audience all hissed when she came on!"

"When she said, 'It might be better for all concerned if the children are—sent away,' somebody got up and shouted, "Go back to Vienna!"

"Wasn't that funny? Now, what is this?"

"Okra casserole, isn't it?"

"I don't know, but there's shrimp in it."

"How long has Helen been away?"

"She hasn't been back here in, oh, it must be five years now. No, no, you take more of it."

"I've got enough. Cranberry sauce?"

"Just a bit."

"Oh, I got some on your plate."

"It's all right. Where was it she went away to school?"

"Some art school in Michigan."

"Interlochen School of the Arts."

"Is that what it was?"

"I think so. I just know it must have been so hard on Hope. Her husband died of cancer; then a year or so later there was that car wreck, and all she had left was her little granddaughter, Helen. And then about two years after that, there was this great offer to go and study acting. Helen was only seventeen. It was exciting, but it meant Hope would be all alone. Could you just hand me a piece of that chicken?"

"Here; do you want a slice of ham to go with it?"

"I shouldn't."

"Oh, go ahead. It's the Potluck."

"All right; just one slice though. Now who did Helen marry?"

"A big-name New York actor; I don't know his name. It was in the paper though—it happened last September. Here, I'll give you a little bit of this dressing, too. Samantha Slaughter made it."

"She makes such good dressing."

"I know."

And so on and so on and so on.

Nina, her pancreas no longer bothering her, had made her way to a table where John Giusti was seated by himself.

"May I," she asked, "sit at the captain's table?"

He smiled, rose, smiled more broadly still, and gestured to one of the empty metal chairs:

"Are you always so much trouble, Fraulein?"

"Oh much more, Sir!" she said, setting the sixteen inch plate filled with indeterminate and multi-colored foods on the table before her.

"John," she said, "you were just wonderful!"

"Thank you. High praise from a teacher of literature."

"No, I don't have anything to do with it. You were just good. You all were."

"It was very moving, wasn't it?"

"Oh! That last scene, the last song—everybody in the little theater, singing...of course, we barely could sing, we were all crying so hard."

"Me too. I was choked up. I didn't realize they'd all sing along like that."

"Well. Everybody over the age of thirty knows that movie so well. Who in the United States of America doesn't know "Edelweiss?" It's like an alternate national anthem."

"Yes, I suppose it is."

She deliberated a while about eating, not knowing whether to begin with the plum pudding, the raisin soufflé, the crab bisque, the green beans with onions, the crawfish etoufee, the sardine vinaigrette, the roast beef with hollandaise sauce, or the foods lying hidden under the ones she could see.

"Oh by the way, Nina, I meant to ask you today: when am I seeing Furl again?"

"Do you need to?"

"I think so; it's been six months, hasn't it?"

"Surely not!"

"Yep. I was checking my calendar."

"How could I have forgotten?"

"Well," he said, smiling, "you had a lot on your plate."

"You're not talking about the Pot Luck—"

"That too. And in addition to that, there's the fact that, around the time Furl was getting his last round of vaccinations, you were helping to catch a murderer."

"My God, John. It's true. Just a few weeks before that whole thing happened, we were in your clinic."

"How is old Furl, anyway?"

"Same as always, as far as I can tell. Runs the house."

"Nature of cats."

"And how have you been, John? Apart from your difficulties with the Third Reich, I mean?"

"I've been well, really well."

"Still splitting time between here and Vicksburg?"

"More here than Vicksburg. I go to the Medical Research facility there once a month, and they let me watch. It's the technical aspect of veterinary science. I like to fool around with it and they give me gadgets."

"I'd ask you to describe them, but I know I wouldn't be able to understand a word."

"It's not that hard. Mainly they make things to calm animals down. Comes in handy."

"Well, it will come in handy. You know how Furl likes shots."

"We'll make him the happiest cat in the world."

"I'll believe that when I see it. But anyway, when should we come, John?"

"What about Tuesday at ten o'clock?"

"Perfect. We'll be there."

Silence for a time.

Should she bring it up?

Would it be painful for John?

Or was he sitting there thinking about it anyway, knowing the question would have to be asked sometime.

Oh, the hell with it.

"So John, the news about Helen—"

He looked over her shoulder, as though seeing something no one else knew was in the hall. Then he shrugged, smiled a smile that was not quite a smile but too resigned to be a frown, and said:

"That was kind of a shocker, wasn't it?"

"Yes, it was."

More silence.

She amused herself to think that she was sitting here with Captain von Trapp while, all around them, tinkle tinkle scrape scrape scrape chew chew chew gossip gossip gossip—The Hills Were Alive With The Sound of Eating.

"You've not seen her in a long time, I guess."

"No. Not since she left for Interlochen."

Something seemed to strike him as funny and he hummed:

"She was sixteen going on seventeen…"

"Was she, really?"

"Yes. Turned seventeen three days after she left."

"That has to be right. You had both taken my sophomore world literature class."

"Which she aced, I remember. I barely passed."

"Barely passed indeed. You got a strong B +."

"Although I didn't deserve it. By the way do you remember all the grades of all the students you ever taught in thirty or forty years here?"

Yes, she was forced to admit to herself, simultaneously terrified and appalled by the thought.

"No, of course not."

"I think you gave me a gift. I was just not able to get into those plays."

"Well, you were always a scientist. You were winning science fairs. When you weren't making the all regional football team."

"Yeah. It seems like a long time ago. Helen and I were–"

He shook his head, and munched some salad.

"We were very close. We'd dated for two years. But then that offer came..."

He shook his head.

"—and she knew there was a lot more in the world than John Giusti. But still, I remember the last night."

He remembers, Nina mused, his last romantic night with the most beautiful woman in the history of Bay St. Lucy. I remember world literature grades.

How fair is that?

"I can visualize it," he continued. "We were out on the rock jetty. It was August, but there was a wind, and spray kept coming up from the rocks. We just sat there, not caring very much how wet we got. She told me very calmly that it was over between us. She was, she knew, never going to come back to Bay St. Lucy. She didn't want a long distance thing. I pretended to agree, because you didn't really disagree with Helen."

He was silent for a time, looking at the same point he'd been looking at, which was nowhere in the dining hall of course but in another decade, another life.

"Did you," Nina asked, "ever try to contact her?"

John nodded.

"I wrote a letter. Then another, a few weeks later. She didn't answer. So I gave up. And that was that."

"Well. It would have been hard to..."

"Nina! Tom!"

Hope Reddington had materialized like Glenda the Good Witch at a spot one foot behind Nina, who now turned to address her while looking for and not seeing The Ruby Slippers.

"Hope!" she said. "What wonderful news!"

"Isn't it?"

"Everybody in the church is talking about it."

"Actually, dear, everybody in church is eating."

"That too. But between bites, they're talking about Helen. That's the 'occasion' you were talking about in Margot's shop yesterday."

"Yes. That was my secret. I felt I should keep it to myself until church. But, John, you were wonderful last night."

"Thank you, Hope."

"Nothing to thank me about. I'm just telling the truth. And Nina—"

She put her hands on Nina's shoulders and bent closer.

"One 'thank you' is necessary. I do have to say 'thank you' to you."

"Well—"

"None of this would have happened, of course, without you."

"I'm just glad I could help, Hope."

"I knew sometime, somehow, that Helen would come back. And now you've made it possible."

"It was my pleasure."

"If there was anyone in Bay St. Lucy who could have done this, who could have made it possible for Helen to return, I should have known it would be you."

"You're too kind, Hope. I only did what little I could."

"Thank you, Nina. Thank you for bringing my granddaughter back to me."

So saying, she turned and disappeared into a puff of casseroles.

"Wow," said John, still looking for Helen, who'd disappeared into the past. "She's very grateful to you, Nina."

"Yes. She is."

"You brought her granddaughter back to her."

"Yes. I guess I did."

"How? hat did you do, that had anything to do with Helen Reddington coming back home?"

Nina shook her head:

"I have no idea."

John, startled, bent forward:

"What?"

"I haven't the slightest idea what the woman is talking about."

She continued to look around the dining hall.

But all Hope was gone.

CHAPTER 5: NEWS

Nina had not been back to the Robinson Mansion—
which, despite the fact that its official name was "Auberge
des Arts," would always be the Old Robinson Mansion to
her—since the events of Christmas. Nor could she walk
through the grounds without shivering a bit, despite the heat
of the day.

Eve Ivory. Standing up there, above the assembled group,
making that shocking announcement.

Her "security forces" standing grimly at her side.

The town envisioning its future as a gambling mecca.

And then, days later, she and Moon Rivard making their
way through the escape tunnel. Emily Robinson's doll, down
there buried for years and years, rotting, its button eyes
having seen nothing for decades but toads and spiders, its
clump of cloth nose smelling must and decay.

So why wouldn't there be chill about the place?

"Champagne, ma'am?"

She had, much as rubes in Chicago attract scam artists
wanting money to send to their families stranded in Indiana,
attracted a waiter.

She could not drink champagne in the early afternoon.

But it seemed rude simply to say no, for this young man,
white jacketed and bow tied just as everyone else seemed to
be white jacketed and bow tied, was beaming at her so
eagerly, as though his entire future depended on completing
this small transaction.

An excuse.

She needed an excuse.

"I'm sorry," she said, "but I don't have any money with
me."

Great excuse!

Not only that, but it was true!

"It's free," he responded.

Darn.

The only other excuse she could think of (also true) was "It makes me throw up," but she did not want to say that, and so she was left with:

"Sure."

He gave her the champagne.

So now she had a glass of champagne.

Too bad it was in this glass. If it were in a paper cup with a top on it she could carry it back to Furl, whose personality was more in keeping with champagne than her own.

"Nina!"

"Nina!"

Who was that?

Oh!

Macy and Paul Cox.

"Hello you two!"

"Nina," shouted Macy, making her way past a strolling accordion player, "I saw you in the audience last night!"

"Of course I was in the audience. I wouldn't have missed it!"

"What did you think?"

"You were all superb!"

"Weren't they great?" chimed in Paul.

"They certainly were!"

The conversation addled its way on for a few more sentences about the play and then it went into how excited everyone was at Alana's announcement and then into the progress of the new high school, with Nina beginning every question with, "So how is…." and the MacyPaul tandem answering only:

"WE'REHAPPYWE'REHAPPYWE'REHAPPYWE'RE HAPPY!"

no matter what words they actually chose to say or how they arranged them.

This went on for a few minutes and then Nina, like a bit of refuse after a disaster at sea, found herself floating along with the prevailing currents, looking first this way and then that, trying to avoid anything particularly destructive.

Finally, she felt drawn toward the mansion itself, as though somewhere just inside the main entrance was Niagara Falls and both she and everyone around her were going over them.

"Who are all these people?" she found herself asking.

Because, although she knew a good many of them (the usual gang of town dignitaries), there were others thrown in as well. People who genuinely did look comfortable in white jackets and bow ties, and who had silver hair that stayed in place. People who wore dark glasses because it was fashionable and not because they were out on the ocean all day; people who wore perfume and women who wore perfume, too.

Not like the strange folk who populated her little seaside village and loved their mangy existence, most of which was carried out sipping coffee in bed and breakfasts or painting seascapes in refuse-filled attics or helping tourists catch redfish or just lying around drunk.

Some of these people, she found herself noticing, wore socks.

The whole mass of them did not go over the falls but rather oozed out into the small swamp of folding chairs that had been set in precisely the same manner Nina remembered from the night of Eve Ivory's announcement. Perhaps, she found herself thinking as she set the still full champagne glass beneath the chair and on the stone floor, perhaps Alana had planned it that way simply to infuriate Eve Ivory's ghost.

Things were to be different now.

How different?

Well, soon to know.

For Alana herself had risen, come forward on the dais elevated above the entrance hall, and now addressed the group spread out below.

It was, Nina discovered almost immediately, a very different Alana.

More conservatively dressed now, in a dark blue suit which, though still capable of rendering a mild electric shock, had nothing like the Fusion-Reactor voltage usually emanating from Alana's wardrobe.

"My Dear Friends…"

The voice was somewhat quieter now, and there was even a slight promise that all vowels would be treated equally and not whipped and stretched out to the point of exhaustion.

"My Dear Friends. The occasion that brings us here today is very different from the one that brought us here months ago. This is a time—"

She looked down at the podium, shook her head, smiled at the audience, and said quietly:

"I have written eleven speeches to try to convey the wonderful news I have to impart. None of them do it justice. So I'm simply going to say it."

Then say it, thought Nina.

What's happening?

"The first production to done in Theatre des Arts, our major stage here—will be William Shakespeare's *Hamlet*, premiering August first."

Wow, thought Nina.

So who's going to play Hamlet?

It's a little harder part than Stanley Kowalski.

And you better get Ophelia's name right and not start calling her Ellen.

An appreciative murmur was still rolling around in the crowd.

Nice idea, Alana.

Start with something ambitious.

Bay St. Lucy might not be able to produce the best *Hamlet* in the world, but we can sure as heck give it a try.

"The production will be mounted by The New York Shakespeare Company."

Silence.

What?

Now it was not silence anymore; it had moved forward to a kind of Advanced Stupor.

"The entire production will be filmed by the Public Broadcasting Company. The role of Hamlet will be played by the incomparable Clifton Barrett, who will also direct.

The role of Gertrude the Queen will be played by Constance Briarworth, who, as many of you I'm sure know, is given credit for discovering Mr. Barrett over a decade ago, and was Gertrude in his breakthrough performance at The New Globe Theatre in London. And the role of Ophelia, will be played by the town's own daughter, and of course the wife of Mr. Barrett, Helen Reddington."

It took a while of course for this all to sink in.

And it was not made any easier by the fact that everyone was still standing and buzzing around and laughing and saying "How did you do this?" and so on and so on.

While Nina was still seated.

Thinking.

But now it began to make sense.

The new people up there in the real clothes were producers, and film makers. And publicists, and—well, those kind of people.

They had been drawn here by a world class facility. By a world class ocean.

Well the Gulf of Mexico wasn't exactly the North Sea, but it could be cooled down a few degrees by an enterprising director.

And by money.

A lot of money.

Robinson money.

Which the town now had access to because of…well, because of what Nina had done.

This was the reason for Hope saying what she did.

Nina had, in a way, drawn Helen Reddington home.

The first thing to do was—no she could do that later—the very first thing to do was go and congratulate—no, she couldn't because of the crowd, no, the first thing of all she had to do was—no that could come later, too…so what was the first thing she had to do?

Stand up?

No, sitting here was ok because everybody else was standing up and why do just what everybody else was doing?

Then she realized what the first thing to do was.

She reached under the chair, grabbed the glass, and, in three good swallows, drank the champagne.

Then she stood up, made her way through the crowd, then through the greenhouse, then past a radio reporter who was interviewing somebody who had to be a producer or an agent or a writer or a director or The President of France—and out into the gardens.

Where was—

There! There he was!

"Waiter!"

"Yes, ma'am?"

"I need another glass of champagne!"

It was still exactly the same price as the other one had been—free—but it tasted much better.

Sip slowly, make it last.

Or just gulp it down and get another one.

What the heck.

She began to wander through the azaleas.

There was that waiter.

"I'll have another glass, please."

"Here you are, ma'am."

"Still the same price?"

"Yes, ma'am."

Ha ha ha!

She was much funnier when she was drinking champagne.

She took the first sip, realized that she was moving from the azaleas to the roses, and then remembered teaching *Hamlet* all those years. Bobby Jacobs that time standing in front of the class to recite one of twelve or fourteen famous lines she'd asked them to memorize.

Not all of the lines, of course.

Just—just choose one of the lines, come up in front of the class and recite it.

Bobby Jacobs had chosen, "There is a divinity that shapes our ends, rough hew them though we may."

"There is...."

"Go on, Bobby."

"There is..."

"You can do it."

"There is a divinity that shapes our ends rough."

She had lasted something like fifteen seconds before, explaining to the class that something had caught in her throat, she had rushed out of the room, down the hall, and into the teachers' lounge.

"What's the matter with you?"

No way to answer of course, just have to laugh uproariously for five minutes or so, and finally try to get one's breath back.

Now Clifton Barrett was going to come here and say those lines with her in the audience.

Would she dare approach him for an autograph?

How, how in heaven's name, had Helen Reddington from little old Bay St. Lucy, approached the deity that was Clifton Barrett? And made him fall in love with her?

And marry her, to boot?

When had that marriage taken place? Ten months ago? Yes, she could remember having read about it in both *The Bay St. Lucy Courier* and *The New York Times*, it being one of the few stories common to both of those illustrious publications.

And now Helen was coming home—

—bringing him with her.

Not only him, but a world class Shakespeare production!

She thought about the question and marveled about it for a time.

Then it began to rain.

Rain comes differently in Bay St. Lucy—and probably all coastal towns—than it comes elsewhere. It does not warn of its approach. There are no sinister black anvil clouds stretching their way across the prairie sky far to the north, no distant rumblings of soft and ominous thunder, no warnings on Weather Telefacts, no fun involved in preparations, no remembering to take one's umbrella, and no running wildly through the streets to get home and under shelter.

No, in a seaside community the sun was shining and then it wasn't; it wasn't raining and then it was.

Hard.

Straight down. No wind involved in the operation.

Drenching rain.

The rain water, she could see, was pelting down into her champagne and diluting it.

Can't have that.

She drank the rest of the champagne.

Then she set the glass on a table that happened to be next to her.

Then Jackson Bennett put his massive arm around her, turned her gently so that she was facing a different direction than she had been, and roared just enough louder than the roaring rain...

....that was a funny phrase, wasn't it, *roaring rain*...

...all those 'r's...

Champagne, champagne!

The night they...invented...champagne...

Maybe they could do that play!

"Nina, come on! You're getting drenched!"

"Come on where, Jackson?"

"Over here! Come with me! We'll get under this little trellis thing!"

It was, she found herself thinking, actually a gazebo. But it was exactly in the right place—ten feet away—and it had a roof, and it had chairs and a table.

Within a few seconds they were seated, Jackson dripping and beaming, Nina burping and dripping and beaming.

"Where did this come from?"

"I don't know, Jackson."

"Are you all right?"

"I think so. I've been drinking all afternoon so I'm drunk as a skunk."

"All afternoon? Really?"

"Well, let me look at my watch. It's one twenty three. I started drinking at one sixteen."

"Ok, I guess that's pretty much all afternoon. How much have you put away?"

"Three glasses of champagne."

"My God, that's more than six ounces."

"Well. I knew it was a lot."

"I didn't know you had it in you."

"It probably won't be in me for long. I generally throw it up."

"Thank you for telling me that, Nina."

"It's the least I could do."

And so they simply sat there for a time, laughing and watching sodden shapes bent over and scurrying madly through the watery maze that the old Robinson gardens had become.

Jackson, the young running back out of LSU, the struggling African American recent law graduate whom Frank had taken in as junior partner...

...the young man whose family they both had come to love and admire...

...this Jackson was now leaning toward her and asking:

"So what do you think of the news, Nina?"

"Stunning."

He nodded.

"I know."

"But Jackson..."

She would have leaned forward too, but she probably would have fallen unconscious on the metal table and been unable to rise.

"...Jackson, how could this happen? Surely the city council must have been involved in this."

He nodded.

"We missed you, Nina. We could have used you on the council."

"I'm not sure I would have been much help. But anyway, after the Robinson thing, I just felt like I needed a break from major decisions."

"We all understood. But I think you would have been excited about this particular project."

"I'm sure I would have. So tell me everything."

He smiled.

"Alana Delafosse is quite a lady."

"Yes, she is."

"The mayor called me in March, and told me he wanted a small subcommittee—actually it turned out to be me, Tom Landrieu, and Mary Phillips—to listen to Ms. Delafosses's proposal concerning what she was characterizing as a summer festival."

"Yeah. I'd heard her mention something like that."

"Well, we met in the old library. She talked, and, I admit, we were skeptical. We had already voted money to redo the mansion, but so much was going on. And when she really went into the particulars of the scope of the thing: New York actors, major national film companies—for a while we were just looking for a nice way to tell her 'no.'"

"I can imagine."

"But she didn't quit. And we kept having meetings. And the numbers she kept bringing in were—frankly, they were astonishing."

"What kind of numbers?"

"Ten million dollars."

"Jackson, we're spending ten million dollars to put on this production?"

"No, we're making ten million dollars."

"What?"

He grinned.

"I know. It's hard to believe. But—well, you were at the play last night, weren't you?"

"Yes."

"That whole thing at the end, that Salzburg thing?"

"The Salzburg Music Festival. It's famous."

"Apparently. But what Alana pointed out to us was, that it didn't always exist. Salzburg in the early nineteen hundreds was just a sleepy little village, almost dying, because nobody could make money mining the salt beneath the city. The salt that had made it famous centuries before."

"I didn't know that."

"Neither did we."

"Alana probably learned it in Russia when she was training to be an assassin."

"Alana never was in Russia and she never trained to be an assassin."

"You're no fun. But go on."

"Salzburg got to be Salzburg because of a guy named Max Reinhardt, who looked at the city and said, 'Hey, let's put on a play!' And they did. And they are still."

"What did Salzburg have that Bay St. Lucy doesn't have?"

"Maybe a few old castles, Jackson pointed out, "but we've got the ocean. We've got a beautiful little town full of artists."

"And we have money."

"That we do. Anyway, it turns out Alana had already started contacting people—she's good at that—and a miracle happened. Whole bunch of them, actually. Alana somehow made contact with The New York Shakespeare Society and offered them a cool million dollars if they would come down here and produce *Hamlet*."

"Had you authorized her to make such an offer?"

"Of course not; you think we're crazy?"

"My fault. I'd just forgotten for a second or so that Alana was Alana."

"Well, she is. Anyway, apparently the New York Shakespeare Company has bills to pay too, and the Reddington/Barrett couple has their ten thousand dollar a month upper West Side apartment to maintain—and they all just said, "We could use a million dollars, let's go to the beach!"

"Ok, but I still don't understand…"

"Other people got wind of it."

"What other people?"

"The Arthur M. Vining Foundation."

"Who are they?"

"A foundation. They give money to support art. So, by the way, does Amalgamated Petroleum, who just happens to have an offshore drilling rig two miles out from here."

"Publicity, publicity."

"Everybody found out about it; and everybody wanted to be involved, nobody more so than the entire state of Mississippi."

"The state is involved?"

"Of course. That's why the governor is here today."

"The governor of Mississippi is here today?"

"Nina, you just walked right past him."

"I thought that was the president of France. I guess I should know those two people apart, shouldn't I?"

"Well, you're retired."

"I guess that justifies it. So why does the state want to get involved in a Shakespeare production?"

"Mississippi is sensitive about our reputation."

"Our reputation?"

"Yes. The word around the country is that the people of Mississippi are, well…"

"Stupid."

"Well, intellectually challenged."

"We have learning differences."

"Yes, or at least that's the reputation. So a great cultural event by the sea could be extremely valuable."

"Wow! So Alana Delafosse waved a million dollars around…"

"And we're going to make ten times that."

"Incredible."

And, just as she said that word, the rain stopped.

And after it did, nothing noteworthy happened in the rest of the month of May.

Except there was one memorable event.

It happened Thursday evening, when she visited Hope Reddington, for a light dinner.

She and Frank had always fit into the Reddington's circle of friends, so mutual invitations had been frequent. She had been in the house several times, and had always loved it. It was not the Robinson Mansion. It was in a different section of Bay St. Lucy, where the trees were not as stately and magnificent and the people were not as stately and magnificent. But both sets of living creatures—trees and people—had done all right for themselves. They were upper middle class trees and people, who exuded in comfort and conviviality what they might have lacked in lineage and wardrobe. They shaded each other. Low to the ground, hard working, and efficient, they shared a flora/fauna appreciation for cracked-with-time sidewalks, ambulatory and not decorative. The trees shaded these sidewalks not because they were obligated by God to do so, but because the sidewalks seemed to attract them down, invite them as it were. And the people walking on the sidewalks shared something in common with the trees themselves, not passing helter-skelter over the concrete on their way to some encounter or another, but standing rooted in it, as the sun set, and they chatted aimlessly about the turning of the earth.

It had been their neighborhood—Nina's and Frank's—for the last twenty years of their lives together.

"Nina!"

"Hello there, May Belle!"

Since Hope was in her eighties now, she was aided in many aspects of housework and the daily obstacles to living by various members of the church. It was not a formal arrangement, nor would these ladies, Nina knew instinctively, ever have accepted money.

But they were there often, getting a bit of breakfast together, making coffee for Hope and whoever happened to stop by at eight in the morning.

Bringing by a spot of lunch.

Offering rides into town and back.

And making a light supper for Hope to offer Nina.

"Isn't the news about Helen exciting?"

This from May Belle Witherspoon, tall and gaunt, her silver glasses stuck absent-mindedly upon a bun of hair, her apron flopping busily as she walked down the front stairs and out onto the driveway, where her own stately Buick sat behind the Reddington Oldsmobile, which had sat motionless for the last several years.

"Hope is fit to be tied, you know!"

"I'm sure," Nina answered, "that she is."

Nina approached the house. It was all porches and gardens, various brown-brick Georgian columns sprouting here are there, seemingly not supporting anything at all but just keeping the building planted deep into the earth.

"Do you like cucumber salad?"

"Love it," she lied.

Cucumber salad being the only salad in the world that Nina actively disliked.

She had no idea why.

"You know they're going to stay here!"

"What?"

"Helen and her husband. The actor. They're going to stay here!"

"Really?"

"Yes, Hope just got a call from Helen a few days ago! The two of them are going to stay in Helen's old bedroom. It's being fixed up now! No one has slept in it since Helen left Bay St. Lucy five years ago."

"That's incredible. Hope must be so excited."

"Oh, she is, she is! Come on up—watch the front stairs, they're a little rickety. I've set dinner out on the back porch so the two of you can watch the sun set over the bayou. I must tell you, I don't know which one Hope is more excited about: her granddaughter coming home or Nina Bannister coming to have dinner with her!"

"Well. It's been a long time. Frank and I used to come over all the time. I have a lot of memories of this place."

And she did, and they all came flooding back as she walked into the entrance ante-room and then into the main living room itself.

The house was possessed by the past and had no role to play in the present. It was musty, of course, as such houses always are, dust particles whirling and dancing like little chains of DNA molecules in light beams thick as tree trunks that always seemed to be glowing golden through great six foot high windows, no matter what time of day it happened to be.

But the air's lack of movement was secondary in importance—at least in terms of placing the house in any chronological relation to the rest of time—to the fact that all of the people living in it were dead.

They were not mournfully dead.

They were simply happy to be what they now were, pictures hanging on walls, or sitting on grand pianos, or propped on coffee tables, or hanging down on gold chains from the vaulted ceilings—and smiling in gray, muted tones that exuded good memories.

It was a happy house, and always had been.

Outside of it had occurred those things—sickness, fatal automobile accidents—that are both a part of life and the end of it.

But they had not been allowed in here.

And so as Nina walked carefully, almost reverently, through the dining room with its great oaken table and silver tea service, and through the kitchen with its ranges and coolers and cabinets and spices—and through the back parlor where sat a golden harp that had been played by Helen, and before that, her mother—

—as she walked through these places, she could swear she was hearing, mixed with her own breathing and the creaking of wooden floorboards—the sound of utter stillness, laughing softly.

"Nina, won't you sit down?"

They were on the back screened in porch now. A white wrought iron table sat directly beneath an overhead fan, which rotated slowly emitting an almost imperceptible growl of gears. Just beyond the far screen wall, almost close enough, Nina thought, that she could reach out and touch it, flowed Plaquemine's Bayou, making its stately way into the gulf, twenty feet wide here and shining orange/brown in the setting sun.

"Hope is still in her room, getting ready."

"That's all right. Tell her there's no hurry."

"Would you like some coffee?"

"I would, May Belle."

"Of course. Here you are."

The coffee was poured. Nina sipped, then set her cup on the table and looked up:

"You won't join me?"

"I should go and check on Hope."

"But you will be joining us for dinner?"

May Belle shook her head.

"I'd love to. You know I would. But I have to go home and get dinner ready for the family. As for cleaning up…"

"Don't worry about that. You know I'll help her."

A smile of immense relief, like the smile one emits after learning that the tumor is not cancerous.

"Oh would you?"

"Of course."

"Thank you so much! Hope is very independent still. But you know, after a certain point it gets difficult."

"Don't worry, May Belle. I'll be sure she's all right for the night before I go."

"Thank you, Nina. I won't give it another thought, now that I know you're here. But—if you'll just excuse me a small minute, I want to be sure she doesn't need any help."

And May Belle Witherspoon was gone, sucked into what had always been the welcoming arms of Reddington hospitality.

And, Nina mused, sipping happily on the coffee that had been given her, still was.

She sat for perhaps five minutes, losing herself in various memories of various evenings out here, where they would all chat about this or that, the men sometimes fishing for catfish in the bayou, the women content to point at stately egrets standing in foot deep shore water, motionless, watching the current eddy past.

When was the last time?

It had to be ten years ago.

Think, Nina—

Helen is now twenty-three years old

She was seventeen when she left for Interlochen.

The accident had occurred two years before that.

Nine years.

What came into her mind was a summer evening, balmy as this one. She and Frank, Paul and Laura—and the sound of the harp being played by Helen, back there, in the parlor.

While the bayou made its way timelessly toward the gulf.

Helen, the very young Helen—who had no idea about the accident to come that was to claim the lives of her parents, nor the marvelous adventures that were to befall her in Interlochen and New York—had that very night been able to look down on its waters from her own bedroom window.

Moon River.

A bayou and not a river.

Not wider than a mile.

But crossing it in style she certainly would be.

She and her husband, one of the greatest actors in the world.

Coming back to sleep with her in her childhood bed.

And how would she feel about that?

"Nina!"

These reveries were interrupted by the appearance of Hope, who exploded into the doorway and tottered her way out onto the porch, hurtling at two to three miles an hour and panicking both Nina, who thought of jumping up to catch her as she was certain to fall forward, and May Belle, who thought of grabbing her from behind since Nina would certainly be too slow to do any good at all.

"Hope! It's so good of you to invite me!"

Incredibly, nothing disastrous happened, and with a bit of chair scraping and "oh don't bother I'm fine—ing" and "no no it's all right—ing," Hope was seated and pouring coffee into her own cup.

"Are you sure you won't stay and eat with us, May Belle?" she asked.

"I can't, Hope," replied May Belle, who had somehow gotten over her panic and had time to both return to the kitchen and bring the salad bowl.

"Husband calls, I know."

"Yes he does. And big ole' teenage boy, too. Now—salad's out, you've got silverware, and plates and dressing—anything else?"

"No, we're fine! Now you get back home and take care of your family."

"I will. Good night you two."

"Good night."

"Good night."

And, save for a fish plopping near the pier, and a water bird yowling mournfully as it skimmed its way over the bayou current, Nina and Hope were alone.

On her own back porch, Hope no longer seemed to feel the need of looking up and out from under something. She did on the other hand seem to feel an equally pressing need to avoid being heard by something; and so she leaned forward, making the legs of the table scrape against the hardwood porch floors, while, her grinning face poised directly above a serving bowl filled with what appeared to be Bleu Cheese dressing, she paused.

For one second. Two seconds.

Listen, listen...

Three seconds. Four seconds...

...then the secret.

"July 6."

The grin only broadened, while Nina pondered her response to this communication, this number, this enigma.

She could not bring herself to be so stupid as to ask something like, "So what's happening on July 6, Hope?"

Clearly she was supposed to have known the burning question, whose answer was "July 6."

It was like one of those game shows, in which the contestant, having been told the answer, is to guess the question.

But for the life of her she couldn't think of any she could have asked, the answer to which would have been 'July 6,' except the question, "What day comes two days after the fourth of July?"

Which she did not want to ask.

And so she simply waited.

The grin only broadened.

We will be, she told herself, here all night.

Then a stroke of brilliance hit her and she said:

"So that's the big day, is it?"

Hope exploded in joy.

"Yes! Yes, I've only learned of it today! July 6, Tuesday afternoon, at 8:00 p.m.!"

The dazzle of the brilliant idea seemed to have faded a bit by now, but why not ride things as far as possible?

"So then—things will start happening."

Another explosion of joy.

"Yes! Yes!"

But how long could she keep this going? How long could she avoid saying, "So *what* things will begin happening, Hope?"

"Do you think you'll be ready by then?"

The grin disappeared, there replaced it an expression of pure panic, and finally an atmosphere of calm and resignation.

"Yes. Yes, I believe everything will be done. When Helen and her husband arrive, her room will be ready for them. All of the workmen have assured me of that."

Thank God!

Hope and her husband were arriving on July 6, at 8 p.m..

Now maybe they could eat.

They did so, with Hope chattering on about this and that, all subjects fair game and relevant as long as they were Helen and her famous actor husband. Nina got a few words in here and there, mostly about the splendor of the cucumber salad and about how she had always loved cucumber salads and about how her mother had made wonderful cucumber salads and about how much Frank had loved cucumber salads and of course it was all lies, lies, lies, but there wasn't much else to talk about.

So she munched, and listened, and nodded, while the sun set over the bayou, and the shadows lengthened, and every now and then a gray log with one yellow eye floated by, indicating that it was either a very special log indeed or an alligator.

Finally:

"Nina, I wanted to ask you something. It's a bit of a difficult subject; somewhat personal. I hope you don't mind."

"Of course not, Hope."

"I wanted to ask…"

Silence again, except for the drone of an airplane passing low on its way to landing at the Bay St. Lucy Airport, and the sound of wavelets lapping at the pier outside.

"Do you ever feel—well, close to Frank?"

Nina thought for a while, and finally decided to tell the truth.

"Yes."

"It's as though he's—somehow all around you?"

"Yes. Yes, it's that way."

"Well—I feel that way more and more often now, as I walk through the house. Or as I sit out here and watch the water. There are presences. Old friends. Loved ones. They seem to be telling me that something will be happening soon. I shall be 82 in two months, and...well, they seem to be letting me know that my time is coming."

Nina would have commented, except she began to be lost in her own thoughts, which were occasionally similar.

Not often.

Just...

...just sometimes.

Mostly about this time of day.

"It's a very strange thing. They make me feel as though there's nothing to fear. That it will be all right. And do you know, Nina? I don't fear. I don't fear anything at all."

"Hope, I'm sure you're right about there being nothing to fear; but you're going to be with us a long time. You have many years in front of you."

Nina had, of course, no idea how long Hope Reddington had to live.

She had no idea how long anyone had to live, herself included.

But there were certain things one was expected to say.

Or?

At any rate, Hope continued as though she had not heard the comment anyway.

"I just want to be sure that she's all right."

"Who, Hope?"

"Helen. I just want to have her here, and see her with a loving husband who will take care of her. And then I will be ready to go."

"I'm sure..."

But Hope interrupted her:

"As it is, I have concerns."

"What kind of concerns?"

A shake of the head.

"I'm not sure. I was unable to go to New York for the wedding. So far, so far..."

"I understand."

"I've not seen Helen and her husband together. I don't know anything about their lifestyle. Both of them famous now, in such a wonderful city. I assume it to be everything she dreamed of as a girl."

"Of course it is, Hope."

"But...her letters. She writes frequently, as she always did. But...there's been a change in them."

"What kind of a change?"

"It's hard to put into words. She writes about marvelous things, but without joy."

"I'm not sure what you mean."

"Nor am I. It's simply...well, you must remember the nights all of us spent, sitting out here, knowing that we would wake up the next morning and go through our completely routine lives. Lives spent at the pharmacy, or the law office, or the high school."

"Yes. I remember them. I remember them very vividly."

"Of course you do. Because there was a kind of wonder about them. They were filled with love."

"That's true."

"Helen's letters...well, that wonder is missing, Nina. It's simply not there. Perhaps it was during the first month or so of the marriage. But it's gone now."

Nina knew nothing to say.

The conversation stopped, then picked up again, then died by increments, as the night sky darkened.

Finally it was time to clean the dishes, put the remains of the hated cucumber salad in the refrigerator, where it would hopefully go unthought of until it died and disappeared, be sure that Hope was secure for the night...

...and go home.

During her ride back Nina thought about the presences.

Yes, they did hover around her at times.

And yes they did make her feel that everything was going to be all right.

They were not there now, though, and they were not there as she parked her Vespa and made her way up the stairs.

They were not there, telling her that everything would be all right.

She was soon to find out why.

PART TWO: ARRIVALS AND DEPARTURES

CHAPTER 6: WHAT IS SO RARE AS A DAY IN…

One of Nina's favorite lines in literature had always been Tolstoy's opening to *Anna Karenina*.

"All happy families are alike; each unhappy family is unhappy in its own way." Except Nina applied these lines to months. Every miserable month had its own story, or stories. Happy months, though, just rocked along as they chose, day to day, one pleasurable sensation following another, all equally luscious, all completely forgettable.

Such was her June in Bay St. Lucy, following the announcement of The Great *Hamlet,* which was to act as forerunner to The Great Summer Festival.

Every day she rose, breakfasted, Furled, Unfurled, went to run on the beach and ultimately walked on the beach, worked for two or three hours in Margot's shop which meant she chatted for two or three hours with Margot, came home, Furled, Unfurled, lunched, napped, fished with Penelope Royal, dinnered with any one of a number of friends, came home after dark, Furled, Unfurled, had a glass of wine, went to bed resolved to read something truly great (there was a volume of Schopenhauer on the nightstand, where it had lain for several months), read instead a mystery, and then dozed off to sleep.

She remembered each one of these things vividly—how Margot's shop looked, how it felt to catch a fish with Penelope, the lovely shiver of finding out who the murderer was—but she remembered each scene only once, which would have meant that, at month's end, she would have missed something like 29/30ths of her life.

It bothered her.

What had happened to all those moments?

No matter, because this was no longer June.

This was July.

Different story entirely.

Hellzapoppin.

July 4 came and went, big tourist days, much business in the town, all the sea craft booked, fishing as good as it might be expected to be in midsummer when it was at its worst, and the town filled with weaponry. There were fireworks going off everywhere—from offshore oil platforms to high school and middle school stadia to beach condos with fancy rooftop launching pads—and there were battle re-enactments, soldiers on parade, military marches coming from every bandstand in town—everything, in short, to remind the citizens of Bay St. Lucy of how good a thing war was and how lucky we were to have it.

Nina spent most of the day inside.

Furl was too frightened to go out on the deck.

But the day passed, and gave way to July 5, the day for cleaning up used rocket flares and bottle blasters and roman candles and squealies and Whirling Dervishes, all in the hope that they were spent and not live, and that they would disappear into ponderous garbage trucks and not explode into the hands and faces of curious, five year old, would-be infantrymen.

Then came July 6.

At 8 p.m. Helen Reddington was coming home, flown in from New York City, via Memphis, and accompanied by her husband, Clifton Barrett.

The Great Clifton Barrett.

A crowd had begun to gather at Bay St. Lucy's airport around 7:30. It was not a huge crowd. It was not the crowd that a head SEC coach would have drawn, nor the crowd that a star running back would have drawn.

For this was an actor, after all, and an actor's wife.

It was the crowd that a good starting linebacker would have drawn.

But Nina, having been driven to the airport in Margot's Volkswagen, still felt a tingle of excitement as the lights of the small plane—and then the plane itself—appeared, flying in from the East, the sky in the middle stages of twilight, a full moon almost directly overhead.

"Look at Hope, Nina!"

"Yes. She's so excited."

Hope was barely taller than the barrier rope that had been strung to show the crowd its limits.

And it was a crowd that appreciated the effort.

The mayor; Alana Delafosse; several of the people who had been arriving from New Orleans during the previous days to help with the production.

Perhaps twenty five people.

Two newspapermen, their flash bulbs ready.

The plane landed, taxied, and pulled to a stop while Nina and Margot wormed their way forward.

"How are you feeling, Hope?"

For a second Hope had not realized who was standing beside her; when she did, she grasped Nina's hand and held it with remarkable strength.

She could not, though, say a word.

A ramp was rolled to the doors of the small private jet— no commercial jets landed in Bay St. Lucy.

The door of the plane opened.

And there, within it, was Helen Reddington.

"Bravo! Bravo!"

As much applause as could come from twenty five people, mixed with cheers and more shouts of adulation

"Bravoooo!"

Helen stepped forward, and then started down the ramp.

She was, Nina remembered, the tallest short woman she had ever seen.

For she was not large at all. But something about her bearing and grace magnified her. She was much bigger than her size. And her eyes, the deepest most penetrating eyes Nina could remember, sucked the world into them as one, and held it there before mentally digesting it, so that she could decide which parts to keep and which to throw away.

She was dressed in a red suit. But it was not quite the shade of red that Alana would have worn, nor was her belt the same depth of black, nor was her hat anything at all, for she wore none. But all of her coloring, all of her subtlety, all of the immensely sophisticated and still hauntingly elemental simplicity of her bearing convinced Nina that, if ever Bay St. Lucy had ever produced a true princess turned Russian assassin, it had done so not with Alana Delafosse, but with Helen Reddington.

She poured down the steps and into the arms of her grandmother, who hurled herself upward and dangled a foot or so off the ground, green pumps pumping, while she attempted to drive her cheek bones through the skull of the woman holding her.

Flashbulbs exploded; there were small cries, tears, and the circle imploded.

Then—Nina was the only one looking up for a second or so, the only one to see—Clifton Barrett appeared.

He was from New York City.

NEW YORK CITY!

And he looked about him in wonder, much as Spanish explorers must have done centuries ago when setting foot on the New World.

His mouth fell open and his eyes sparkled in amazement; she could almost hear him perceiving THE REST OF THE WORLD and whispering to himself:

"My God! It does exist!"

Then he, too, descended the stairway.

For a time he was engulfed in the same knot of people that was attempting to asphyxiate his wife; but somehow he forced the circle outward, so that a space of some two or three feet came to exist between the welcoming party of Bay St. Lucy, and the two people who stood before them.

Nina got, for the first time, a good look at the man. His appearance reminded her of an adage which she had once heard: whatever you wear, include one truly superb item.

His outfit would have been simple enough: dark blue sports jacket, charcoal gray slacks, black shoes shined so brilliantly that the evening star reflected more brightly in them than it did in the actual sky, but that, otherwise, were simply shoes and not props for a fashion-shoot...

...but in the midst of all of that ordinariness, all of that richness so superbly subtle as almost to achieve normalcy...

...in the midst of all this ensemble, was the scarf.

It lay around his neck like a fat, drugged snake, imported for its color and venom from some hardly known island off the shore of Indonesia. Almost red, almost gold, almost purple, but none of these colors because two tints brighter, it was the only soft article of clothing that Nina had ever been afraid of. It had not been tucked in; it had hidden itself—and any tie or other neck accoutrement that might dare make its way onto Clifton Barrett's neck at the moment—it would have eaten.

This scarf turned, scarcely aware that there was a human being attached to it, took two steps toward the mayor, hesitated, and finally gave its wearer permission to speak.

"My dear Sir—it is a pleasure."

To which the mayor mumbled something inaudible; but then what would not have been inaudible juxtaposed against the voice of Clifton Barrett, which could only have been compared to the roaring of a great waterfall, but amplified and made more elemental?

Whatever the mayor had said elicited the response:

"You are too kind. Far too kind."

"Clifton?"

This from Helen Reddington, who, taking her husband by the arm, all the time avoiding the scarf, which could have uncoiled and sprung at any moment—led him two steps toward Nina.

"Clifton, this is the teacher I told you about."

Oh God, thought Nina. *What is she doing?*

"This is Ms. Bannister, the best literature teacher in the world!"

Her husband's face became one of the first small towns to receive electric current, lamps all over it coming on simultaneously.

"This is the great lady! My dear, my dear—Helen talks of you whenever she talks of her school, her people."

"I learned more from you, Ms. Bannister," Helen interjected, "than from anybody else in school...or from anybody else ever!"

"My lovely Ms. Bannister," intoned Clifton Barrett, bowing slightly. "I wonder if you might agree to teach me something of *Hamlet* one of these days. I must confess—great parts of the play still elude me, though I have devoted to it—well, more than an average amount of time."

He stood, awaiting an answer.

They all stood, the reporters, everyone.

Nina realized she'd been asked by one of the greatest Shakespearian actors in the world to teach him Shakespeare.

And, while asking, Clifton Barrett had placed himself so that the moon rising over the airport's control tower reflected itself precisely in the middle of his azure pupils like an orange in the blue summer sky. While he spoke to her his voice softened and lowered, softened and lowered, so that the sounds he was making translated themselves with perfect clarity to a) anyone who knew chivalry; b) anyone who knew actors; and c) anyone who knew women.

"Will you, dear lady, come to our rehearsals from time to time—and allow us to know your thoughts?"

Upon hearing these words, Nina composed herself, waited just an instant or two before answering, blocked from her mind the unutterable charm of the man so that it would not detract from the wit and sharpness of her reply, and finally said something like:

"Wadawadawada."

Upon hearing which everyone laughed.

"Well! That's answer enough for now! Now, you must accompany us to—well, to home. To Helen's grandmother's house—where, as I understand it, there are to be some revelries!"

She composed herself again, stepped forward, and, with more confidence now, said:

"Wadawadawada."

"Nina," said Margot, pulling her away, "you're making a fool of yourself. Come with me; we'll go to the party."

And they did.

They had entered Margot's Volkswagen and negotiated the small driveways, entrance and exit ramps designed by airport engineers to frustrate people who had only dropped other people off or picked other people up and were thus not constrained to be frustrated by air travel itself, when Margot said:

"What was the matter with you back there?"

"What do you mean?"

"Haven't you ever seen anyone famous?"

"Of course I have."

"Who?"

"At a baseball game in Indianapolis once I saw Colonel Sanders."

"What were you doing at a baseball game in Indianapolis?"

"Don't remember."

"How do you know it was Colonel Sanders?"

"Margot, when you see Colonel Sanders, you don't forget it."

"What would he have been doing at a baseball game in Indianapolis?"

"Don't know. Not my business. But it was him."

"All right, so you've been in the presence of greatness."

"Damned straight."

"That still doesn't explain why you made such a fool of yourself back there."

"How did I make a fool of myself?"

"He asked you if you would teach him Shakespeare."

"Yes, he did. And I said, 'I'd be honored to tell him anything I knew, but that I could learn much more from him than he from me.'"

"You said, 'wadawadawada,' or something like that."

"Did not."

"Did so."

"Why would I have said 'wadawadawada?"

"I have no idea. Except I might point out that he invited you to rehearsals."

"Yes, and I said that I'd be honored to come."

"You said 'wadawadawada' again."

"You're just making all this up. Here—turn here!"

They argued for a time longer as Margot negotiated the darkening streets of Bay St. Lucy, and Nina recounted the witty and urbane answer she had in fact given to Clifton Barrett's questions.

She had said the right things, hadn't she?

Except—why was this blurriness in her memory bank, precisely where 'answers to recent questions' should have been? And why was that space filled instead with only a memory of those eyes, that voice...

...that voice.

"This is it, isn't it?" came a different voice. Margot's.

"Yes. Turn in here!"

And there they were, the words 'Turn in here!' right in that little bank slot.

So it was all right now.

She just had to stay away from Clifton Barrett.

One of her favorite Shakespeare critics had written about the "Green World Comedies." In these comedies the first act consisted of things taking place in the real world—Athens, for example, or some Italian court. The setting soon switched though to Arden Forest, which had, at sunset, become enchanted. Elves and fairy creatures and spirits of the night all manner of supernatural beings haunted it, and by turns vexed, frightened, and enchanted the mortals who had ventured into their lair.

This had happened, she realized, with Hope Reddington's house.

It was the same house she had visited only weeks earlier but it had become magical and now was haunted by deities who, if only watched a bit more closely than normal, could have been seen floating several inches above the ground.

Huge floodlights dotted the gardens.

All of the lights in the house were glowing golden.

People came and went. Some of them were the same functionaries who had peopled the Robinson mansion at the time of Alana's announcement.

But their number had lessened in favor of the theatrical people, who, having played imaginary beings all of their lives, had become imaginary beings, who, besides the fact that they were floating, were transparent.

You could see right through them!

"Nina! Margot!"

Alana Delafosse, who, incredibly, now looked like a post-mistress or a social worker.

"Ladies!"

My God, she was even talking like a mortal.

The contrast was simply too great—she could not be Alana any more!

"Come! There are so many people you must meet!"

And meet they did, Nina eschewing beverages (she had taken three days to get over the champagne at L'Auberge des Arts and so avoided like death the white jacketed waiters whom she continued to blame for the whole thing), Margot eschewing any type of moderation (Gin! Margot's eyes said upon setting one foot into the garden—gin! Everywhere gin!) and the entire conversation elevating itself to POLITEPOLITEPOLITE as they learned that this lighting crew had descended from Memphis, that group of set designers had come from New Orleans, the Polonius standing by the magnolia tree was from St. Louis, the Fortinbras leaning against the bird bath and getting drunk there had been hired from the Chicago Repertory Company—and there was the great Constance Briarworth, stunning in jewelry that made her look like a Christmas tree. She was standing by the grape arbor, speaking with three women who would have been though great beauties in their own rights, but here had assumed simply the roles of minor deities.

The courteous conversation drifted for a time around these porches of Olympus, while Nina watched in wonder as the trees were illuminated by tiny points of flitting, golden light, thought by mortals to be fireflies, but known by English teachers to be Puck and his friends, minor functionaries whose job was to serve Oberon, Hippolyta, and the other major deities.

After a time they were in the house itself, then ascending the staircase—a thing she had never done before, even when she and Frank were regular visitors—and then entering Helen's old room.

"Will you look at what Hope has done up here?"

Another lady from the church—astonishingly, Nina did not know her, for she and her husband had newly joined—was leading a kind of tour.

The tour would have been worth a great deal, even had it not been for all the pictures, banners, ribbons, and Tony awards covering the walls.

No, the tour would have been worth scads of money if it had only shown the bed.

Helen, Nina imagined, had slept on a twin bed as a young teenager.

Now that bed had been replaced by the resting—and, one must not deny, breeding—place of kings.

It was a magnificent bed, a four poster bed, overtopped by a canopy that almost brushed the fourteen foot ceiling.

"My God," whispered Margot.

"I suppose," Nina found herself whispering back, "that's what Helen is going to say, when they both get in there."

By eleven o'clock some of the crowd had begun to leave.

Nina and Margot had separated, Margot now standing in a far corner of the garden, conversing with the magnificent Constance Briarworth.

When Nina, sitting at a table on the small pier that led down to the bayou—which was lapping at the boards two feet in front of her—was joined by Clifton Barrett.

He sat down opposite her and smiled.

Incredibly, she realized, she was going to be able to speak.

Perhaps it was just exhaustion, or the transforming effect of Arden Forest.

She herself had become a goddess, and could speak quite rationally with Oberon.

"I am sorry that I approached you so blatantly this afternoon at the airport."

"Oh that's all right. I was honored."

No wada's.

Incredible.

"I did mean what I said, you know."

"I'm sure you did, but...I have to tell you, I doubt very seriously whether I have any insight that an actor—and director—of your stature has not heard a million times over."

"That may be—but I doubt it. I'm only a performer. You, dear lady, are a teacher."

"Well. Whatever I can do."

Silence for a second.

Or a few centuries.

They were in The Green World.

Time had no meaning here.

"It is," Clifton Barrett went on, "a great honor to be in your city."

"We're honored to have you."

"I'm meeting Helen's wonderful grandmother for the first time. She was unable to come to New York for the wedding."

"I knew that."

"But so much was happening. There are so many obligations that one has to fulfill..."

"I'm sure that's true."

"And in the meantime. Well. I do know how much she means to Helen."

His face, which had become quite serious, brightened.

"Did you see what she has done to the bedroom?"

"Yes, we were taken up in a tour."

"I feel like a king!"

"Well, in a way, you are. You're King of Bay St. Lucy. At least for a while. We all just hope you don't get bored here.

He shook his head.

"No, never. Boredom is simply not possible. In the first place, I love being by the sea. I have a bad back, and walking on the beach is wonderful therapy. In the second place, the play is all-consuming. What a wonderful opportunity. And the people who've been assembled are top notch. Absolutely the best, from all over the country. We're going to create a truly memorable *Hamlet*. And as for the rest, if I have any time at all…well, part of it will be spent getting to know the people of St. Lucy. Helen's people. By the way, though, I do mean what I said about rehearsals. We don't want too many people wandering around in the theater while we're blocking and running lines, of course…"

"I understand."

"But you are one of those special people who should feel welcome at any time. Please do come."

"I will. I'll let you know ahead of time, of course, but…"

Nothing followed the 'but.' Nothing could follow it, because suddenly there was no one on the other side of the table to listen. Clifton Barrett had disappeared.

He had not disappeared physically because the body was still there; but something in him had declared 'time,' and that meant whatever space upon his mental stage that had been reserved for Nina, was now to be occupied by other actors.

He rose—completely ignoring Nina—walked around the table, and stared out over the garden. He scanned the thinning crowd until he saw his wife, chatting with this subordinate or that Neanderthal or that would be ticket buyer. Then his gaze intensified and intensified still more until it riveted itself into the back of her neck—

—and she turned into it, wincing—she was forty feet away, but still Nina could see her wince—and nodding.

She made quick apologies and left the conversation she'd been engaged in and walked briskly into the house.

This magical—and somewhat frightening—ritual accomplished, the man across the table returned to the man across the table and managed a completely impersonal smile downward at the woman he had, only seconds ago, pretended to be conversing with.

"We must," he not-quite-said, "abide by our schedule."

Nina, knowing nothing at all to say, simply nodded.

Then he took a step back, turned, looked up toward the window of his wife's room, and waited until she opened it.

After she had done so, she leaned out, staring down, first at the bayou, and then at her husband below.

She said, simply:

"Ah me!"

But this was enough.

Clifton Barrett seized the cue as though he were an alligator floating by, seizing a rodent caught in the current.

"She speaks! Oh speak again, bright angel! For thou art as glorious to this night, being o'er my head, as is a winged messenger of heaven unto the white upturned wondering eyes of mortals that fall back to gaze on him, when he bestrides the lazy-piercing clouds, and sails upon the lazy bosom of the air."

All of the people remaining in the garden turned, became silent, and converged on the pier.

A stage, Nina thought. And actors to behold the swelling scene.

Nina could see Helen's fingers gripping the railing, while the caves that were her eyes deepened, and the small voice that had come through the laughter in her throat, now retreated, to be replaced by the sonorous tones of soon-filled tombs:

"Fain," said Juliet, channeling through what had been Helen Reddington, "fain would I dwell on form, fain, fain deny what I have spoke; but farewell compliment! Dost thou love me? I know thou wilt say Ay!"

And so saying, Juliet turned and followed Helen Reddington's body back into the bedroom.

The door closed behind her.

Clifton Barrett looked down at Nina, and said:

"Good night, dear lady."

"Good night," she answered, feeling very cold suddenly, and not knowing why.

Helen Reddington's husband—as though the crowd left in the garden were nothing but statuary, motionless figures which, once vaguely admired, could now safely be ignored—whirled and strode purposefully into the house.

And was gone.

CHAPTER 7: FREE EATS!

Bright and early the following morning, Helen Reddington brought Nina breakfast.

"Bread man is here! Bread man is here!"

The world was just waking, morning light creeping like kelp up onto the beach and around the stilt poles of the shack. The pelicans were making their first low level sweep over the balmy waves, and the sun had yet another ten minutes in dawn's great Green Room before making its entrance, to begin Act Four Hundred and Seventy Three Million in the classic play BEING.

"All kinds of bread for you! Baking's done, errands to run!"

Nina had made her way into the kitchen and was just getting the coffee on; Furl had pressed his nose against the sliding glass deck door and was beginning to yowl softly; but the rattle of the front door changed everything, as did the cheerful voice that could have been a mixture of sparrows singing and morning sea breeze tinkling in the wind chimes.

"All kinds of baked goods! Bread for your breakfast!"

She made her way through the living room, opened the door, and saw the face of rejoicing, the countenance of youth, the smile of New Day Coming, and the biggest and ovalest brown bread loaves ever yeasted.

"Helen!"

"Bread man's here!"

"You remembered!"

"Of course I remembered! How could I not remember?"

"Come in, come in!"

She opened the front door; the smell of the bread entered first, followed by the bread itself, and then the bearer of the bread.

"Your lovely home, just as it was!"

"Well...not much potential for decorating, Helen."

"And no need. It's marvelous. You moved in, I remember, in October. I had been in your class two months my sophomore year,—that was world literature—and idolized you, of course. So I made a vow to visit you often, mornings, because mornings are always best—and bring you something that I loved as much as you loved literature. And of course that was bread!"

"And so you did. So you did."

Nina could remember it as though it happened yesterday.

Her move into the shack happened a scant three months after Frank's death; and the sight of this superb young student, the excitement she radiated—

—these things were welcome indeed.

And they still were.

For here was Helen Reddington, the great Helen Reddington, looking precisely as she had those years ago.

A bit too much rouge perhaps.

Why had Helen started wearing so much makeup?

But otherwise the same. The identical lithe and lightly muscled body which seemed to have the consistency and flexibility of spaghetti but the tensile strength of iron ore.

Here she was, coal black hair pulled tightly into a gleaming bun, athlete's body clad only in a bare undershirt and running pants—and eyes glittering like black diamonds.

"Bagatelli's is still open!"

She might as well have said:

"Tomorrow is Christmas—and Santa is real!"

"Yes. They haven't missed a day. Baking every morning."

"And do you go there often, Nina?"

"Yes I do. Three or four times a week, at least."

"I love it! I've just come from there, and they are exactly the same, he always covered in flour, she always bustling around with the same absolutely perfect blue striped apron, both of them yelling at each other at the top of their lungs: 'ADEPENTO! ADEPENTO, DECCOLATERI, SOPALIUSCIA!' or some such gibberish, that nobody in town can ever understand—they still do that and it's so wonderful!"

"Yes they do, Helen. Haven't changed one syllable, or lost one gram of flour. Here. Come on in. Let's slice this bread and get it out to the deck with some coffee and butter and jam and whatever we can find. Then I want to hear everything."

"Everything?"

"Absolutely everything."

"Well, that might take some time."

"You brought two loaves, didn't you?"

And, laughing, they set about confirming that the last years had gone nowhere, and were in fact out there in front of them, as ready to be lived through as the ocean was to be sailed out onto.

At least ten minutes of this newly regained decade were given to the pleasantries of the kitchen; but after these matters had been accomplished they found themselves sitting on the deck, the cat dealt with, the bread smeared with half an inch covering of everything in the refrigerator that came in small glass bottles, and the coffee showing once again why several empires had been made and destroyed just so two women such as these could drink it every morning.

"I'm sorry, Nina, that Clifton left you so suddenly last night."

"I don't know what you mean, Helen," lied Nina.

"It's just—he has very strict ways of doing things. It can be difficult to get used to."

"He simply saw the chance to do a moving exit scene. We were all quite delighted."

This was a lie too, but it seemed to relieve Helen, so, Nina mused, let it go and enjoy the sesame rye.

"When I met Clifton I was so—I was just so inexperienced. I knew nothing. Nina, I didn't even know how to walk."

"I seem to remember," Nina said, pouring a bit of cream, "that you walked quite effectively."

Helen smiled.

"I thought so. I used to think so many things. When I look back…"

She looked back.

After she had done so for a while, Nina asked:

"Where did you meet him, Helen?"

"New Jersey."

"Really?"

"Yes! Yes, I was there doing an off- off-Broadway production of something or other. I'd only known him a short time, and he invited me to go with him to London."

"What a fairy tale story."

"Well it's not…"

She was silent for a time.

Then she leaned forward and said:

"Nina—there are some other things I wanted to talk to you about."

"Certainly, Helen. Anything at all."

"First, I want to thank you for taking care of Grandmamma."

"Helen, I've not taken care of your grandmother."

"Yes, you have. You all have. The whole town. So many wonderful ladies. The people from the church. I know what you've done."

"They more than I."

"All of you. And it was necessary, because I wasn't here. I just—well, I went off and did my thing."

Nina leaned forward:

"But what a thing, Helen! Interlochen, then on to New York—now this! Everyone is so proud of you, your grandmother most of all."

There was a pause. Finally Helen asked:

"Is she all right, Nina?"

"Hope?"

"Yes. I know she's frail. But last night there were times—of course there was so much confusion, and the reporters, and the lights—but there were times when I wondered whether she—I don't know how to put this—I just wonder if she's all right."

"She's fine, Helen. Really she is."

"Excellent then. So that leaves one other thing to be taken care of."

"And that is?"

"Rehearsals. I think it's been decided that you and Grandmamma are to come to rehearsal next Thursday."

"Next Thursday?"

"Yes, Thursday morning at ten o'clock. We'll be blocking then."

"All right. It will be an honor to come."

"Good. It's just that…"

"What, Helen?"

Helen pursed her lips:

"Nina, this visit to rehearsal has been set up by the Bay St. Lucy newspaper as a kind of publicity event. Hometown girl makes it big, comes back, eager to perform for favorite teacher. You know."

"Well, I can imagine."

"So it must be done. But you also have to understand, we don't have too much time to get this production ready. Only three weeks. And it's going to be filmed, so that adds more pressure."

"Should I not come?"

"You have to come; it's arranged. It's one of those things that can't be changed. And Grandmamma has to come…it's just…"

"Yes?"

A longer pause.

And those deep, enigmatic eyes, darkening.

"Clifton can be very demanding. The last year, my time married to him, it's—it's perhaps not all that one might think. If something happens at rehearsal…"

Like what? Nina found herself thinking.

But the subject died, drifting out to sea like flotsam, while Helen, her thoughts forced elsewhere, looked at her watch.

"I have to go now, Nina. But I can come again, can't I?"

"Of course."

She'd just opened the front door when she asked the question that had probably been on her mind the entire time.

"Nina—"

"Yes, Helen?"

"There is one more person I wanted to ask about."

"Who?"

"Is—well—"

"Go on."

"I wondered about John."

"John Giusti?"

"Yes. I just wondered if he ever—"

"Married? No, Helen, he never did."

She nodded.

"I'm not surprised. Is he still here?"

"Oh yes. He's our vet. His clinic is called 'The Pelican Skeleton.' There's a three foot statue of a pelican outside it, with the bones all showing."

She smiled.

"That's like John."

"You never were in contact with him after you left?"

"No. No, but I—Nina do you think he'd be upset with me if I went by sometime today, just to say hello?"

"I can't imagine John Giusti being upset with anybody. He just doesn't have that kind of personality."

"No, he doesn't, does he. Thank you, Nina."

She descended the stairs, crossed the driveway, and strode away toward town.

That was Nina's first free meal of the day.

The second was to be dinner.

She was not planning to have a free dinner; she was actually planning to have spaghetti and meat sauce, the ingredients of which were safely tucked away in the grocery bag which swung freely beside her leg as she made her way home from Greeley's Market.

Seven thirty.

Sun just beginning to set.

Put the groceries away, go and run—no, why kid yourself, walk—along the beach for a mile or so in the twilight, wave and smile at the tourists, wonder why they let their ten-year-old boys swim what seemed half a mile out in the ocean where they would certainly drown or be eaten by a shark, realize that it was none of her business and that it was in the nature of ten-year-old boys to defy rip tides and marine predators—

—and then cook dinner.

But that was not to happen.

She reached her parking lot just as did a vehicle of some kind, which she heard crunching the shells in the driveway behind her.

She turned, taking note first of the vehicle itself, then of the animals inhabiting it, then of the person driving it.

Vehicle first.

It was not a car/truck/or van so much as a military casualty. It was one of the worst and most battered looking mobile things Nina had ever seen. It was a metal box itself of no color—not white, not gray, not off-green—just the color of death or non-existence, punctuated here and there, in stripes and dots and gashes, with the marks of suffering and violence.

The animals inside it were not dead, however, but merely big. There was what seemed to be either a Labrador retriever or a musk ox panting in a cage which occupied the passenger's side in the front seat; there were two weasels frolicking away in a slightly smaller cage in the far side of the middle seat; and there was a parrot squawking in a bird cage in the rear seat.

John Giusti parachuted out from beneath the steering wheel, holding firmly to the door as he did so, insuring that it did not fall off.

"Nina!"

"Hello, John! What a nice surprise! I'm just getting ready to go upstairs and cook some spaghetti; would you like to join me?"

He shook his head, leaned on what would have been the hood of a normal vehicle but was an indeterminate part of whatever this thing was, and smiled broadly.

"Just the opposite: I wanted to invite you for dinner."

"Pardon?"

"You've never been out to my place."

"No, but—"

"I was at Duncan's down by the dock today. I got twenty four barbequed shrimp. You like barbeque shrimp?"

"Of course, but—"

"It's a bit of a drive, but—I'd really like to have you as my guest."

Nina immediately began speculating on reasons why John Giusti would be inviting her to his home for dinner.

The first reason that came to her mind was that he was sexually attracted to her—despite the thirty year difference in their ages—and was going to attempt to seduce her.

She discarded this reason immediately.

The second reason was that he was simply lonely and wanted conversation.

She looked around in the vehicle and remembered that John, wherever he was at any particular time, was always surrounded with animals, which he loved more than he loved human beings.

So she discarded that possibility.

Then she thought about barbequed shrimp.

Which she craved.

She said to herself:

The heck with it.

And she said to John Giusti:

"Sure."

She could not sit in the front seat because, for various veterinarial reasons, the Labrador could not be moved. (It had something to do with his relationship to the two weasels.) She did not want to sit in the middle of the middle seat, because she did not have or expect to have a good relationship with the weasels either.

So she scrunched against the door, used both hands to move aside an automobile part of some kind that sat—oozing oil onto the plastic covered seat—and gingerly placed it on a pancake thin metal box that sat on the floorboard.

Then she simply listened to the animals chatter, trying once or twice to answer questions put to her by John as they made their way out of Bay St. Lucy.

This did not work, his questions and her replies, her questions and his replies, all sounding something like, "RRRRaaaarghhhh arrrrghhhe rrrgggh!"

And so they gave up.

She simply rode along, wondering from time to time what could be happening, reminding herself that she seldom if ever knew what was happening anyway, and making herself forget the whole thing and just enjoy the ride of what must have been ten miles, along coastal and not-so coastal roads that she'd never explored.

During these miles she entered a kind of coma, the not-quite-conscious state that she could recall experiencing—not without a kind of pleasure—as a child, when taken on long automobile trips in the rain. There was kind of a sound the windshield wipers made—which, like the smell of tomato plants on your hands after you'd picked and prodded at the lush green plants, or the taste of morning when it was a perfect morning—there were all these sensations that both isolated you completely while making you one with something else in the universe that was perfectly rare, utterly impossible to duplicate, and unimaginably common.

So for a time she simply breathed softly on the window glass while the yellow-pine forest wrapped itself around her.

The engine, which had seemed to be exploding at first, was now merely growling. The moon rose, horrible-red and massive—and the highway, now roadway, now dirt path meandered inward and downward.

They'd left the coastline for a few miles, she realized, and were now heading back toward it.

There—something darted across in front of them.

A deer.

Had that been a deer?

It was getting darker. Craning her neck, she could see the stars up through the roof of pine needles. The Mississippi sky was ferocious and black, stars glittering in mute and yellow explosions.

It all remained like this for a period out of time, all changes elemental and thus of great and no importance, until they reached John Giusti's house.

"So here we are!"

"John, this is a great place!" she shouted above the roars and chatters and squawks that had heralded their coming.

She had said the house was great because that was obviously the thing to say in this circumstance. In truth, she could not quite see the house, at least not clearly. But it was certainly far different than she'd imagined it to be. The path from the driveway led up to it, not down, and there were thick shrubs and trees everywhere.

Where was the ocean?

She could hear it, rumbling and grating not more than a few yards over the top of the trees; but she could only see a small yard, and the huge Labrador, released from its cage, jumping on John as he wrestled open the door.

"This is home!"

"How did you find this?"

"I had a client who lived here. I drove out to take care of one of the animals that was too sick to move. Fell in love with the place. The client moved away a few years ago and asked me if I was interested in buying it. I've been here ever since. Look, would you mind waiting outside just a minute or so? There are some animals inside that I need to pen up."

"Definitely pen up the animals."

"It won't take long, and I'm sorry to make you wait..."

"Definitely pen up the animals."

"All right. I'll leave you and this big guy to get to know each other."

He helped Nina down from the van, then strode off toward his house.

She walked a few steps behind him, still quite unable to see the shape of the dwelling, so masked was it by vegetation.

She noticed a bench by the walkway; she sat down upon it and began communicating with the Labrador Retriever.

"Hello, boy," she whispered, petting a head which resembled a bowling ball.

"I love you," replied the dog in its own language, resting the remainder of its head upon her knee and salivating on the hem of her blue jeans.

"What's your name?" she asked, creating several in her mind and rejecting Prince, while the Labrador, breathing as hard as a motionless animal can breathe, answered, also in dog (Nina spoke dog as well as cat; she did not know why, or remember where she had learned the language):

"It doesn't matter; just keep petting me—right there, right on that particular spot on my head, while I drool on the bottom of your pants."

They sat that way for a while, the summer air of the Gulf Coast filling her nostrils with as many aromas as human senses could recognize.

"Rex," she decided, would not work either.

What about 'Marcel?'

No, that was just stupid.

This big, friendly, slobbering beast of a dog could not be named 'Marcel.'

How did other people come up with such clever names?

"Could I be your dog?" importuned Certainly-not-Marcel, gazing up at her with the eyes of a desperate, starving child. "And go ahead, keep petting me—it's SO GOOD!"

"I'll come up with a name," she said, sliding a finger under the animal's leather collar and scratching its neck.

"Who cares?" answered whatever the animal's name was, snuggling closer to her.

"Nina!" came a shout from the house, "You can come on now. Just stay on the concrete path, and don't mind the trees!"

She rose.

The dog, grief stricken, worked his way between her legs, planting a paw the size of a bullfrog atop one of her shoes and driving it into the soft earth.

"That's all right; that's all right, boy."

"No it isn't!" he protested through horrified eyes. "You're LEAVING!"

"Just for a little while."

"NO YOU'LL NEVER COME BACK! I'M KEEPING MY PAW ON YOUR SHOE!"

"Gotta go now, boy. Gotta go!"

And she did, making her way back toward the door of the house, while Marcel ran around and through her like a canine mountain stream.

"Come on through here! It's a little tricky!"

She made her way along a twisting narrow sidewalk, the limbs of pine trees reaching out to brush against her, and she felt as though she were walking through the Black Forest .

Finally the trees gave way and she could see.

"Wow!" she could not help exclaiming.

For there, laid out before her, was a wide, long, pier, at the end of which glowed what would have been a magnificent beach house, had it been on the beach.

It was not.

It was an ocean house, perched as high above the surging waves—twenty feet or so, she judged—as her own shack was perched above the beach.

He stood in the doorway, beckoning.

The house, all vast glass windows, seemed to reflect a thousand images of him, the animals around him, and the sea beneath him.

She started forward, feeling the pier wobble a bit under her, boards swaying ever so slightly as she walked upon it.

The moon, which could be seen just over the jutting roof of the whatever it was because it certainly wasn't a house because houses aren't pure glass and they don't hang suspended high in mid air above the sea—that moon, perfectly jovially white, laughed at her, enjoying her shock at seeing the thing.

"Come on out, Nina! The pier won't fall!"

"John!" she shouted back, trying to make herself heard over the grating and roaring of the waves, which became deeper more sweeping as the water deepened. "John, this is magnificent!"

"It's a good place, isn't it?"

"I've never seen anything like it!"

She turned. The beach was behind her now, narrow but perfectly white, dark pine forests impinging upon it, as though the trees were trying to drive the sand into the water.

"Come in! Come in!"

She stepped inside.

And in so doing she stepped outside.

For there was, strictly speaking, no inside.

There was furniture. Heavy, mahogany, leather, couches tables chairs rugs and things a man would have to sit on and lie on and put things on and have some woman come in from time to time and clean.

But she was still more outside than inside, the vast glass walls magnifying everything on the coast, from birds that skimmed low over the ocean to lights twinkling miles to the south in Isle au Pitre, to slowly moving freighters that made their way like moving oil splotches hurled upon the clean azure evening sky and now oozing horizontally along it—to the waves, always the waves, swelling, throbbing, falling, and rising again, having vowed never to allow stillness to anything in the universe.

"How far out are we, John?"

He beamed.

"Maybe a hundred and fifty feet."

"This is incredible."

"I know. Like I say, I fell in love with it when I saw it."

He was standing in the kitchen—for it was a kitchen, and a modern one, with soft white light coming from a fluorescent tube above the oven, and a vast glass wall to his left showing an epic film version of The Ocean by Moonlight.

"It was supposedly built by an architect who drank himself to death."

"But not while he was designing it, I hope. We're not going to fall into the water are we? The poles aren't going to give way?"

"Haven't yet!"

This place is wonderful!"

And it was. The walls were doors, the roofs were walls, and air seeped in from everywhere, delightfully cool, whispering out of hidden crevasses that served as ventilation ports. There were animals all around, of course, most of them dogs, but cats here or there, and slinking little reptiles that peered around crags in the wall structure or out from gurgling fissures.

"Come on out!"

He opened a massive sliding door and stepped out into empty space.

She followed, expecting to fall to her death, sucked into the surge below.

This did not happen, though, and she soon realized that, if she were in fact to drown, it would be as a result of spray flying up from collisions with the support poles beneath.

John's beaming face glistened with moisture.

"You like it?"

"It's amazing! I didn't know trees came so close to the water."

"The Mississippi coast," he said proudly, "is one of the most diverse in the country, in terms of pure ecology. Forests everywhere."

She realized she was in fact standing on a deck.

She walked closer to the edge of it and craned her neck.

"My God is that a lighthouse?"

"Yep. Quarter of a mile down the beach. It's called Two Mile Point."

"It's dark, though."

"Hasn't been used in three decades. No shipping anywhere around here now. But there are fifteen lighthouses like it on the Mississippi coast, and, except for the one at Biloxi and a couple of others, most people don't even know they exist."

He took two steps toward what Nina took to be a point of no return, leaned over a rock ledge, and flipped a switch that, hanging as it were in mid air, she had failed to notice. Six feet above them a spotlight flashed on, illuminating the sea beneath.

"It's ten or fifteen feet deep here. Look down; when the light hits it, it's so clear, you can see fish."

"I do! Look! That's a big one, just swimming next to the pole. What is that?"

He leaned over farther and seemed to think for a time.

"Hard to say. Could be a sea bass."

Then he looked up, and out toward the horizon, which now was marked by a slender line of lights from the beaches near Gulf Shores.

"Sometimes I sit out here and train the light further out. I've seen Manta Rays, six or seven swimming together, maybe four feet from wingtip to wingtip. Sometimes you see schools of tuna."

He shook his head:

"There are lots of things out there that no one would ever think about. You can't see them from a shallow beach, but here, where it's deep—and where nobody seems to come—I don't know, it just hypnotizes me. Even when there's nothing in that light—just the ways the sea keeps changing color."

She could feel it herself. After the fish disappeared she continued to watch, enjoying the soft stinging of the spray and lulled by the roaring of the relentless waves.

Finally he said:

"I can bring a table out here. Then I'll just heat up the shrimp; we'll have them with a little salad."

He did so, and within some minutes Nina was enjoying her second free meal of the day.

"The shrimp are to die for."

"Yeah. They do a good job at Duncan's. Well, look: Nina, I felt guilty on Tuesday after you brought Furl in."

"Guilty? Why would you feel guilty, John?"

"You've always been one of the people I had the most respect for, and I just…I haven't spent any time with you. I thought I would bring you out here and—well, just ask you how you were doing."

"I'm doing fine, John."

"That's good, that's really good."

They chewed for a time.

The shrimp were really good.

He brought out a jug of iced tea.

It was really good, too.

They ate in silence for a time, he having ascertained that she was in fact doing all right.

Then—finally because Nina was getting tired of waiting—he asked:

"So, how do you think she is?"

"Who, John?"

He looked at her not comprehending the question.

Finally Nina, realizing that it had been a massively stupid question, forgot she had posed it and answered the question as she should have answered it in the first place.

"I think she's fine, John."

"Really?"

"I think so; I'm not actually in a position to know."

"She came into the clinic today."

"Yes. She told me she was going to."

"You talked to her?"

"This morning. She brought me bread."

"That's right, I remember she used to do that. And you think she's really all right?"

"I don't know why she wouldn't be."

But at the same time she could not stop herself from thinking of certain things.

The way Helen had winced as her husband's glare—for there was nothing else to call it—had shot into the back of her neck, telling her—

—well no matter what it was telling her.

The main thing was she had felt it before.

And it hurt.

That and the sense of coldness she'd felt when the man had decided that she, Nina, no longer existed, and thus was not worth spending even a second's worth of time with.

That and Helen, this morning, all smiles, except for a moment's hesitation before saying:

"He taught me how to walk."

What could that have meant?

What kind of a husband feels it necessary to teach his wife to walk?

Everything that Helen had said this morning concerning the rehearsal...

...she is, Nina thought, afraid of her husband.

But she did not say this, answering simply:

"I'm sure she's all right, John."

"Good. If you really feel that way, then—yeah, good. Look!"

He lifted his head and gestured out to sea; then he rose, reached high, and adjusted the spotlight so that it was now pointing some fifty yards out.

The ocean was alive, sparkling, as though a shower of diamonds had been dumped from some low-scudding invisible cloud, and were now being churned about in the incoming waves.

"What's that?"

He shook his head.

"I'm just a veterinarian. It might be shrimp; it might be mullet; it might even be some kind of phosphorescent plant."

"Is that all one plant? Or animal?"

"No. Thousands of—of something."

"What's it doing out there?"

He smiled.

"Just what we're doing here. And what everything else is doing out there—eating."

"You're kidding."

"No. All that brightness, that sparkle—it's just tiny fish or tiny anemones or tiny sardines or tiny crabs or tiny sea urchins, all called together in one circle, because something smaller had been there before in a similar circle—just waiting to be eaten."

"Amazing."

"You fixed us up, remember?"

"What?"

"Helen and I—you got us together."

"How could I have done that?"

"That September; sophomore year."

"John, that was a long time ago."

He shook his head.

"It was yesterday."

"All right, it was yesterday a long time ago. What did I do that was so important?"

"Want some more shrimp?"

She shook her head.

"Suddenly, watching that feeding frenzy going on out there, I'm beginning to lose my appetite."

"Don't. It's just nature."

"I suppose," she said, taking a sip of iced tea. "Unless you're the thing being eaten. Then it's nature plus a little more."

"You asked us to do a report together. Write about whether Oedipus was innocent or guilty."

"Oh yes. I do remember something about that assignment."

"We went over to her house and sat out in the garden. We argued. I can't remember which side I took. Anyway, that was our first date. We went out together for two more years. I was thinking so hard about proposing to her. I knew I should wait through our senior year though. Now I think about it and...I mean, if I had, maybe Interlochen wouldn't have happened. But of course she would have just had a life here. None of New York would have happened either. It's just me, being selfish. But Nina..."

"Yes?"

"Do you think it would be all right if I saw her again?"

She looked at him.

The vast silver circus of feeding and sparkling that had been staged simply for their benefit had disappeared.

The spotlight now illuminated only turquoise swells, darker blue, lighter green, now almost black.

"I don't know, John. That has to be up to you. Just...you have to realize she probably isn't the same person you knew five years ago."

He was looking at the same blank spot in the ocean, as though waiting for the lights and the spectacle to begin all over.

"Of course. It's just—"

"Just what?"

"When she came by today—well, it was just to make small talk."

"A normal thing."

He shook his head.

"I don't think she's all right."

"Why not?"

"I don't know. I got to know Helen very well. I know about her ambition. I know her expressions. I know when she's—"

He hesitated.

"When she's what, John?"

Then he shook his head.

"It's like," he whispered, "out there in the water. I can tell when something's happening. I just can't tell always, what it is."

"Helen's not out in the water, John. She's not being eaten by anything."

He simply looked at her and said quietly:

"I think she is."

There was silence for a time.

During the rest of the dinner and during the ride home they talked about other things.

Nina forgot what they were.

CHAPTER 8: THE IMPORTANCE OF E:14

The following Thursday Nina attended a rehearsal of *Hamlet.*

She was never to forget it.

There was, of course, a most obvious reason why she would not—and could not—forget it.

But there were other things, too.

She could not forget how two major rooms in the old Robinson mansion had been melded together, their ceilings obliterated, their walls and windows darkened—in order to make a stage reminiscent of the one she and Frank had seen in Chicago, where they'd spent their tenth wedding anniversary.

Lights everywhere, all of them high over the stage, pointing in different directions out of black shiny tubes that looked like weaponry.

In the back of the stage, a back wall and behind that another back wall and above that ten back walls that could be dropped from ropes and pulleys and various mechanical wonders.

No, these things she would not forget.

But also not to be forgotten was the fact that this was not community theater.

She'd never acted in any of the community plays done by Alana Delafosse and her minions, nor in any of the plays done in Bay St. Lucy before her coming. But she'd helped out. She'd been on the refreshment committee or the publicity committee or the costume committee or the parking committee or the sets committee or the animals committee or the prompters committee—

—because a small town—its churches, its schools, its government, the very fabric of its existence—cannot exist without committees.

So Nina was always on one committee or another, whatever the time of year, whatever the holiday, whatever the festivity, or whatever the time of grief.

She'd been on committees for *Oklahoma, South Pacific, Streetcar Named Desire, My Fair Lady, Cabaret, Harvey, Arsenic and Old Lace, Desire Under the Elms* (which the community had not liked very much), and, for several Christmases running, the combined church choirs' production of Handel's *Messiah*.

But it was always very different.

People mingled and had coffee and laughed. Somehow rehearsing got done.

But a good deal was eaten and there was uproarious laughter, and there was much gossiping.

Here, even as she entered, propping up Hope with a palm under an elbow until they found seats in a far back corner, here it was different.

In the first place, she could not tell the men from the women.

It was not a question of being gay or not, for Bay St. Lucy, artistic community that it was, had long since dealt with this question with a casual wave of the community's hand and the words:

"As long as it doesn't hurt anybody…"

—no, it was something different.

These people all existed in a world in which sex did not exist, or at least during working hours. They all looked the same. Their hair was the same. It was a little too short in the women (if those were women up there) and a little too long in the men (if people with skin like that could be called men). They had on what at first seemed enormous amounts of clothing; but, since the temperature was always 72 degrees in this sarcophagus of a theater, that would have been impossible due to the probability of heat stroke. No, this clothing was not remarkable because of its excess but because of its bagginess. The sweaters melted into the shirts which melted into the pants which melted into the one thing everybody had on that was precisely the same, that being brown sandals.

"This is so exciting!" whispered Hope.

"I know. For me, too."

There were more differences. For one thing, there was no conviviality here. People did not eat. There was no anteroom where a huge coffee pot had been set up. True, there were a few isolated small cups of coffee being sipped from time to time—it was, after all, ten thirty in the morning—but the knots of genderless beings huddled in different parts of the stage, and, high above, back in the balcony, and, over there, by the very last seat in the first row—were not laughing and were not here for fun.

They spoke very quietly and intensely, pointing here and there, and carrying notebooks, which they seemed constantly to be fighting for, as though everyone had written something down to which the others had been denied—and desperately needed—access.

"What," asked Hope, bending to whisper in Nina's ear, "scene will they be rehearsing?"

"I overheard someone at the entrance say Act I, Scene 3. That's Polonius's big scene with his son, Laertes."

"Oooh, I see. Is Helen in it?"

"Yes, it's Ophelia's first scene."

And the scene did in fact come together.

She watched as various main players detached themselves from the groups they'd been conversing with, and gravitated toward the stage, onto which they climbed with a kind of trepidation, warily scanning and then assaulting it, as Mrs. Throckmorton had assaulted the community theater piano some six weeks earlier.

There, young and virile, gray sweater, dark hair, sideburns—that must have been Laertes.

Yes, he had just flashed Laertes' smile.

And there, entering from stage right, slightly baggier, slightly darker gray sweater, sandals flopping just a bit, hair the exact shaggy style as everyone else within sight but starting to turn white—or was that dye? No one knew with these people—that must have been Polonius.

"Look Nina! There she is!"

And it was true. Helen Reddington had materialized as a ghost materializes, standing completely motionless, an Ophelia-statue in her sweater-slacks uniform, center stage, but as far back as she could plant herself.

Her eyes were closed.

She simply stood, breathing.

It was as though she were meditating.

She saw nothing, nor seemed to look at anything around her.

She looked, Nina found herself thinking, so small.

Then, movement from behind them.

She turned, as did Hope, as did the few other people seated in the audience, as did all of the other people hanging above the audience, or working behind blinking electronic consoles overlooking the audience, or wherever else they might have been or whatever else they might have been doing in relationship to the audience.

For into the theater had walked Clifton Barrett.

He strode down the center aisle.

"Clifton."

"Morning Clifton."

"Hello Clifton."

All of these comments were directed toward—by people who happened to be sitting or standing or kneeling or reading or conferring or scribbling or whatever else—three feet of the man's path.

He made no gesture of recognition to any of them.

He simply strode to the stage, mounted it, and took control of it.

All of the groups on stage were now doing something or other in relation to him.

He had become the sun; they no longer worked but orbited.

He looked, she thought, quite different than he had the last time she'd seen him.

Smaller, but...

Somehow that did not matter.

No scarf now; but no sweater either. He was a slender man, not quite six feet tall. His black hair glistened like a raven's in the floodlights that poured down on the stage; he had a pencil-thin goatee which descended to the point of a dagger just below the cleft in his chin.

He was dressed in elegant simplicity—white dress shirt, superbly pressed, with gold cuff links.

He took from the pocket of this shirt a pair of wire rimmed glasses, whose frames were barely detectable, and he moved his face toward or farther from each sheet of paper that was shown him, while he either nodded or scowled or shook his head or nodded curtly.

He did not smile.

Finally, like debris sucked down into various drain spouts, the superfluous people on and around the stage huddled together and prepared to do what they had to do while Polonius said good bye to his son and Ophelia said good bye to her brother.

"Ready?"

This was the first audible word Nina had heard from Clifton Barrett, and it was directed not at the three actors who stood around him but at two monstrous green eyes glowing in the balcony.

"We're ready," answered either the eyes or some spirits of the machine that had hidden themselves behind them.

"Run the block code once through, all right?"

"All right."

These mysterious voices continued, and it hardly came as a surprise that they spoke an incomprehensible language.

"Line 867-1,098 Polonius will be R-21, move to O-56 on 965, finish M-32."

The four figures on the stage stared at the area around their feet, as though they expected snakes to crawl up their legs.

Finally, there seemed to be general agreement, and nodding of heads.

Clifton Barrett raised his gaze to the balcony and said.

"All right so far. Go on."

And the same type of gibberish continued to rain down.

"Laertes' lines 1,125-1,246 will be M-46, finishing O-18. Ophelia's lines…"

Etc. etc.

"What," asked Hope in a whisper, "are they doing?"

Nina shook her head.

"I'm not sure, Hope. I think they're blocking the scene."

"What does that mean?"

"They're making sure of where everyone has to stand when a certain line is delivered."

"Is it that important, as long as the audience can see them?"

"I think it is because—oh I don't know, Hope, but it may be that those lights in the balcony are from TV cameras. They're not just going to perform this play. They're going to film it."

"Yes, I know."

"It's costing everybody a lot of money; but it all has to be perfect. When the camera thinks Laertes is going somewhere, he's got to be there. Exactly there."

"Well, I wonder what would happen if…"

"Wait, Hope! I think they're starting!"

"All right."

Astonishing, absolute quietness.

Polonius speaking to Laertes:

"And these few precepts in thy memory, see though character…"

Then the great speech; *costly thy habit, neither borrower nor lender…*

Polonius himself was not giving the lines though, nor was there being made on the part of the actor any effort to call the old man forth. These lines were spoken without dialect, dryly, with no emotion, flat affect.

Important to each actor, Nina could finally see, was only position.

To the right of Laertes and just slightly between his shoulder and the audience.

Now circling him…

…coming to a stop just there, stage right, so that Laertes must bend slightly to hear.

Now in motion again, making circular gestures with a long staff that he was not actually carrying at the time.

And all the time Clifton Barrett, some ten feet away, looking hard into Polonius' eyes, then turning and gazing at the balcony, from which Nina could see, from time to time, behind the great green eyes, a positive hand wave or an encouraging gesture.

Until, those last great lines:

"This above all—to thine own self be true…"

And, while saying this line, this crucially important line—Polonius forgot where to go.

He hesitated ever so slightly, and stepped to his right.

Pause.

Voice from the balcony:

"No. J32."

There was silence onstage for a moment.

Finally Clifton Barrett pursed his lips and said quietly, to the man who was standing no more than three feet from him.

"Do you understand J32?"

"Yes, Clifton."

"Do you know what that means?"

A slight smile, then a nod.

"Do you?"

"Yes, Clifton."

"Point it out for me, please."

Absolute silence in the theater.

The sound of Polonius' feet as he turned, pointing to a spot on the stage behind him.

"There."

"Are you certain?"

"Yes, Clifton."

"Are you sure you understand what you're supposed to do, and where you're supposed to go?"

"I do."

"You do?"

"Yes."

"You definitely do? Because you didn't, only some seconds ago. Where did you think you were going?"

Silence.

The question repeated:

"Where the hell did you think you were going?"

"Sorry Clifton."

"You're sorry?"

"Yes. Won't happen again."

"Are you certain of that?"

'Yes."

"Yes what?"

"Yes, I'm certain."

"That's good! That's good to hear."

Then Clifton Barrett took a long step forward and bellowed straight into the man's face, which now had begun to blush vividly:

"Because we open IN TWELVE DAYS, YOU BUFFOON!"

Silence again, except for the shout, echoing through the theater.

"If you want us to run through it again, Clifton…"

A shake of the head.

"No. You obviously don't know what you're doing. Let's move on."

And they did.

Oh my God, thought Nina.

Oh my God.

Clifton Barrett nodded to Laertes, who said:

"most humbly do I take my leave, my Lord."

Somehow, the actor who was to play his father, and who had just been completely humiliated, managed to go on, replying gamely:

"The time invites you. Go your servants tend."

Laertes to Helen Reddington:

"Farewell, Ophelia; and remember well what I have said to you."

To which Helen, replying:

"This in my memory locked; and you yourself shall keep the key of it."

Laertes:

"Farewell."

Laertes exits, stage left.

Polonius:

"What is't Ophelia, he has said to you?"

Ophelia:

"So please you, something touching…"

Voice from the balcony:

"No."

Silence.

The voice again:

"No, it's K-14. It's K-14, Helen."

No one breathing.

Two steps from Clifton Barrett, who was now standing directly before his wife.

And with a quick deft motion, his right arm jerking upward, he slapped her hard on the right cheek.

POP.

"Oh!"

Nina did not know if the short burst of air and sound had come from herself, or from the collective crew, or from Helen, who now stood motionless as the statue she had been to begin the scene—

—or from Hope Reddington, whose hands now covered her mouth, and whose eyes were wide with horror.

Clifton Barrett wheeled, leapt down from the stage, and strode out of the theater.

And that, Nina thought to herself, explains the rouge.

They sat there for some instants.

There was nothing to do.

Finally, Helen having disappeared backstage, and the various crews beginning to mill and worry and chatter as they had been doing, Hope said quietly:

"Perhaps we should go now, Nina."

"Yes. Good idea."

They rose and made their way out of the theater, then out of the mansion, then into a waiting huge car driven by one of the ubiquitous ladies who always seemed prepared to drive Hope—and anyone with Hope—anywhere she needed to go.

"So how was the rehearsal?" said the woman driving.

"Oh fine," said Hope, who seemed perfectly at ease.

"Hope—" began Nina, not knowing exactly where she was going with whatever it was she was going to say to an eighty year old woman who'd just seen her granddaughter physically assaulted...

...but she did not have to say anything, for Hope interrupted her like a cheerful little blue and babbling stream flowing into a muddy and stagnant river.

"It's remarkable," she said, "how complicated it all is. All of the things they have to remember."

"Yes, it is."

"Thank you for coming with me, Nina."

"It was my pleasure."

"I hope we were not in the way."

"I'm sure we weren't."

Then they were silent.

They remained silent until the car disgorged both of them; Nina made sure Hope was safely in the house; the two women had made the necessary conversation leading to parting; and Nina found herself, Vespa putt-putting dependably along, traversing the Mean Streets of Bay St. Lucy.

Oh my God oh my God oh my God, she found herself thinking, while wondering whether to turn on Coastal Boulevard or keep sputtering along Bay Drive or stop and get coffee somewhere—or just drive straight into the sea and drown and get the whole thing over with.

What could Hope be thinking now?

Nina, Nina, Nina...

...Nina, should you have left the woman alone to wander up the stairs into that bedroom to stare at the pictures of a sixteen year old girl who had at one time seen her entire life in front of her?

...but what could you have said, if you had stayed?

What was there to be said?

That slap—a brutal slap, the sound of it having echoed through the space, as it was echoing now through Nina's brain—

—and the thing about it that was worse, that being the knowledge that it was almost certainly not the only one of its kind.

There had been others before it.

There before her loomed Margot's shop, and there out of the shop loomed Margot, who, perceiving Nina, smiled and waved and thus brought back into the world some semblance of normality.

"How did it go?"

She parked the Vespa, locked it, stored her helmet, and straightened.

Margot was about to get into her Volkswagen.

"How was the rehearsal, Nina?"

It was, she did not say, the worst single experience of my entire life. She continued not saying, I don't think I will ever get over it. Furthermore, she did not add, I'm going to be sick to my stomach and I may never sleep again, because I will keep having nightmares about that insufferable jerk humiliating that beautiful and fragile young woman there fifteen feet in front of her aging grandmother.

She did not say any of these things.

"It was okay," is what she did say.

"Good. Want to come with me? I'm visiting a few studios around town. Stock is getting a bit bare, and I need to buy some pieces."

"I'd love to come."

"Good. Get in."

She did, immensely grateful to have something to do, and also wondering if she and Hope had been the only citizens of Bay St. Lucy to have seen the slap, everyone else being 'theater people' and thus unable to communicate with the town itself.

"We'll pop by Laura Redmond's studio first. She does divine things. They keep selling, too. Then we'll head over to Bob Fiske's place. He told me he'd be throwing a few more clay pots this morning. Those always move nicely. Then we'll..."

Thank heaven, thought Nina.

Margot had been in her shop all morning.

The slap had taken place, when?

She looked at her watch.

Fifty-five minutes ago.

If Margot, bustling about in the center of Gossip Center Bay St. Lucy, had not heard about it, no one had.

Which meant it did not exist.

It had not happened.

So Nina could allow herself to be drawn into the same flow of meaningless chatter she always engaged in with Margot and avoid using a string of profanities to describe Clifton Barrett, because she hated profanities and never used them anyway.

But then, thinking back on what she'd seen, perhaps that was a mistake.

One or two choice profanities right now…

They turned into Laura Redmond's driveway.

Then they were in Laura Redmond's shop, gazing at the paintings that were hung and were propped up and were hidden and were half finished and were just being started and were—at least three of them—just purchased by Margot and destined to be delivered to her shop the following day.

Then they were somewhere else

Clay pots were all around them.

Except Nina was nowhere other than that accursed theater, which kept drawing her mind back into it.

The worst thing about it, she decided…

…oh hell, there was no single worst thing about it. It was all worst.

But one of the contenders for Worst Thing in the Universe Ever Prize was the fact that Clifton Barret and his quick short brutal right cross to the jaw had ruined *Hamlet* forever.

"Oh that this too too solid flesh could…"

SLAP!

"To be or not to…"

SLAP!

"The air bites shrewdly; it is very cold."

SLAP!

"My hour is almost come, when I to sulphurous and tormenting flames…"

SLAP!

And then they were gone and on their way to some other place.

It was just in front of this other place, where they'd just gotten out of the car, that Helen Reddington found them.

At first, she thought that Helen had simply materialized, as she had seemed to do on stage some hours earlier.

But then she saw a bicycle, a sole bicycle, in the rack beside the door, and knew how the materialization had been accomplished.

"Helen!" exclaimed Margot. "Helen, Nina has been telling me how much she enjoyed the rehearsal!"

Let's see, thought Nina, *how good an actress you really are.*

Helen beamed.

"We were happy to have her there! Yes, yes, I think things are coming together nicely!"

Pretty damned good. Pretty damned good.

"Nina…"

"Yes, Helen?"

"I wondered if…well, I wondered if we might talk a bit."

Margot, sensing the 'in private' that hung two feet above a small mimosa tree and seemed to have nowhere to go or anything to do, dissipated it by saying:

"I'm going to be inside here for a time; why don't the two of you wander through that magnificent jungle of statuary in the back, and chat there?"

Which is what they did.

It took them some time to make their way through a maze of hedges that guarded whatever ramshackle center of craft and hand wizardry that Margot had now brought them to—for Nina had now lost track of their comings and goings and had no idea where they were—but get through it they did, and they were rewarded by the sight of a massive football field of statuary lying seemingly discarded in front of them.

"Good grief, look at all this!" Nina found herself whispering.

Helen, younger and therefore more cynical, simply moved her head from side to side, narrowing her gaze.

They took several steps forward, then more steps, until finally they were surrounded by what would certainly have been the largest most massive, most wonderful cemetery lawn in the world except that there were no dead people under it.

To begin with, there were birdbaths. Big birdbaths, wide birdbaths, petite little cute birdbaths, ornate birdbaths, Greek birdbaths, simple rustic birdbaths, birdbaths for eagles, romantic and flowery birdbaths, obscene and dirty and vulgar birdbaths—it seemed such a shame, Nina found herself wondering, that, just as there were apparently no corpses buried in the most wonderful graveyard in the world, there were also no birds bathing in the thousand million or more swimming pools that had, by dint of light gray limestone and loving workmanship, been offered up to them.

Perhaps because there was no water.

There were not only birdbaths, of course.

There were tiny little concrete rabbits the size and shape of bowling balls with frozen ears; there were ornamental flowers weighing fifty pounds apiece. There were little shepherd boys and girls, ogling each other, and there were lambs and cows and deer and dogs and cats and animals of indeterminate nature.

There, far across the—what? Yard? Football field? Memorial Park?—at any rate there across it was a monstrous concrete horse, at least ten feet high, and certainly able to hold the entire Greek army, which was just waiting until another Troy could be built for the chance to jump out and wreak havoc.

Somehow they found themselves attracted to this beast, and had been making their way toward it for some time, avoiding rock toad frogs that had somehow made their way onto the narrow sidewalks, when Helen said:

"I went to Margot's shop after rehearsal. Well, no...I went home first and made sure Grandmamma was all right. Then I went to the shop. They gave me a list of the places you and she might be going this afternoon. Finally, I got lucky."

"Well, I..."

There was nothing to say, of course, and so she simply let the sentence die, aware as it expired of the somnolent growling of an airplane engine high above them.

Nina looked up. There, circling lazily overhead, was a World War I vintage biplane pulling behind it a large red banner upon which had been written, in old English script, the words HOT SAUSAGE!

How strange, she found herself thinking, as she stared out over the field of monuments around her. *How strange it all is.*

"Nina, I wanted to explain to you about...well, about what you saw today."

"You don't have to do that, Helen."

"I want to."

"It's really not any of my business."

"I know you must be concerned. I'm sorry you had to see that."

Again, nothing to say.

The horse grew larger as they approached it.

The airplane continued to circle.

"My world is difficult to describe. Clifton can be...well he can be quite demanding."

They reached a strange and distrustful looking oasis in the desert of statuary. Tropical palms of some sort now ringed around them. There was a wrought iron table with two chairs.

An unseen power pulled them to the table and forced them to sit down.

"When I arrived in New York—my God, what was I, nineteen? I had one year at Interlochen, but even after that I knew nothing. Nothing at all. I got hired by a repertory house off off off off Broadway—so far off Broadway it was probably in Illinois or at least it seemed that far. It was actually New Jersey, as I told you a few days ago. The subway didn't even go out there. But anyway, someone told Clifton about me and he came to watch a performance. After that, it all changed."

"I'm sure it did."

"After that...well, the world was different."

Silence for a time.

Then...

You have to ask it, Nina.

You have to ask it.

"Does he hit you often?"

"I need...I need discipline."

"You need what?"

"Discipline."

"That's what was happening today? That's what we saw? Discipline?"

'Yes."

"Helen, your husband hit you."

"I deserved it."

"You what?"

"I deserved it. We're twelve days from opening. Missing a spot like that—professionals can't do that. Not in Bay St. Lucy, not on Broadway, not in London—I think it may have been Paul—the actor playing Polonius—I think Paul may have thrown me off. Or having Grandmama in the audience. I don't know. But I deserved to be slapped."

"No you didn't."

"Nina...artists, at the highest level...well, there has to be a..."

"Divorce him."

"What?"

"Divorce him."

"Nina, he's all that's ..."

"Divorce him. Right now. This minute."

"Hey, you two!"

This from Margot, who was making her way along the paths toward them.

"We've got to go! I've got four more shops to visit!"

Nina rose.

So did Helen.

"Divorce him, Helen."

Whereupon Helen Reddington looked at her, shook her head, slowly, and said:

"I can't."

Then she turned and walked away.

During the following shop visits, and the ride back to Margot's, and the ride back to her own shack, Nina could think of only one good thing about the entire situation.

That was the fact that no one in Bay St. Lucy knew that Helen had been slapped, except for Nina and Hope.

She arrived home to find John Giusti's van parked in her driveway.

John himself was sitting on her top step.

He rose as she ascended the stairs, looked down at her, and asked:

"Did he hit her?"

Nina hesitated for a second.

John asked again:

"Did he hit her?"

"Yes," she answered.

He walked past her down the stairs, got into his vehicle, and drove away.

"Oh, bloody hell," she whispered.

She found herself wondering if she had any gin.

CHAPTER 9: THE AUTOGRAPH HUNTER

Nina spent most of the rest of the evening and all of the following day waiting to hear that John Giusti had assaulted Clifton Barrett.

This news did not come.

Clifton Barrett was in fact assaulted.

Just not by John Giusti.

The assault took place in the following manner:

The new income pouring into the town, plus news of its soon-to-be status of The French Riviera reborn into The Southern Mississippi Cannes Summer Festival—had lured various art entrepreneurs to attempt new ventures, some of which only a few months earlier might have been deemed imprudent, unwise, or just ridiculously stupid.

But people, Nina had surmised upon hearing of the plan, often did stupid things, and if a young man from somewhere in New Mexico wanted to open a coffee house/wine cabaret/cinema playhouse, featuring foreign films (especially French foreign films) in the upstairs portion of The Stink Shoppe (two hundred yards down the street from Margot's own emporium)—why, that was his business.

It might even have been a good idea.

At any rate, people such as she and Margot were the kind of citizens who needed to patronize French films, if such films were ever to gain their rightful place in the hearts of the people of southern Mississippi; and so they planned to go together to the Wednesday evening performance of Claudel Desmoulins' *Le Renouvillier*, a work which purported to be fabulous entertainment for anyone who enjoyed the films of Alfred Hitchcock.

Nina had always enjoyed the films of Alfred Hitchcock.

Dial M for Murder.

North by Northwest.

Psycho.

(Well, *Psycho* was a little scary, and there was that scene in the shower, which had caused Nina to take only baths for several years…but which was now stored far enough back in her memory bank that it did not directly affect her life, except for the troublesome fact that she almost had a heart attack every time Furl nosed open the bathroom door and came in to use the litter box while she was taking a shower, making her expect a tall shadow to appear outside of the shower curtain, and an otherwise prim churchgoing woman to start hacking at her with a butcher knife and screaming: "EEEEEEEEEEEE! EEEEEEEEE! EEEEEEEEEE!"

So 7:30 on the evening in question found the two of them at their tables. There were no rows and no theater chairs, just small circular tables that might have come from the Rue Montparnasse and upon which had been placed the small glasses of Chardonnay they had ordered.

They had not talked a great deal during the course of an afternoon spent selling some of the newer purchased items that now graced the walls and nooks and crevices and porticos and junctures and door jambs of Elementals: Treasures from the Sea and Earth.

There were, when one thought about it, only two things to talk about.

They learned about the less important thing at 3:30 in the afternoon when Officer Moon Rivard (head of Bay St. Lucy's police department) parked his squad car in the parking lot, waddled up the driveway (Moon was not an obese man, although he had a kind of barrel chest; it was just that his short and powerful legs resembled parentheses rather than human limbs, and turned what would have been 'walk' for most people into 'waddle' for him)—and approached the shop.

He smiled broadly upon entering. He bent as he passed through the doorway—a fact which always surprised Nina, since the top of his head was two feet shorter than the door itself)—and he made his announcement somewhat like a father who'd just learned of the birth of his healthy child.

"Did you ladies hear?"

Oh God, thought Nina.

She hated it when people said that.

One of the possible answers was always: 'Hear what?'

But that sounded so dumb.

And, whatever it turned out to be, whatever it was, she had not in fact heard of it.

So why bother with that answer?

The better answer was the one she gave Moon Rivard now.

"No."

His smile became broader, and the wild, iron gray-eyebrows which sat atop his gleaming blue eyes like barbed wire protecting beach fortifications, seemed to glow somehow, as though the excitement inherent in BRINGING NEWS had electrified it.

Anyone who touched it during this one instant would have been shocked.

"Hurricane!"

Well, Nina found herself thinking, that's just the hell what we need.

A hurricane.

Helen Reddington's husband beats her.

John Giusti is probably going to kill him for it.

It's her fault, for having told John Giusti about it.

And we're having a hurricane.

That's just the hell what we need.

Margot took a step forward and placed the object she was holding—a thing that was golden and black, but had no function that Nina could recognize—on a thing that Nina could not recognize either, and said:

"This is the first we've heard."

Moon nodded.

"Just got word from the Weather Service. Named Deborah. Hurricane Deborah."

"It's coming here?"

"Naw."

He shook his head and stared at the things around him, much like a diver might look at the long sunken artifacts of a lost civilization.

"Naw, they think it will hit over by the Florida panhandle. They're warning Pensacola."

"I see. When?"

"Couple of days, the way it's looking now. I thought I might drive around town and let people know though: if it follows the path it seems to be on now, and grows a little— they think it will—we might get some heavy rain on Friday and Saturday."

"Flooding?"

"Don't know. All the shops that have basements, though—well, be good not to have something too valuable down there. If it's two, three inches of rain, there'll be lots of runoff. You might want to warn your boarders. Shouldn't panic or have to leave town. Nobody's evacuating or nothing. But it won't be very good down on the beach, and the fishing boats will be moored up tight. Those are two days when folks might want to rent a movie, maybe just stay in their rooms."

And so there was that bit of news.

It produced little conversation between Margot and Nina, neither of whom knew anything to say about hurricanes and both of whom avoided mentioning the weather except to say "A tornado is coming!"—which it clearly was not.

As for the other bit of news—

—it was, of course, the fact that Clifton Barrett had struck his wife.

Nobody knew how this information had leaked out.

Nina had thought it might remain a "Production Company Secret" until John Giusti had questioned her about it the previous day.

But of course that would have been too much to expect.

Somebody had talked.

Or maybe not.

Maybe 'news' was like late-spring pollen, which, try as you might, could not be kept out of people's hair and off their breakfast tables.

But the strange thing about this 'news' was that it had not been allowed to turn into gossip.

There were, even in towns as inquisitive as Bay St Lucy, untouchable subjects.

No one, incredibly, talked about it.

It was as though the minister's zipper were down.

It must be noticed; could not be missed; was horrible to contemplate; and foretold dire consequences.

But there was simply no appropriate time in which to talk about it, and no words with which it could adequately be expressed.

No one was going to stand up during the scripture reading from Second Timothy and shout: "Zip up!"

Anyone who had, during the first minutes of The Fellowship Hour, started a conversation with the words, "Did you notice that Brother Daniels had forgotten to…"

…would have been stared down, and would have been forced to return home for the afternoon carrying an unopened bowl of green beans and French onion sauce.

And so, time had hung on their hands.

And so they found themselves here, waiting for Alfred Hitchcock to begin speaking French.

The film began.

A few characters, two at first, then two more, entered an apartment.

They sat down on a couch where they began smoking cigarettes and talking.

They continued to talk for twenty minutes.

After thirty minutes Nina went to sleep.

She awoke to find Margot punching her in the knee.

"Wake up."

"What?"

"Wake up."

"Where am I?"

"The Cinema Verite."

"The what?"

"The Cinema Verite."

"There is no such thing."

"Of course there is; we're in it."

"Doing what?"

"We just watched a movie, Nina!"

"You're kidding."

"No, it's over now and we have to go."

"What was it about?"

Margot was tugging and pulling and hauling at her now, and so she rose.

"What was it about?"

"I don't know, Nina."

"Why don't you know?"

"I was asleep."

"You too?"

"Yes."

"I thought you were just concentrating."

"I was concentrating for a while, then I went to sleep."

"Why didn't you say something?"

"I thought *you* were concentrating."

"What time is it?"

"Ten-thirty."

"Ten thirty? We slept for two hours?"

"Well. We had a hard day."

They were descending the stairway now leading down into the 'foyer,' which was really The Stink Shop, which sold bizarre dresses the size of handkerchiefs, and which was now closed.

They made their way outside, moving slowly in a line of movie-watchers who were all rubbing their eyes and looking at their watches.

"That was the worst thing," said Nina, "I've ever seen in my life."

"You didn't see it; you slept through it."

"Yes, but I could hear it in my sleep. They just kept talking and talking and talking…"

"Don't think about it."

"Why did you make me do that?"

"Me? You're the one who suggested it!"

"Did not!"

"Did so!"

"What," asked Nina, feeling somewhat faint and wishing that the hurricane had struck some two hours ago and abolished the building, "can we do now?"

Margot's response was immediate.

"Let's go get drunk."

"Where?"

"Doesn't matter."

And so they went to get drunk.

(This meant, invariably, that they would allow themselves two drinks apiece, and that Nina's would consist mostly of papayas or strawberries or crème de menthe or apple strudel or whatever needed to be added to mask the unpleasant taste of alcohol, while Margot, sipping a martini or a Scotch on the rocks, would make fun of her.)

But the phrase, 'Let's go get drunk!' was such an enjoyable thing to say that it invariably made her wish she'd been a 'bad' girl in high school, and had done more than spend innumerable nights studying, so that she could now be a retired English teacher.

They decided to drive out to McGee's Landing, which was an improbable place on the 'Bay' side of the community. It lay on the far side of a great earthen levee which kept the Bayou Fourche out of the town, and it tripled as a slightly disreputable bar nights, an unhealthy restaurant afternoons, and the Center for Swamp Tours! mornings.

It had very little fame except for its drink menus.

It offered a remarkable variety of alcoholic beverages, a fact which delighted the fruit loving Nina and appalled Margot.

It was dimly lit now as they entered it, walking beneath a huge stuffed alligator which had been clamped by massive concrete rods to the wall above the door.

They were taken to a table by a window that overlooked the bay.

The water was placid in the moonlight, and lamps glowed on various platforms or fishing huts that dotted the murky, moss laden, swamp surrounding them.

Menus soon sat before them.

"What are you going to drink?" asked Margot.

"Let's see what they've got."

Margot ordered a gin, which came immediately, along with a small glass of tonic water.

She splashed a drop or so of the tonic water into the gin and then asked Nina:

"So what are you ordering?"

"I'm investigating the menu."

"I hate it when you do this."

"Oh, be quiet."

"You're the worst person to drink with I've ever known."

"Look. I can get a Bacon Old Fashioned, with either Gran Classico or Curacao as an inversion."

"Nina, do you even know what an inversion is?"

"Of course I do; it's when you put one of the things over the other. Or I might want a Green Chartreuse. That's served with either Strega or Branca Menta. And look, they have Dolin Blanc Vermouth."

"You may need to sit at a different table."

"There's also…"

She was interrupted by Margot, who was gazing across the room, at a corner booth.

"Will you look at that."

"What?"

"There. Over there."

She forced herself to look up from the menu which, had she been forced to admit it, had in fact begun to sound like dialogue from the film she'd just slept though.

"What?"

"Look who's here."

Then she recognized the couple.

The man was Clifton Barrett.

The woman—blonde-haired and radiant and gorgeously attired, with diamonds or something else sparkly hanging around her neck and over her bosom—was Constance Briarworth.

"His first Queen Gertrude," whispered Nina, in a kind of awe.

She'd seen the woman at the party in the Reddington's garden.

But that was from a distance.

The effect was much more intense now.

"How nice," said Margot, "and they seem to be having such a good time."

They were in fact, Nina realized, sitting on the same side of the booth.

And laughing.

And laughing louder.

She at whatever he was saying.

He at whatever she was saying.

And then they were holding hands.

Then he had cupped his hands behind her neck.

And pulled her head gently toward his.

And kissed her, lightly on the lips,

After which they began laughing again.

"This is an excellent chance," Margot said, "to get an autograph."

Nina stared at her.

"What?"

"Oh, I'm an inveterate autograph hunter."

"Margot, don't…"

"Do you have a pen?"

"No. NO! Margot…"

"Come on! I'll get one for you, too!"

"Are you crazy?"

"Come on; bring your drink! I'm sure they're going to want us to join them. Oh, that's right; you don't have a drink yet, do you? Well, no matter, I'll take mine over."

"Margot, sit down!"

For Margot was in fact standing up, her gin and tonic in one hand, a menu in the other.

Worse—much worse—Nina was, inexplicably, standing up too, and now following Margot across the room.

She found herself asking mentally how large the restaurant's floor was, and how long it would take them, given the length of Margot's storklike strides, to reach Clifton Barrett's booth.

Not long at all in fact.

As it turned out, they were there now.

With Margot beaming down and saying:

"What an honor! Mr. Barrett?"

Who looked up, half smiled, and said:

"I'm sorry. I don't believe I've..."

"I'm Margot Gavin. Big fan of yours."

"Well, that's fine. It's just that..."

"I wondered if I might have an autograph!"

"I...well, certainly, if you have a ..."

"Where's your wife?"

Silence.

Everyone in the restaurant was looking at them now.

The smile disappeared from Clifton Barrett's face.

"I think it probably inappropriate to..."

Then Margot threw the drink in his face.

Swoosh.

A small sound. A smattering of ice and liquid.

Which now was oozing from his glasses.

There was a gasp from the people who'd been customers of the restaurant, and now were spectators at the drama.

He breathed very deeply, took off his glasses, and began to dry them with the napkin that had sat in front of him.

Quietly, he said:

"It would be best now if you would..."

Then Margot slapped him three times. WHAP WHAP WHAP, forehanded backhanded and forehanded...

...after which she leaned to within a few inches of his face and hissed:

"You like to hit women? Hit me."

Silence.

Clifton Barrett's mouth opened and the tip of his tongue, like a lizard peering out from a cave, showed itself and disappeared.

The restaurant breathed one time—as though it had been transformed into a single creature—then relapsed into silence.

"Hit me."

More silence.

"Stand up. Stand up and hit me. I'm a woman. You like to hit women, I hear. Okay. Stand up, and hit me. Please. I like to be hit. Show me how much you like to hit women. Right here."

She pointed to her right cheekbone.

"Right here. You like to hit women. Stand up. Hit me right here."

Silence.

Clifton Barrett could not stand up, of course, because Margot had effectively trapped him in the booth.

He could only look down at the sodden napkin in front of him.

That, remain silent, and continue to breathe.

"I'll be outside," whispered Margot.

Then she wheeled and left.

Nina did nothing.

There was nothing to do.

CHAPTER 10: DOWNTOWN!

The following morning Margot Gavin was taken to court for assault.

Nina learned about it from Moon Rivard, whose squad car pulled up in her driveway at a little after 8, just as she was washing from her skillet the remnants of a small helping of scrambled eggs.

"They asking for you, Ms. Nina."

"Who is?"

"Just about everybody. Ms. Towler, the District Attorney. Mr. Bennett. I guess he's gonna be Ms. Gavin's lawyer. And then there's the other lawyer."

"Which other lawyer?"

"The one representing Mr. Barrett. He got in from New York early this morning."

"All right. Give me a second."

She put on something or other, not quite certain what to wear to the arraignment of one's best friend, but remembering her parting words to Margot the previous evening:

"I don't know what will come of his, Margot. I hope nothing will."

"Don't worry about it. What could happen?"

"You can't go around hitting people and expect not to get in trouble."

"Actually, my dear, precisely the opposite is true."

And, so saying, Margot had driven off.

But she had been wrong, of course.

One might go around hitting other people and not get in trouble, but when one began hitting the great Clifton Barrett...

...so now here Nina was, getting into Moon Rivard's squad car, and wondering what was going to happen, while also noticing with the easy familiarity of a lifelong coast dweller the fact that the pre-storm sky had turned lemon, the sea had changed its texture somehow, and the birds had disappeared.

They pulled out of her driveway.

"Why do they want me down there, Moon?"

"Well. They say you saw it."

"Yes. I saw it."

"Mr. Barrett says Ms. Gavin came over to him, asked him for an autograph, threw a drink in his face, and then slapped him three times. What is your version of what really happened?"

"Margot went over to him, asked him for an autograph, threw a drink in his face, and then slapped him three times."

"All right. Then that means the two versions are pretty close."

"Pretty."

A crowd of people had begun to form around city hall. Nina saw the all-purpose beige van belonging to *The Bay St. Lucy Courier,* a young woman she did not recognize who could have been a reporter, and a young man she'd taught when he was in the fourth grade but whose name she'd forgotten because he was such an average student, and who, she was happy to realize, had followed the path set out for completely average people and become a photographer.

"Right through here, ma'am."

She made her way behind Moon and into the building, noticing as she did so several shiny black automobiles parked almost touching the door.

"Take a right, and then in here. They're in the courtroom."

She had rarely been in the courtroom itself, a strange thing for the widow of one of the town's most respected attorneys to admit, but the place had always made her nervous. She was not absolutely certain why. One possibility was, of course, that Frank was competing here almost every day of his life, and that this staid, immensely high ceilinged chamber with its paintings of dead people and photographs of living ones, was for him little more than a burnished oak boxing ring.

The other possibility was that daily, weekly, monthly, one of several judges whom she'd come to know through the years as party guests or country club bridge partners, sat up there on the ten foot tall ebony chair at the far end of the hall and told people that they had to be put in a cage for the next portion of what had heretofore been their own lives, and now no longer belonged to them.

"Hello, Nina."

This from Edie Towler the District Attorney.

Edie, tall and unassuming, was dressed in soft shades of gray and walked toward her in soft shades of gray and spoke to her in soft shades of gray.

"Nina, thank you for coming."

"No problem."

"We have, as you know, a situation."

"Yes."

Behind Edie's shoulder she saw Margot, who was sitting on one side of the room with Jackson Bennett.

Margot, who was dressed in what appeared to be the flag of Norway, waved cheerfully to her and smiled.

Opposite the aisle sat two more people: Clifton Barrett, wearing a dark blue dress shirt and what was almost certainly the only conservative tie that he—or for that matter the New York Shakespeare Company—possessed.

And his attorney, God.

The man, Nina mused, was probably not God, for that would have been unfair.

But he looked like most people wanted God to look. He wore a charcoal gray suit that no one except God could have afforded and that had almost certainly been custom-tailored because God could not go into stores and buy clothes off the rack. He was God's height, which meant that he was a little larger and taller and more impressive than all other human beings—who had merely been made in his image—but not so big as to be completely unrecognizable or unapproachable.

And he had superb silver hair.

Nina had always preferred to imagine God as having silver hair.

How could God have, say, red hair?

"Come on down front, Nina," said Edie Towler.

I don't want to, thought Nina.

But she followed anyway.

Edie, somewhat improbably in Nina's view, pulled what seemed little more than a folding chair up facing the front row of seats, so she was sitting just in front of the accused and the accusers.

She cleared her throat, sat, and made her face into something like a smile.

"Thank you all for coming."

As though, Nina thought, this was a bridge party.

"We have a difficult matter before us here."

Nina looked at Margot, who seemed completely at ease, sitting there beside Jackson, who seemed completely ill at ease. Then she looked at Clifton Barrett, who, black eyes glinting like diamonds, looked like a snake, and then she looked at God and remembered where snakes came from in the first place.

This was not good.

Edie was speaking to Margot now.

"As I understand the charge here, Ms. Gavin, it appears that you assaulted Mr. Barrett last night."

Margot said nothing.

"Did you?"

Margot nodded.

"I did."

Silence for a time.

Then Edie:

"Why?"

God:

"That isn't really relevant, is it? The fact is that the assault took place."

Edie breathed deeply and said:

"Strictly speaking, I see your point. But I do think it might be in the best interest of everyone here, if we could just talk this matter out, so that we can find out what really happened and why."

"Apparently last night the defendant wasn't in a talking mood."

"I know," said Edie. "It's just—if we can hear from Margot—"

God nodded and sat back in his chair, so that the universe continued to exist.

"Margot, did you hit him?"

"Yes."

"Why?"

"I wanted to."

"Ms. Towler…"

"I know. Margot, you're going to have to be more forthcoming than this. If this is true, if you assaulted him…you can be fined, or you can go to jail."

Don't try to be funny, Nina found herself mentally yelling at Margot, all the while remembering their conversation in the car last night on the way home from McGee's Landing:

"Margot—you hit him!"

"Yes, I did."

"You can go to jail for that!"

And the answer:

"The worst thing about jail is they don't let you stay there. Just when you've started to make real friends they say you have to leave."

Don't say that now, Margot. Don't say that here.

"I hit him," said Margot, "because he deserved it."

"He what?"

"He deserved it."

"Why did he deserve it?"

"Because he likes to hit women. So I thought I'd give him a chance to hit a woman who hits back."

God rising now, standing, his full wrath poured out upon the Israelites, who had been just plain stupid to disobey him.

"Ms. Towler this is simply absurd! Apart from the fact that it's the purest nonsense, it also constitutes slander! My client is one of the best known artists in this country, if not the world!"

"We're aware of that, Mr. Tomlinson."

Tomlinson?

It wasn't God?

If this incredible entity standing in front of her—both hands outstretched, voice rumbling like thunder—was only a human being named 'Tomlinson,' then God must really be something!

"This man could be performing on the most prestigious stage in London right now!"

"Yes."

"His services are in demand all over the world. Literally all over the world."

"We know."

"And yet he's come to spend a month in this small community. Why? Because his wife grew up here. He wants to get to know her community. And, in so doing, he's offering the town a chance at international publicity. Bay St. Lucy, Ms. Towler, can be on the map for decades to come. Some of the world's top stars and movie makers may well choose to summer here."

"That's all true."

"And now we have to sit and listen to these slanderous fairy tales about him doing harm to his wife? Putting this story out alone would be grounds for a major lawsuit, even if the assault had not happened."

"Yes, I'm aware of that."

"But the assault did happen! And something must be done about it! As District Attorney, you are responsible for seeing that something is done about it!"

"Well, that's what we're here to straighten out."

"As far as I can tell, this defendant is not even sorry about what she did!"

"She isn't a defendant yet, Mr. Tomlinson; she hasn't been formally charged."

"Then why hasn't she? She needs to be incarcerated! Fined and incarcerated!"

Edie Towler seemed to ignore these orders, and chose to address Margot again:

"What do you mean, Margot, about Mr. Bennett abusing women?"

"I mean he likes to hit his wife. Isn't that abusing women?"

"By 'his wife,' you mean Helen Reddington?"

"Yes."

"And when did he abuse her?"

"At their rehearsal two days ago. He slapped her."

"And you know this how?"

Margot shrugged, but said nothing.

"Margot—how do you know this?"

"It's common knowledge."

Upon hearing this, Clifton Barrett's attorney threw up his hands in despair.

Clifton Barrett himself merely smiled, and shook his head.

An unstoppable train, Nina thought, is coming right toward me.

And I can't do anything about it.

"Common knowledge? What is that supposed to mean, Margot."

"It was seen."

"Seen by whom?"

Traaaaaaain Comin'! Comin' Round the Bend!

"Well, for one, Ms. Bannister there saw it."

The train was in fact stopped by Tomlinson, who sat down, seemed to gather himself together after suffering, along with his client, through the monstrous indignities that were being ladled out. Then he opened a briefcase that sat in front of him on the desk, took out a sheaf of perhaps twenty papers, and held them up.

"Ms. Towler, before this goes any farther..."

"Yes, Mr. Tomlinson?"

"We need to deal with a spate of pure vicious rumors that seem to have been circulating for the past hours, about some bizarre and completely imaginary event that, as far as my client and I can gather, is supposed to have happened at one of the last rehearsals."

"Go on," said Edie.

You're going to deny it, aren't you? thought Nina.

Why you...

...oh where was profanity when one needed it?

"To begin with, I need to point out that, for reasons that will very quickly become obvious, attendance at the professional rehearsals is almost invariably strictly limited to cast members and other crew personnel who are a part of the production."

"I can understand that; go on."

"This is not true, of course, of community theater, which by its very nature exists as a social event for the community. The point of it is, everyone comes together, everyone gossips a bit, eats a bit—has a good time."

"Yes."

"But the professional theater is an entirely different matter. Rehearsals can be extremely intense, and are not to be attended by the general public. On the other hand..."

He now turned and looked back over his shoulder at Nina.

"...due to a special request from Ms. Reddington, her mother was given an invitation to attend a rehearsal the day before yesterday. She was accompanied by this lady now sitting with us, whose name is, I believe, Ms. Bannister."

"Nina Bannister, that's right."

"At this rehearsal, Mr. Barrett somehow was perceived to have struck his wife. An event that purely and simply did not happen."

"That's a lie," said someone in the courtroom.

It was Nina.

Clifton Barrett's attorney now turned in his chair, rose, and leaned toward her, so that his shadow, like that of a great mountain in the early afternoon, began to creep across the flat and unspectacular land that was her.

"I beg your pardon?"

They were all looking at her now, of course.

"I beg your pardon?" came the repeated question.

"That's a lie."

"You're saying that Mr. Barrett did in fact strike his wife?"

"Yes."

"You saw it?"

"Yes."

He pursed his lips, nodded, and continued:

"You are close friends with Ms. Gavin here?"

"Yes."

"Did you tell her about this alleged 'attack'?

"No."

"Are you certain of that?"

"Yes."

"Did you tell anybody else?"

She thought of John Giusti, standing there on her stairway, asking:

'Did he hit her?'

She remembered her reply.

'Yes.'

And she listened as Clifton Barrett's attorney asked once again:

"Did you tell anybody else?"

She said nothing.

"Did you enjoy telling about this alleged 'assault'?

No reply.

"How many people in the community of Bay St. Lucy did you entertain with this fairy tale, Ms. Bannister?"

"It's not a fairy tale; I saw it."

"Really? You were the only one who saw it?"

"No, everybody there saw it. Everybody on stage, everybody in the balcony. The whole company saw it."

"The entire company?"

"Yes."

He nodded, then turned to Edie Towler and handed her the rest of the sheaf of papers.

"Then," he said, the back of his neck now talking to Nina, "can you explain how I happen to have twenty eight sworn affidavits here, all from people in attendance at that morning's rehearsal, all swearing that nothing such as you described ever happened?"

Silence in the courtroom.

Silence silence silence.

Silence until something or other was heard.

But whatever it was, Nina wasn't listening.

She sat as though hypnotized for what must have been an hour. Back and forth, back and forth, with Edie doing everything she could to keep Margot out of jail, and Clifton Barrett, who apparently had to leave town early in the afternoon and fly back to New York for a brief time, finally agreeing to let matters rest, if given Edie's assurance that any such similar behavior from townspeople would be harshly dealt with.

There was an apology from Margot, who, Nina realized, could never have given it herself, and had to slip into the role of Mother Superior to manage it.

Then they all left the courtroom.

They walked down one hallway, around another, and through the door leading outside.

There was a crowd of fifty or so people awaiting them.

Flashbulbs, pictures of the great Clifton Barrett, pictures of Margot.

No pictures of Nina.

Thank God.

This from Barrett's lawyer:

"We can take one or two questions from the press."

Question:

"Will Mr. Barrett be pressing charges at this time?"

Answer:

"No. This has been a terrible misunderstanding, stemming from malicious and untrue rumors. As far as Mr. Barrett is concerned, the matter is dropped."

"Will this have any effect on the play?"

"No. Mr. Barrett must fly to New York this afternoon. He will return early tomorrow morning. Then he will be following the production schedule as will the entire company."

Next question:

"Could you tell us…"

"I'm sorry, we're on a bit of a tight schedule. If you'll excuse us…"

Press conference over, making their way through the crowd…

Don't anyone notice Nina. Don't anyone notice Nina.

Almost to the waiting patrol car.

And there stood John Giusti.

At the edge of the circle of spectators.

Blue denim shirt, blue jeans.

Simply standing and staring.

Clifton Barrett no more than ten feet away now.

Five feet.

And both men simply stare at each other.

When John Giusti says, flatly, with no trace of emotion, and so privately that no one except for Nina seems to hear.

"If you hit her again, I'll kill you."

Clifton Barrett shows no sign of recognition or emotion.

John turns away and leaves.

Barrett enters his car.

The door closes.

And the car drives away.

CHAPTER 11: BY THE SEA BY THE SEA...

Slightly before noon, Nina was dropped off by one of the town's squad cars.

She made her way up the stairs, pushed open the door, which she'd forgotten to lock, and went out onto her deck, where Helen Reddington was smoking a cigarette.

"Hi. Welcome back to where you live."

"Hello, Helen."

"I made myself at home. The door was unlocked. Hope you don't mind."

"No, I don't."

Helen was wearing a black bikini and had propped her feet on the rail. She'd pulled a small end table up beside her. On the table was a glass half filled with water, a package of Marlboro cigarettes, and a small dish that she'd taken from the kitchen to use as an ashtray.

"Like my abs? I have great abs."

This was true. There was no fat at all on her stomach, and the softly curved tan muscles looked like dunes in a quiet desert.

"No boobs of course. But that gets taken care of."

"Really?"

She drew on the cigarette, then exhaled smoke over the rail and half-smiled.

"I have a contract to do a film next year. I'm some sort of super heroine. Powers and all that. I get to beat people up."

"Good."

"Yeah, I enjoy it, except it isn't real. Same thing with my body. If the upper part needs to be bigger, then they make it bigger. All illusion. All, all illusion. I'm sorry for what just happened to you in court, Nina."

"You know?" asked Nina, drawing up a chair and sitting down.

"Overheard. Overheard Clifton and his lawyer talking when they got back to Grandmamma's. He wins again, of course."

"I don't think they're going to do anything to Margot. She apologized. It almost killed her, but she apologized."

"That's good."

She drew hard on her cigarette, then stubbed it out.

"I didn't know that you smoked, Helen."

"How could I not smoke? Given everything. The way things are, the way I've made them—how could I not smoke?"

They were silent for a time. Finally Nina asked:

"So how bad is it? You don't have to pretend anymore that things are wonderful. I'm your friend, Helen; you know that. How bad is it, really?"

Helen shook her head while lighting another cigarette.

"It's hell."

More silence.

Then:

"The great actress, Helen Reddington. Come down to Bay St. Lucy to convince everyone that I'd achieved it all. Great career, New York, fame, London. Wonderful marriage, wonderful husband—heaven. But Nina—be careful what you wish for."

Nina could think of nothing to say. Finally Helen gestured out toward the ocean.

"Look, porpoises."

"Yes. The two of them swim by every day about this time, going south, toward Hatteras. I suppose they pass by the other way sometime. During the night. I don't know."

"I used to love watching the porpoises. I'd name them, like kids do."

She took a deep breath and said:

"I had it all out there. It was waiting for me. The whole world. And now...now I've ruined it. I've lost it all, and I've ruined it."

"Helen, you have your career."

She shook her head.

"No, he has my career."

"You mean Clifton Barrett? But that can't be true."

"What is true, what is not true—that's more confusing than you might think, somehow."

"Helen—Helen, you have to leave this man."

"Really, Nina? Do I?"

"Of course you do. He beats you!"

"No, he doesn't."

"He does; I saw him!"

"No, you didn't."

"I was there! I saw him hit you!"

"But twenty-eight people saw him not hit me. And that's the reality, don't you see?"

"All right, so twenty eight people are scared to death of the man."

"Cross him and they'll never work again."

"It doesn't matter. You can still leave him."

"But I can't."

"Leave him!"

"I can't! I can't!"

"Why not?"

"Because he has my money!"

They sat for a time, Nina remembering something that Frank had been told about unforgivable mistakes in interrogating witnesses:

'Never ask a question you don't know the answer to.'

Good, she thought, that the two of them were not in court now. Of course she'd been in court two hours ago and had made a fool of herself.

Somehow that seemed unimportant now.

"How—how is this possible, Helen?"

A shrug. "Lawyers."

Nina nodded. "I know about lawyers."

"Not the kind of lawyers Clifton has."

"All right. I guess that's true. But still…"

Helen leaned across the table:

"The long and short of it is this: a year ago Jackson Bennett called me and said there were—well, concerns, about Grandmamma's age. She was fine mentally, but at over eighty…well, he suggested that there be a power of attorney giving me control of her business affairs. So such a document was made out, and signed by all parties. Grandmamma had no objection."

"All right. So you have her power of attorney."

"Which means Clifton has it, as my husband."

"Helen, you kept none of your property?"

"No. It's all in his name."

"But why would you…"

"Why would I what? Say 'no' when the smartest lawyers in the world are telling me how rich the man was already, and how Grandmamma's funds would be tripled within six weeks if placed together with Clifton's fortune and invested wisely? Would I say no to that?"

"But…if he has that wealth…"

"He has nothing."

"What?"

"He's a fraud financially."

"He's one of the most successful actors in the world!"

Helen smiled:

"Yes, he is, isn't he? Yes, he is."

"But he must have made a fortune as an actor!"

"And lost it. Several times over. Lost it, Nina. Most of what he has now is Grandmamma's money."

"All right. So divorce him and get that money back!"

"And why would he allow me to do that?"

"Threaten him! Threaten to tell the truth about him!"

"The way you just did?"

"But surely someone…"

"I've had three affairs, Nina."

Shocked, Nina could only stare for a time across the table.

Never ask a question you don't know the answer to.

Except, Nina found herself thinking, there is a better version of that piece of advice.

The better version:

Just shut up and never say anything at all.

"Helen, how could you do such a thing?"

"Nina, how could you lie in court about having seen Clifton hit me?"

"I didn't lie."

"Everybody thinks you did, so you did."

And, finally beginning to understand, Nina shook her head slowly.

"The affairs you had were fictitious."

"Oh what a thing to say! Fictitious! Why, there are pictures of the men! There are hotel receipts! If I have a hard time remembering ever having done these things, taken part in these assignations, slept with these men—and by the way, one of them is quite famous, the story will break next month, it will be fabulous for his career—if I forget these things, it's because I have Alzheimer's Disease. Just setting in early."

"You didn't do it? You didn't have these affairs?"

"No. Of course not."

"But he'll convince the world that you did."

"Yes."

"And then…"

"Then he'll divorce me. "

"When will this happen, Helen?"

"When he gets tired of me. I'm already twenty-three. Clifton, I've found, prefers younger women. He was with a thirty-five year old—Constance—at the restaurant when Margot slapped him. But that's not like him. I've heard that he has a twenty-year old in mind. His next 'minion.' So the story about my affairs will break. He will, in tears, announce the divorce, we will separate—Grandmamma and I will receive a small settlement, he will keep the rest—my career will be over, he will see to it—and that will be that."

Nina was silent for a time.

Finally she said:

"I believe I understand now, why the two of you agreed to come and do this play."

"Yes, you probably do. We came for the money. A million dollars."

"Are you going to get any of it, Helen?"

She shrugged.

"We've talked about it. Clifton has...well, he's held out some hope."

"Nice of him."

"There's a possibility that we will simply split it, and go our separate ways. But he hasn't agreed to that formally. He says he's being advised concerning his options. We'll see. Knowing him, the way I have come to, we'll see."

"I hope it goes all right. I hope he agrees to split the money."

"That third wish," said Helen, softly. "The third wish, in most stories about deals with the devil, when one is granted three wishes—is always for death."

"You can't wish for death, Helen."

"Oh, but I do, Nina. More than you know."

"You have too much to live for."

Then Helen smiled at her.

"You misunderstand. I don't wish for my death. I wish for his."

"Helen..."

"Somebody needs to kill him."

CHAPTER 12: THE SOUP KITCHEN

Friday, August 1, the opening day of *Hamlet*, Hurricane Deborah's western edge brushed over Bay St. Lucy. Clouds were low and would have been gray/black had they been visible at all and not obscured by horizontal sheets of rain.

The entire community looked like a 1950's film, viewed on a broken TV.

There were no people, cars, dogs, birds—

—there was only static, punctuated by the occasional fleeting image of a living thing running as fast as possible toward a structure that could not be seen.

By six a.m., rain had begun pouring against Nina's window; it drummed, rattled, drove, and spattered, as though a group of malicious little boys were standing just below with a fire hose, which they had trained upon her deck and house.

The wind howled like a large sick dog.

The ocean was directly beneath her, lapping happily at the base of the long poles upon which sat her precarious little shack.

She did not mind it, though.

She knew that the water would be no more than two or three inches deep, and she had, ever the experienced coastal dweller, taken pains to tie her freezer, her barbeque grill, and a couple of other storage boxes, fast upon solid ash platforms that had been built for just this purpose.

And so she would have been able to sequester herself in the bedroom and read more novels, had she not been forced, every half hour, to go to the door, open it, and talk to people.

Moon Rivard arrived at seven thirty a.m.

"Ms. Nina?"

"Yes!" she shouted, barely able to make herself heard above the expiring beast that was actually a nicely maturing wind.

"What is it, Moon?"

Howl! Howl! Howl!

Spatterspatter!

Roooooarrrrr!

Moon just outside the door, drenched in black oil slicker; she just inside the door, drenched in the spray of his black oil slicker.

"WHAT IS IT, MOON? HAS SOMETHING HAPPENED?"

"STORM, MA'AM!"

"YES! I CAN SEE IT! WHAT ABOUT IT?"

"I CAME BY!"

"YES, YOU DID!"

"I NEED TO KNOW IF YOU'RE ALL RIGHT!"

"I'M ALL RIGHT EXCEPT I'M A LITTLE WET NOW!"

"HOW'S THAT? NOT SURE I UNDERSTOOD WHAT YOU SAID, MS. NINA!"

"I'M A LITTLE WET BECAUSE OF HAVING TO OPEN THE DOOR!"

"YOU OUGHT TO GET BACK INSIDE!"

"THAT'S TRUE, MOON!"

"YOU SURE YOU'RE ALL RIGHT?"

"ABSOLUTELY!"

"BECAUSE I CAN..."

"GOOD BYE, MOON! THANK YOU FOR COMING BY TO CHECK ON ME!"

"IT AIN'T NOTHING AT ALL! NOW IF I CAN..."

"GOOD BYE MOON!"

And she closed the door, careful not to catch his nose in it.

At eight fifteen, Jackson Bennett came by.

Jackson was larger than Moon, and so she was forced to open the door a bit wider to talk to him.

He had on the same kind of raincoat Moon had been wearing, but there was more of it, so more water sprayed off it and, first, onto the half open door, and, then, onto her.

"NINA!"

"JACKSON!"

"ARE YOU ALL RIGHT?"

"YES, I'M FINE!"

"ARE YOU SURE?"

"YES, I'M SURE!"

"THEY SAY THIS IS GOING TO LAST ALL DAY, MAYBE INTO THE EVENING!"

"I KNOW!"

"YOU'RE SURE YOU'RE ALL RIGHT!"

"I'M SURE!"

"DO YOU HAVE ENOUGH FOOD?"

"YES I DO, JACKSON!"

"YOU HAVE EVERYTHING YOU NEED?"

"ABSOLUTELY EVERYTHING!"

"YOU HAVE COFFEE?"

"I DO."

"MILK?"

"JACKSON…"

"ANYTHING YOU NEED, YOU JUST TELL ME!"

"I WILL! I DEFINITELY WILL!"

"YOU HAVE MY NUMBER?"

"I DO."

"DO YOU WANT ME TO WRITE IT DOWN FOR YOU?"

"NO, I'VE GOT IT."

"YOU HAVE SOMETHING TO EAT FOR LUNCH?"

"LUNCH, DINNER…GOT EVERY THING I NEED."

"THEY SAY IT'S GOING TO LAST ALL DAY."

"I THINK YOU TOLD ME THAT, JACKSON!"

"THEY SAY THE PLAY IS STILL GOING ON TONIGHT, THOUGH."

"GOOD! GLAD TO HEAR IT!"

"NOW, ONCE AGAIN—IF YOU NEED ANYTHING…"

"HAVE A GOOD DAY, JACKSON!"

And she shut the door on him.

A little before ten o'clock Alana Delafosse came by.

She had on enough rain gear to make her look like a small walrus.

"ALANA, WILL YOU COME IN?"

"NO, NO, I'VE COME TO TAKE YOU AWAY!"

"I DON'T WANT TO GO AWAY!"

"YOU CAN'T STAY HERE!"

"I'M FINE, ALANA!"

"PEOPLE ARE GATHERING AT THE CHURCH!"

"WHY?"

"WE HAVE A SOUP KITCHEN!"

"I DON'T WANT TO GO TO A SOUP KITCHEN!"

"YOU DON'T NEED TO BE PROUD!"

"I'M NOT PROUD!"

"YOU CAN TAKE FURL WITH YOU!"

"FURL IS HAPPY WHERE HE IS!"

"ARE YOU COLD?"

"I'M A LITTLE COLD NOW."

"THIS IS HOW PEOPLE CATCH PNEUMONIA, NINA!"

"I KNOW."

"WE HAVE ROOM IN THE BUS!"

"TAKE THE BUS AWAY!"

"I HATE IT WHEN YOU'RE LIKE THIS!"

"I HATE IT WHEN I'M LIKE THIS, TOO!"

"HAVE YOU HEARD THE FORECAST?"

"YES, IT'S RAINING!"

"AND YOU'RE SURE YOU WON'T COME TO THE SOUP KITCHEN?"

"I HAVE SOUP IN MY OWN KITCHEN!"

"YOU'RE NOT JUST TELLING ME THAT BECAUSE OF PRIDE?"

"I HAVE NO PRIDE, ALANA. I PROMISE I HAVE NO PRIDE."

"YOU'LL BE AT THE PERFORMANCE THIS EVENING?"

"IF I'M NOT DEAD!"

"WHAT?"

"NOTHING!"

"DO YOU KNOW IF MARGOT HAS HAD ANY MORE TROUBLE WITH CLIFTON BARRETT?"

"NO, I DON'T KNOW IF SHE HAS OR NOT."

"BECAUSE IT WAS REALLY IMPRUDENT OF HER TO..."

"ALANA..."

"YES, DEAR?"

"THE RAIN IS COMING IN THROUGH THE DOOR!"

"THAT'S WHAT I'M TRYING TO TELL YOU, NINA! IT'S VERY DANGEROUS FOR YOU HERE."

"IT'S NOT DANGEROUS, ALANA, WHEN THE DOOR IS CLOSED. THEN THE RAIN DOESN'T COME IN."

"ARE YOU CERTAIN THAT YOU HAVE ENOUGH FOOD?"

"I REALLY AM! I REALLY DO!"

"DO YOU HAVE MILK?"

"ALANA..."

"BECAUSE DOWN BELOW, IN THE BUS, WE HAVE..."

"HAVE A GOOD DAY, ALANA!"

And she shut the door on her.

This went on all day.

No one would come in and sit with her and have a cup of coffee, because they were frightened that her shack would blow away.

She would not leave and go somewhere else, because her little place was warm and dry—except when the front door was open—and she did in fact have coffee and milk and innumerable other little items of food, so that she was fairly confident of her ability to get through the next six hours or so without having a sudden attack of starvation and dying from it.

Furl slept comfortably on the corner of her—now partially his—bed, and she envied him.

No neighboring cats came to the door and forced him to go answer it and get wet, while they pleaded with him to leave his dry little nook to go out in the storm with them and go to the basement of a cat church.

"Lucky Furl," she found herself muttering.

Around noon she gave up trying to read in the bedroom.

She pulled a straight chair to within a foot of the front door, dragged a standing lamp to within a few inches of it, turned on the lamp, and tried to read there, close enough that she could reach out and answer the door after only one knock.

From time to time she would stand, glare out through the small window that had been made in the door, and say to whatever troop of well meaning Bay St. Lucy neighbors and friends who had probably gathered at the base of her stairway and were preparing to come up:

"It's in Florida! The hurricane is in Florida!"

Then she would sit down and be mad.

Seven people during the course of the afternoon offered her a ride to L'Auberge des Arts, to see the evening's performance of *Hamlet*.

She agreed to go with all of them.

This was not absolutely fair, she initially told herself, but there was no other choice. How could you turn down Moon Rivard, or Alana Delafosse, or Tom Broussard the Writer, or his wife Penelope Royale the Specialist in Obscene Languages, or Jackson Bennett, or Edie Towler, or blah de blah, blah de blah, blah de…

…how could you turn these people down?

So she said she'd go with all of them, and resolved actually to go with whichever one got there first.

This person, as it turned out, was a total stranger.

He arrived at her door at six thirty PM dressed in a nice charcoal gray suit, despite which he still looked like Ichabod Crane, noted that the rain seemed to be decreasing—which was true—and said that his wife had given him orders to come over and give her a ride.

She had already dressed for the occasion. She wore her New York/London Opening Night Gala outfit, which was a black and white dress with black pumps covered by rubber boots that came halfway to her knees—

—and so there was nothing left to do but tape to the door the note that she had already written saying:

THANKS—GOT ANOTHER RIDE!

And descend the stairs with this man, whoever the hell he was.

The buildings, signboards, restaurants, curio shops, florists, dogs, cats, people, and roads of Bay St. Lucy had all become part of the ocean, and, although the rain had decreased slightly in its intensity, it was still not so much falling as attacking. Falling implied dropping vertically, as in parachuting; attacking implied straight-on-over the hill DADADADADADA DADAAAAACHAAAAARGE! coming right at you, as though each individual drop were running as fast as it could and carrying a bayonet.

She kept her eyes closed during the five minute drive, not knowing whether to be more frightened that Ichabod Crane would slide off the road—which was only a sheet of fast flowing dirty gray water—or that he would be attacked by the Headless Horseman, in which case where would she be?

They reached the mansion. She'd always pictured the restored Robinson place as The Titanic raised and turned upright, so opulent were its furnishings. Now though, it was as if they'd gone back a notch farther in time to watch the raising itself. The huge building lay on the bottom of the ocean. Water was everywhere, blowing from the Spanish moss, which stretched horizontally in the still brutal winds like gray wrapping paper—and figures moved about like divers, all of them carrying weakly glowing searchlights as they paddled here and there, unable to speak, and communicating by feeble gestures.

Finally, she realized they'd come to a stop beneath a huge canopy, which she could hear drumming with the rain.

The main entrance door opened, and, an instant later, her own car door swung out, revealing a teenage boy dressed in a suit several sizes too big for him, and wearing black rimmed glasses several sizes too big for anybody.

"Ms. Bannister?"

"Yes."

"Could you come with me?"

"Sure."

"Just right this way. I'm Justin—I'm kind of an errand boy with the company!"

"Hi Justin!"

She followed through the entrance hall and along a corridor that snaked into the interior of the mansion

"Bad storm," remarked Justin.

"Yes, it is."

"Can't postpone the play, though. Too many technical issues. Too many people here."

"I understand."

What I don't understand, she heard herself wondering, is where I'm going.

She found out quickly.

"Just a second, Ms. Bannister."

Justin knocked softly on a door which had magically appeared to their right.

"Ma'am?" he asked.

"Yes!"

"Ma'am, it's Ms. Bannister."

"Bring her in."

The door opened.

She stepped forward into a dressing room, with mirrors everywhere, and a thin stream of cigarette smoke rising from an ashtray which sat on a counter covered by jars of makeup.

The reflection of Helen Reddington stared at her.

Helen was not alone.

Seated in the far corner was John Giusti.

This is not good, Nina found herself thinking.

It wasn't.

The door closed.

"John and I wanted to see you, Nina. To tell you something."

"What is it, Helen?"

"Clifton talked to me half an hour ago. Just before we went into makeup."

"What did he tell you?"

"It's over. He doesn't want me any more."

"Oh, Helen…"

"We're supposed to go back to New York tomorrow. We'll seem happy. The perfect married couple. Then next week his attorneys will announce the divorce. There's still some question as to whether it will be mental cruelty or infidelity, but it will be my fault. The bottom line is that most of it will be kept out of the papers, on the condition that I take what he condescends to give me. And no more. All the money that the company—which is basically him—has been paid to come here, will go to him. I shall get a small monthly allowance. Grandmamma will be allowed to keep the house until she…"

"Yes."

"But the rest of Grandmamma's money—the money grandfather made—will be gone."

"Helen—have the proceedings begun?"

"No. They will be initiated next week."

"Then perhaps someone can reason with the man."

She shook her head.

"No. No chance of that. Interesting that he told me about this thirty minutes ago. Before the performance. He'd like me to have it in my mind as the play moves forward. Perhaps he wants to experience a truly mad Ophelia. He may have the chance."

"Helen, if there were anything I could do."

"There's something I can do," said John, quietly.

"John," Nina said. "You can't be violent with this man. He has all the cards."

John shook his head.

"I'm not going to be violent with him. But I'm not letting him have Helen, either."

Helen interrupted him.

"John and I have spent time together in the last few days. It's been…well, very special to me."

"We've been careful," added John. "With all the press, a husband like Barrett…we couldn't be seen. And we weren't. But we've talked about a lot of things."

"Oedipus," smiled Helen, weakly.

"Yeah. That too."

"But," Helen continued, "the bottom line is that I'm staying here. That will be all Clifton needs, of course, to have the perfect divorce. 'Old flame rekindles for young actress.' That sort of thing. And, despite that, he'll be furious when I tell him."

"When are you going to do that?"

"Tomorrow morning."

"We'll do it together," John added.

"Be careful when you do it," said Nina.

Helen nodded.

"We will."

"If he tries anything…"

She shook her head:

"Don't even think about that, John. That can't happen."

He nodded.

"I know."

Silence for a time.

Then Helen to Nina:

"You'll be sitting with Grandmamma, won't you?"

"Yes."

"Take good care of her during the show. I must tell you…she knows about all of this. I was hoping to keep it from her, hoping against hope that the divorce could be put off. But the way things are now, with my having decided to stay…I simply had to tell her. As far as she's concerned, no one else knows."

"How did she take this news about you and Clifton Barrett?"

"She was very angry with him. She saw the slap, too, and can't forget it. But she's taking it bravely. She would, of course, have every reason to be outraged at me. I'm the one who made the disastrous marriage and lost the family's money; but she's been kind and understanding."

"Of course. That's Hope's nature. She couldn't hurt anyone, and she would certainly never be mad—or stay mad—at you, Helen."

"No. I suppose not. But sit with her tonight and be a comforting presence, will you?"

"Of course I will."

A bell rang. The door opened.

"Five minutes, Ms. Reddington."

"All right."

"I have to go, Helen," said Nina, getting to her feet. "John…"

"Yes, Nina?"

"Are you going to see the play?"

He shook his head.

"I don't think I could take that. I don't want to see the man. Onstage or anywhere else."

"What are you going to do then?"

"I don't know. Wander around the garden. Sometimes when I walk, well…I'm not so angry."

"And then?"

"I'll probably stay in town tonight. I have a bed at the clinic. It's necessary sometimes when there are emergencies. I'll sleep there, then go over to the Reddingtons tomorrow morning. Then we'll tell that…"

"John," said Helen, quietly.

He checked himself, then continued:

"We'll tell her husband about the situation. If he wants to get furious, then let him. But Helen never gets on that plane with him. As for money, I've got enough of it. I can give the Reddingtons all the help they need."

"All right, John," said Nina, opening the door. "Just promise me that you'll be careful tomorrow morning."

"I will. I really will."

"All right, then. And Helen, good luck tonight."

"Thank you, Nina."

Nina left, closing the door behind her and thinking:

"Good luck to both of you. You're going to need it."

CHAPTER 13: GOOD NIGHT, SWEET PRINCE

Hamlet began in and not in the rain, after the curtain went
and did not go up, and Francisco and Bernardo got and did
not get wet.

Elsinore. A platform before the castle.

Bernardo: "Who's there?"

Francisco: "Nay, answer me: stand and unfold yourself!"

Which Bernardo did, causing the crowd in the theater to
crane their necks and peer upward, the opening action taking
place in midair, at least twenty feet above what should have
been the stage.

Ooooohh!

Aaaaahhh!

An appreciative and collective gasp from people who'd
never experienced a production paid for by tons of Robinson
money and designed by experts who, a bit strange though
they might be, still knew a thing or two about sets and
lighting.

It was, thought Nina, the lighting that was so unearthly,
so unlike anything she'd ever seen before. If soldiers and
guards wanted to walk about on platforms hanging in mid
air, why that was their business, and she was not so naïve as
to doubt that gravity could be defied by a mix of strong
scaffolding and invisible wiring.

But the eerie green lighting that bathed them as they
strode about in their armor plates and visored helmets; the
incessant rain that poured down on their glistening armor—

—she knew where the rain was coming from. It was the
same rain that still engulfed Bay St. Lucy, but it had been
hired by The Company to perform in the play; and so, the
roof of the theater having been rolled back and three
mirrored sheets of Plexiglas inserted in its place, an outlying,
dying, fringe of Hurricane Deborah was now drenching and

not drenching the parapets of young Prince Hamlet's castle, making the audience say softly to themselves:

"How can they not be getting wet? It's pouring all around them!"

And Hope, seated in the front row beside Nina, whisper:

"It's very realistic, isn't it?"

It became more than realistic when Horatio and Marcellus entered from the back of the hall—except another twenty feet higher than they were supposed to be standing—waved to their countrymen still hanging somehow above where the stage should have been, and shouted:

"Friends to this ground, and liegemen to the Dane!"

It was off and running.

Motion. Constant motion, nothing stationary on or below or about or behind or outside of or inside of or even having to do with the stage itself, which disappeared while the Cosmos of Norway floated around it. Trumpets sounded from Heaven, drum beats rolled up from Hell, lights came and went like meteors and then it all stopped. Stopped completely still, the storm itself extinguished, the green coral reef lights disappearing beneath a now quiet sea, the elevations flattened, the stage back again and tightly compressed, one candle only burning…

…and Hamlet alone, thinking.

"Oh, that this too too solid flesh would melt, thaw, and resolve itself into a dew! Or that the Everlasting had not fixed his canon 'gainst self slaughter!"

My God, he's good! thought Nina.

They were all good.

Claudius was good Horatio was good Laertes was good Voltimund Cornelius Rosencrantz Guildenstern Osric the Gentlemen the Priest Marcellus Bernardo the Players Fortinbras Gertrude and Ophelia were good they were all good scene after scene after scene after—(To be or not to Be!) scene after scene—so that it was only slightly surprising that when— Act III, Scene IV—Hamlet exclaimed:

"How now! A rat?"

And followed it with:

"Dead for a Ducat!"

And thrust his sword through the mammoth tapestry that now constituted the north wall of The Robinson Castle of Norway...

...making a figure stagger out, mortally wounded and uttering the words:

"Oh! I am slain!"

... that when all of these things happened...

...Hope Reddington would spring to her feet, horror stricken, one hand slapped upon her forehead, another pointing, trembling, at the stage, and shout:

"It's Polonius!"

—and no one would be surprised.

Since the same rules apply in the theater as they do in church (Never be the only one laughing)—the audience remained silent.

The actors remained silent for a third of a second.

Hope sat and whispered to Nina:

"Polonius didn't have any business being there!"

Nina nodded, and whispered back:

"I think the play affirms that."

Then the action continued.

As it had to continue. And as it wound towards its inevitable end, an observer of the theater might have been tempted to comment on the most essential difference between amateur and professional productions. For in the former, Hope Reddington's outburst might have been the highlight of the evening. People, all in love with Hope, would have said for months afterward:

"Did you hear Hope? Wasn't that precious?"

Whereas this particular performance made everyone forget Hope, since the highlights occurred onstage and not off it, and since they simply kept coming.

They kept coming partially because of Helen Reddington herself. The community felt a sense of pride during the early scenes, when the young woman they remembered as a precocious teenager bounded onto the stage in the guise of the youthful and enthusiastic Ophelia, who was simply another precocious teenager who happened to live in

Norway and was enamored with a strange and moody man who saw himself not as a jock but as a Goth.

But then Ophelia went insane, taking Helen with her.

Or perhaps it was vice versa, only true actors knowing which was which.

So that when the queen said "Let her come in," in the fifth scene of Act Four, and Ophelia/Helen crept in from stage left, the audience could not withhold a gasp.

The woman before them moved like an animal, insinuating herself by Horatio as though she were nothing but a shadow passing through him. No, her hatred was for the queen, and Nina could not help thinking of Clifton Barrett kissing this woman when she heard Helen intone, in a voice deep enough to be guttural but smooth enough to be serpentine:

"Where is the beauteous majesty of Denmark?"

Where indeed?

The queen was afraid of her and stepped back.

The actress playing the queen was afraid of her and stepped back.

The town in the audience was afraid of her and would have stepped back but the seats didn't go anywhere.

"How now, Ophelia?

That was a lot, Nina found herself thinking, to ask Helen Reddington at this point.

How now?

Her husband was leaving her and ruining her, her life was in shambles, and she wanted the man dead.

'Perhaps he wants to experience a truly mad Ophelia; he may get the chance.'

They all were getting the chance.

But there was no way to answer, 'How now, Ophelia?' in the sane world and so Ophelia/Helen descended/ascended into another world, and began to sing.

There was no accompaniment; there could not have been, for the 'song,' if one could call it that, was played not by an instrument but by a glare—fixed, haunting, black, and merciless:

"He is dead and gone, lady."

Oh my God, thought, Nina. She's talking about her husband.

"He is dead and gone.

"At his head, a grass green turf.

"At his heels a stone."

The audience, stunned, had no choice but to remain seemingly motionless while the tide that was Ophelia's madness sucked them into Helen's eyes and voice and body, and then spit them out again.

She was gone. They could breathe for a second.

Then she was back again, 'fantastically dressed, with straws and flowers.'

It was a horror of a gown, splattered with horrible orchids, and almost sprouting death weeds, white and blighted; it seemed to have eaten half of Helen, who peered mournfully out of it as though it were quicksand.

She should have been picking flowers for Laertes, but she crept downstage, knelt, and began picking them for the audience.

Except that they—the flowers and not the audience—were invisible.

They were not invisible to Helen, though. She took petals off each, one by one, and blew them out to people on the first two rows, letting her voice sift whispering through the breaths that carried the petals:

Then, looking straight at her grandmother, and no more than a few feet away, she stretched her hand forward, looked at another invisible blossom, studied it, frowned at it, and finally, terrifyingly, let a smile grow around it and take root in it.

Then she whispered:

"There's rosemary; that's for remembrance."

Nina forced her mind to go blank for a time.

When she was able to refocus, the Helen/Ophelia creature had left behind both the stage and an audience of empty shells that had come as people.

The play was never the same, of course, but it did not give up. It had plenty of fight left in it, even after Ophelia's drowning.

And if, in fact, anything could have caused a sane person to forget Ophelia's forgetting, it was the final scene.

Hamlet is killed by the poisoned sword of Laertes.

The stage begins slowly rising toward the roof of the theater, and Hamlet begs Horatio:

"If thou dids't ever hold me in thy heart, absent thee from felicity awhile, and in this harsh world draw thy breath in pain, to tell my story."

Rising, rising…

…then stop the stage…

…and open the roof…

…completely.

No Plexiglas.

There is the summer sky of Bay St. Lucy.

Completely clear.

And precisely in the middle of the opening above the crying Horatio and the dying Hamlet.

The moon.

The full white moon.

With not one cloud passing over it.

While Horatio says, first to the figure who has just died in his arms and then to heaven:

"Good night, sweet Prince. May flights of angels sing thee to thy rest."

Utter silence in the theater.

And all the lights go out.

Pandemonium.

Voices voices voices voices and people getting up and going this way and that way and trampling over each other on the seats and in the aisles and everyone moving out of the theater and everyone moving back into the theater towards the stage and some people shouting and some people crying and the technical people up on catwalks congratulating each other and gradually, gradually, the whole thing getting louder and more raucous because people were beginning to drink.

Clusters of conversation flying around like scraps of confetti:

"How did they do that?"

"How could they know the rain was going to stop?"

"Isn't there some more to the play?"

"I think so, but who cares? The way they ended it was wonderful!"

"Wasn't Helen magnificent as Ophelia?"

"Yes, and Hamlet was superb!"

"He was, he was—and, and, there's going to be a video of it."

"When?"

"I don't know, next week they said."

"Yes but we can't buy it until the national TV production airs."

"Is the town going to be in the production?"

And on and on and on.

Nina had somehow made her way outside, astonished by the warmth and succulence of the still-drenched air, and trying to choose between rides home, when she noticed that everyone had turned and was now facing a wooden platform that had been hastily erected by the fountain that sat before the mansion's entrance.

Floodlights on the platform.

Striding up onto it were Helen, still in her whitefordrowning robes, and Barrett, still in Hamlet's blackbutredstainedfromswordfighting Shakespeare suit.

"My dear friends! I thank you, and my darling wife thanks you!"

Thunderous applause.

Then Clifton Barrett talked about how wonderful Bay St. Lucy had been; and about how wonderful all the people were; and how sorry he was that they were going to have to leave tomorrow—

Someone, one of the other actors, handed him a glass of Scotch, which he drained. Then he talked about...

...how marvelous it was that the weather had changed, and that the moon had agreed to be in the play...

—laughter at this—

Another glass of Scotch.

And all the time, Helen, there by his side, looking up at him with...

...what emotion was that?

It seemed to be respect and love.

But Helen was a good actress.

And she knew how to wear makeup.

It was midnight when Nina got home.

She was hungry but too tired to eat; excited by the play, depressed by what Helen had told her, and utterly drained.

She walked out onto her deck, watched the sea, watched the moon, thought about Hamlet, and listened once again as the monstrously good lines filled her brain.

Then she changed into her nightgown and went to bed, turning restlessly this way and that.

During this time she thought about the situation, and tried to be as optimistic as possible.

Perhaps Barrett, a human being despite everything, would not make a terrible scene the following morning.

Perhaps he'd be persuaded to handle the divorce discreetly, and let Helen go.

Perhaps John Giusti would control his temper.

And perhaps Ophelia's lines in Act Four...

"I hope all will be well."

..would prove to be true.

Maybe things would all turn out well.

By the time Nina had begun to doze off, she'd made herself believe these thoughts.

And she was completely wrong about every one of them.

PART THREE: SOLUTIONS

CHAPTER 14: CHERNOBYL

She was awakened at 6:30 the following morning by the simultaneous sounds of a car horn blowing and several dogs barking, the cause and effect nature of this cacophony doomed forever to remain obscure.

She propped on an elbow, kicked Furl off the foot of the bed, and looked back through her window.

Margot Gavin, dressed only in a floppy gray sweatshirt and dungarees—this in itself was quite an event, something like the equivalent of a reborn Vincent Van Gogh having decided to devote years of his new life copying all of Norman Rockwell's Thanksgiving portraits—was making her way toward the stairway.

Nina, still morning-woozy, had just reached the door and opened it, when Margot ascended on the platform, breathlessly gasping out the question:

"Have you heard?"

Nina frowned, turned, and rasped over her shoulder, while taking the first steps toward the kitchen and tripping over Furl:

"Never ask me that at this time of the morning."

"But..."

She could hear Margot entering and following.

"...but, I didn't know if you'd heard."

"I've never heard. I don't hear."

"Then you don't..."

"No. I've been asleep. Now go on out on the deck. I'll get coffee going."

"You're not going to believe this."

"Then don't tell me."

"I only found out myself about thirty minutes ago. Eve Thornberry came by the shop. I couldn't believe she'd be there so early. But it's like that all over town. Everybody's wandering around shocked. From what I can understand…"

"Don't talk. I have to have coffee. Then, whatever it is, you can tell me."

"I've just got to get all of this off my chest. I can't believe it."

"Is it good news?"

"No! It's…"

"Then please don't talk about it. Go out on the deck."

Margot did so; Nina made a pot of coffee, and, within five minutes, was sitting with her back to the wall of her shack, and her face turned to the incoming tide.

The smell of the sea mixed with the aroma of coffee, and made her, she felt, the equal of whatever news was to come.

This was not true, of course, but she enjoyed believing it.

Margot sat facing her, face somewhat akin to a slab of granite that had been eroded by the sea and was waiting to sink ships.

"All right," Nina asked/slurped. "Tell me."

"I can't believe this has happened."

"Tell me."

"Nina, Clifton Barrett is dead."

A bomb blast.

But somehow, somehow, not surprising.

Nina immediately flashed back to Helen Reddington sitting exactly in the chair where Margot was now, saying:

"Somebody needs to kill him."

John Giusti grabbing him and saying:

"Touch her again and I'll kill you."

And now he was dead.

Too much. Too much to digest.

First though, just get the facts straight.

"What did you say, Margot?"

"Clifton Barrett is dead."

"How?"

"I don't know."

"I mean, what did he die of?"

"I don't know."

"Who found him?"

"I don't know."

"When did this happen, Margot?"

"I don't know."

"Margot, did somebody do something to him?"

"I don't know."

"Did John Giusti have anything to do with it?"

"I don't know."

"Is Helen all right?"

"I don't know."

"What about Hope?"

"I don't know."

"Does Hope even know?"

"I don't know."

"Where is Helen now?"

"I don't know."

"Do they suspect foul play?"

"I don't know."

"My God, I saw him—we all saw him—last night, right after the play. He looked fine. What could have happened to him?"

"I don't know."

"Margot, I'm sorry I keep peppering you with all of these questions."

Margot leaned forward, so that the small table rocked, and took both of Nina's hands in her own.

"It's all right, Nina. It's just so good to get this information of my chest"

The residents of a small community that had been hit by a hydrogen bomb would have had no cause to complain about a shortage of light or heat.

But the amount, the amount...

This was the gossip situation in Bay St. Lucy as the sun rose huge and orange out of the sea at just after 7 a.m.

There was simply too much of it to bear.

It was beyond the levels of human consumption.

Bay St. Lucy had become gossip's new Chernobyl.

On Friday, August 1, the town had been partially flooded by the fringes of Hurricane Deborah.

That was something to talk about.

Then, that evening, a nationally acclaimed Shakespearian production company had mounted a world class production of *Hamlet*, which had been filmed by the Public Broadcasting Service, and was destined to be viewed for years thereafter, if not decades, by theater lovers around the world.

That was something else to talk about.

Two hours after the end of this performance Clifton Barrett, one of the best known actors in the country if not the world, had been found dead, cause uncertain, time uncertain, place uncertain, and anything else even remotely relevant equally uncertain.

That was something to talk about, too.

All of this news had the effect of making normal gossip impossible.

There was simply no place to start.

People would run into each other on the streets and stand mute.

Nothing would come out.

Then, shaking their heads, they would shuffle away, frustrated.

This led to a morning routine of most Bay St. Lucyans breakfasting on something or other, putting on something or other, going downstairs, thinking about the possibilities of things they could do, deciding against them, and resolving instead to spend the morning walking aimlessly through the streets like zombies.

Which Nina and Margot were doing, shaking their heads at a stream of strange looking cars and vans pouring into town, craning their necks to get a good look at the strange helicopters now hovering overhead...

...that one had NBC News printed on it!...

...when somehow or other they got news that a press conference was to be held at 8 AM in the old Bay St. Lucy High School Gymnasium.

In two months there would be a new high school gymnasium, courtesy of Robinson money, but the building was not yet finished.

And so at seven fifty five, they found themselves, along with every other Bay St. Lucyan, crammed into the same space she and Frank had once frequented to watch basketball games.

In the middle of the court three metal chairs sat in a row.

In these chairs sat Edie Towler, District Attorney; Dr. Paul Dawkins, physician and County Coroner; and Moon Rivard, Chief of Police.

A flood of reporters had ringed the people who were to hold the press conference, with more arriving all the time and making their way through the crowd.

Among these reporters was Tomlinson, Clifton Barrett's lawyer.

Edie approached the microphone, setting off, as she did so, a thousand flash bulb explosions.

The microphone squeaked, as it always did. She adjusted it, making it squeak still more. She shook her head and mouthed something incomprehensible to someone sitting at a console of some sort behind the scorer's table.

He nodded and turned some dials.

The microphone died completely.

Then four or five men in janitors' uniforms came and took it away, replacing it with another one, which worked.

Edie's voice now echoed, but it did not squeak.

"Ladies and gentlemen..."

Flash flash flash pop pop pop.

Whrrrrrr of recorders.

Murmurmurmurmurmur of whispers in the crowd, the ability to gossip effectively still not quite back.

"Ladies and gentlemen, as you all know by now, I'm quite sure, there has been a tragedy in Bay St. Lucy."

She paused, took several deep breaths—along with the crowd, which took one collective deep breath—and then continued:

"The great actor, Clifton Barrett, guest in our town and husband of Helen Reddington, was found dead early this morning."

For an instant the silence seemed to become more profound.

Now there was no deep breath.

There was no breathing at all.

The flashbulbs continued to pop.

Several reporters crowded in closer, holding their microphones not more than two feet from Edie's

Edie:

"You all know our County Coroner, Dr. Paul Dawkins. Paul has by now had a chance to make an examination. He will tell you of his findings."

Edie sat down.

Paul Dawkins, tall (once a basketball player in this very gymnasium), slender, wearing a white sport coat and dark blue denim shirt, adjusted the microphone.

He peered at some notes through his wire rimmed glasses.

Sound of an airplane landing, passing low over the building.

More reporters, thought Nina.

"These are the facts as clearly as I can tell them to you now. At precisely five fifteen this morning the emergency unit based in Bay St. Lucy Community Hospital received a 911 call. This call came from the number 415-678-3942. That is the residence of Ms. Hope Reddington. The caller identified herself as Ms. Helen Reddington. The caller went on to say that her husband, whom she identified as Mr. Clifton Barrett, could not be awakened, and was not, so far as she could tell, breathing. A unit was immediately dispatched to the aforesaid residence. Paramedics arrived at five twenty one. They were shown into the residence by Ms. Helen Reddington, who took them upstairs. An immediate check for life signs in Mr. Barrett proved negative. It was determined that he had in fact expired some time earlier that morning. There was no need for any type of emergency cardiac therapy. The body of Mr. Barrett was, accordingly, taken not to the hospital, but to the Jefferson County Morgue, where it now rests."

The reporters could not restrain themselves now.

"What was the cause of death?"

"What did he die of?"

"What happened to him?"

Gestures of restraint from Edie, and then from Moon, who simply rose, and, palms turned outward, activated an invisible force field that pushed the ring of reporters a foot or so back.

"I've had the opportunity to perform a preliminary examination on Mr. Barrett. The official cause of death is cardiac arrest. To the best of my knowledge at this time, the arrest probably occurred between 2:30 and 3 this morning."

"Doctor, was the cardiac arrest the result of any type of drug overdose?"

"I cannot tell you that at this time."

"Were drugs present in Mr. Barrett's blood?"

"Again, I cannot comment on that question."

"You don't know, or you just won't comment?"

"Again, I can only say…"

Tomlinson now on his feet.

Suit just as exquisite, but black now and not charcoal gray.

That superb head of white, perfectly combed hair, glistening in the morning light streaming through a row of windows just behind where Nina was sitting.

"I'm sorry, Mister Coroner. You've had a chance to examine the body?"

"Yes."

"And you don't know any more to say than, 'his heart stopped'?"

"No."

"How is this possible?"

"Sir, all I can tell you is…"

Tomlinson, face flushed, another step forward.

He was almost in Paul Dawkins' face, and even Moon seemed unable to hold him back.

"This is absurd! My client, Clifton Barrett, was attacked two nights ago in a local restaurant."

Edie, half standing:

"Mr. Tomlinson..."

"...no no, let me finish here! And everybody in this building needs to hear this. He was viciously attacked by some deranged woman, and nothing at all was done about it. Now this man, who I can tell you all because I've been for some time his personal attorney, has never had any history of heart disease, is found dead in his bed. He routinely took an over the counter pain suppressant and a mild sedative. But he had been following this routine for years with no problems. And now all you can say is, 'his heart stopped'? That's all you know about the exact cause of death?"

"Sir, we will ascertain the cause of death."

"When?"

"I'm sorry but I can't say more at this time."

"Why not?"

"There are things—that's really all I can say."

"You haven't said anything. May I ask a question of Officer Rivard?"

Moon Rivard rose.

"I'm here."

"Are the police looking into the prospect that there may have been foul play involved here?"

"When a death is sudden, and unexpected, we always have to make a report."

"Make a report?"

"Yes, Sir."

"That's all you're doing?"

"At this time."

"You've not arrested anybody?"

A shake of the head.

"Not any reason to, at this time."

"All right, then, I'll ask the Doctor again," bellowed Tomlinson. "Doctor, is there a possibility that Clifton Barrett may have been poisoned?"

At this Edie Towler stood, and gestured for the coroner to stand.

"This concludes the press conference."

So saying, she strode out of the gymnasium, leading Paul Dawkins and Moon Rivard out through the visitors exit.

For the rest of the morning, Bay St. Lucy found itself plagued by small cancers that kept breaking out in the form of press conferences. This was probably natural, since the city airport was jammed to capacity by private jets flying in carrying more and more reporters, and these reporters had to file stories. Every citizen, every shop owner, seemed fair game.

"Did you know Clifton Barrett?"

"Do you have any comment on an alleged assault that took place some nights ago?"

"Did Mr. Barrett abuse his wife?"

"To the best of your knowledge, was the Barrett's marriage in trouble of some sort?"

"Did Mr. Barrett use drugs?"

"We're from *People* Magazine, and…."

"I'm from *The New York Times*, and…"

On and on and on.

Nina found herself drawn here and there by these abscesses, watching them grow, smiling inwardly at the stupidity of the questions, feeling a bit of pity for the townspeople who struggled vainly to provide answers—for the whole thing was impossible to make sense of—and feeling an equal amount of contempt for people who seemed to enjoy themselves simply because they wanted to be on national TV.

Finally it was ten o'clock in the morning. The sun had climbed halfway up a sky that no longer had anything to do with hurricanes coming or going, and was just blue-shimmering and hot.

The hospital drew her like a magnet. Word was that Helen and Hope Reddington had been taken there for observation, and that both were about to be released (They could not stay in a small private room forever) and she wanted to be there when they were.

She had no idea why she wanted to be there.

She could not invite them to stay in her one room shack.

(And, as she had earlier told John Giusti, every family in Bay St. Lucy had already made such an offer.)

She could not help them with any kind of advice.

The simple truth was, she finally found herself admitting mentally, that she was motivated by morbid curiosity.

So she arrived at ten and waited, standing around, overhearing bits of gossip.

"How is Helen holding up?"

"I don't know. The minister is in there now."

Another voice.

"I heard she's just being real…you know, quiet. Marge Peterson had gone in with flowers and was just out in the hall. She said Helen was just real quiet, and asked to be left alone for a little while."

This kind of talk made Nina face a question she'd been avoiding.

What did Helen Reddington think about the death of her husband?

She could remember Helen lying there on the deck, cigarette smoldering, her dark and enigmatic eyes focused on the horizon—talking about the hell her life had become.

Made so by this man.

"Somebody needs to kill him," Helen had said.

Now he was dead.

But how?

"She was just real quiet…"

I'll bet, thought Nina, *that she was.*

By ten thirty, the people-tumor that was spreading in front of Bay St. Lucy's hospital had metathesized alarmingly, so that ambulances would have been blocked from approaching emergency rooms, had there been any ambulances out at this particular time, which there apparently weren't, the town having during the past ten hours exhausted the daily supply of emergencies it was allowed to have.

"Ms. Bannister?"

This from a whispered voice close behind her.

"Ms. Bannister?"

She turned and saw a short and sandy-haired young woman whom she did not recognize, but who, to judge from her starched white uniform, appeared to be a hospital orderly of some sort.

"Yes?"

"You're Nina Bannister?"

"I am."

The young woman leaned closer.

Her whisper was barely audible.

"Would you mind to follow me?"

"What…"

"They're going to be releasing the Reddingtons."

Nina still did not comprehend what role she was to play in this, but the woman took her arm gently and began to pull.

They had begun to make their way through the crowd.

The whispers continued, over the woman's shoulder.

"There are too many people out here at the front entrance; they're taking them out at the rear of the hospital. All these reporters…"

"Yes, I see."

"But…well, Ms. Helen is asking for you."

"Why?"

"I think she wants you to do some things for her, ma'am."

And so Nina followed obediently as they left the main part of the crowd, made their way around a corner of the building, and came to a halt behind a nondescript pale blue door which sat in the middle of a nondescript not-quite yellow wall.

The words "Do Not Enter" were stenciled in white on the door.

Which immediately opened.

Standing within it, frozen, motionless for an instant, were Helen and Hope Reddington, dressed as if for church (where, Nina wondered, had the dress clothes come from?…then she remembered the fifty or so lady church members standing at the other side of the hospital and she began to get some idea)—and ringed by one or two doctors, one or two policemen, and one or two of those people who never seem to have a real function but who always pop up at important events.

It took a millisecond for Helen to recognize Nina.

Then she dove out of the doorway and tackled her as though sacking a quarterback.

Neither she nor Nina fell down, but the embrace was so strong, the capture so complete, that the play would have been called dead, and Nina would have lost five yards.

Helen was sobbing.

After a few seconds, Nina realized that she was sobbing, too.

"Nina..."

"It's all right."

Finally Hope was standing beside them. She beamed up at Nina.

Yes, it was Hope, the real Hope, because once again she was looking up and out from under something.

"Nina, dear!"

"How are you Hope?"

"I'm fine, dear. They're taking such good care of us!"

"I know, Hope!"

Then Hope, turning to Helen:

"Can we go home now, Helen?"

"No, Grandmamma, not quite yet."

"I'm just a bit tired."

"I know, Grandmamma."

"I'd like to lie down in my own room."

"It won't be long now. But..."

She pulled Nina away a foot or so and whispered:

"Things are going to be very difficult for a time."

"I know, Helen. Whatever I can do..."

"There's a crowd on the other side of the building."

"Yes."

"I'm sure they'll be here, and soon. I know reporters. When there's a scandal..."

"I understand."

"There's one thing I want you to do...really for Grandmamma."

"Whatever I can do."

"All right. It's as I've been telling Grandmamma. We can't go back—we can't go back there, right now. It's just...I can't stay..."

"I understand."

"So we'll be staying elsewhere for some days. I don't know how long."

"All right."

"Here is a list..."

She handed Nina a folded slip of paper.

"These are toiletries, a few items of clothing, some sentimental things...they should all be easy to find, and can fit in two small suitcases. If you'd gather them from the house..."

"Of course."

"Several ladies from the church have keys."

"It won't be a problem."

"it will be such a comfort for..."

But by then the crowd had discovered them, and came rushing around the corner.

It had soon pinned them against the back wall of the hospital.

It was as though they were an exhibit at the state fair.

"When was the last time you saw your husband, Ms. Reddington?"

"Had he been drinking?"

"Does he take drugs?"

"Do you think he died of an overdose?"

"What can you tell us about his last moments?"

"Is it true that he'd been abusing you?"

All of these questions were interrupted by Tomlinson, the attorney, who pushed through the crowd, made his way to Helen and her grandmother, put an arm around each of them, and said in a bullhorn voice:

"Ms. Reddington will not be answering any questions at this time."

"Can you tell us where she will be going now? Where she's going to be living for the next days?"

He nodded:

"Arrangements have been made for Ms. Reddington and her grandmother to stay at a hotel in Vicksburg. I'm not at liberty to divulge the name of the hotel. We will be leaving Bay St. Lucy soon, by helicopter. That's all I can say now about that matter."

"Can you tell us anything more about what happened to Mr. Barrett?"

"Not at this time. We are insisting, of course, on an autopsy."

"Has foul play been ruled out?"

"Nothing has been ruled out."

"Excuse me!"

Helen Reddington extricated herself from the attorney's grasp, took a step forward, and, ignoring him, addressed the crowd:

"I'd like to make a statement."

Tomlinson, obviously taken aback, reddened:

"Helen, you don't have to say anything."

"I know, but I want to. I want to get this over with."

"I have to advise strongly…"

"I understand your advice, but I intend to make this statement. Now please allow me to do so."

Silence.

Helen Reddington continued:

"My husband and I, along with my grandmother, returned to our house around 11:30 last evening, after the performance of *Hamlet*. We were driven home by friends. Several people stayed for some minutes to wish us well, but we were tired, and Grandmamma was exhausted, and so we made our excuses. We went up to bed. My husband routinely takes medication for back pain. He also takes a mild sedative to help him sleep. Within a short time I could tell he was sleeping normally. I went to sleep almost immediately myself. I slept soundly. I knew nothing until first light came through the window, a bit after five. I could tell something was wrong. I'm not even sure how. Clifton was…well, too still. I touched him, and he was cold.   spoke to him, and then shouted to him, and then shook him. After that, I knew. I had a cell phone that's on the nightstand. I called 911, and said that my husband was not breathing. I then continued to shake him and try to make him talk to me. But he was…just cold. After a minute or so I could hear the sirens coming. So I got up, put on a robe, went downstairs, and woke Grandmamma. I told her not to worry, but Clifton was ill, and would be taken to the hospital. After that, the vehicles arrived, and you know the rest."

Silence for a moment.

Tomlinson stepped forward and was about to speak, but Helen Reddington interrupted him.

"Now there is something further. I'd like to announce that, as of this moment, Mr. Tomlinson is no longer our attorney."

Stunned silence.

Finally Tomlinson:

"Helen, you can't fire me. I'm your husband's attorney."

"My husband is dead."

"But…"

"And you're fired."

More stunned silence.

Tomlinson spoke.

No words came out of his mouth.

Helen Reddington again, to the crowd.

"My grandmother and I will be staying with a friend in Bay St. Lucy. As for the autopsy—if the coroner's report deems that foul play has been a possibility, then ordering the autopsy is, as I understand it, his decision. If he does not, then my husband's body will be cremated day after tomorrow, and it will be done here. Now if that is all…"

It was, of course, not all, but during the moment's lapse required for the known universe to resume motion according to its eternal laws, a vehicle of some kind rounded the corner of the hospital.

It worked its way through the crowd, honking once, but not needing to honk a second time, its two ton weight and battered bumper constituting enough force to move *The New York Times* easily, and—albeit with a bit more of a struggle—even *People* Magazine.

The vehicle—it was a battered van—stopped five feet from the Reddingtons who, Helen with an arm around Hope, made their way up and into it.

Helen dragged the heavy panel door closed behind the two of them.

And they drove away, John Giusti at the wheel.

Within half a minute, they had disappeared around the corner.

In another ten seconds, Moon Rivard was standing at the same corner, a bullhorn in his hand.

The bullhorn brayed:

"I want all of you to listen."

All of them did.

"The Reddingtons deserve their privacy. They been through a lot. Now I'm going to have two squad cars go with them. Anybody else wants to tag along, we gonna arrest. I hope that's clear."

It was.

And the crowd dispersed.

CHAPTER 15: MEMORIES OF AGATHA CHRISTIE

The rest of the day disappeared somehow in a welter of errand running, question answering, confused blathering, and wondering what in heaven's name could be happening. But by nightfall, Nina had succeeded in filling several suitcases with items from the Reddington home, borrowing Margot's Volkswagen which would be used for a pack-mule trip out to John Giusti's home the following morning, eating eleven or twelve (she'd forgotten which) small meals at various shops and coffee stands scattered throughout town as she dispersed, re-gathered, and dispersed again whatever new gossip happened to be floating around at that particular hour—and in general succeeded in using her brain as much as possibly without actually thinking about anything at all.

It was dark when she returned home. The moon had begun to rise over the offshore drilling rig, which now seemed to serve as a rack for it to sit on, as though it were a white and shining bowling ball ready to be picked up and hurled underhanded toward some as yet invisible heavenly pins.

Barrett's attorney, Tomlinson, was sitting on the top step leading up to her shack.

He was, incredibly, wearing only slacks and a short sleeved sport shirt.

He smiled down at her.

"Hope you don't mind. Several people told me where you live."

"I don't mind. I don't think."

"Don't worry; I won't bite."

"All right. Come on in then."

She unlocked the door, and he walked in behind her.

In five minutes they were sitting on her deck, sipping iced tea, watching the moon make the waves silver.

A candle burned on the table, flickering orange, its flame dodging subtly this way and that, either blown about by or successfully avoiding a weak breeze from the sea.

Tomlinson was a florid man, and he would always be imposing.

She wondered if the straight chair he sat in would support him, and winced as he leaned forward to put his perspiration-soaked and gleaming forearms on her rickety table.

He smiled.

"I want to thank you for seeing me."

"Not at all," she said, knowing very little else to say.

"I'm told you are a very knowledgeable person about the town and about what goes on here. I've had talks with Mr. Bennett."

"Yes, Jackson."

"He admires you a great deal."

"Well. My husband Frank hired Jackson a good many years ago."

"So he said. You know, I assume, that Mr. Bennett has been employed by the Reddingtons to handle their affairs now."

"I didn't know that."

"There were several calls made this morning and afternoon; it's all official now."

"And you are…"

"I'm fired."

"I'm sorry."

"Goes with the job sometimes. I'm sure your husband could sympathize. I've been told that he was an attorney."

"Yes. That happened from time to time. We always made it through."

"I'm sure you did."

He paused, looked around.

"It's marvelous out here. I wish I had such a place."

"You live…"

"In an apartment, Upper West Side. Business requires it."

"I understand."

"Someday though."

They were silent for a time.

Finally he continued:

"People around town seem to trust you. I thought you comported yourself admirably in the courtroom several days ago. I had to make you look bad. I'm sorry for that."

"It's all right."

"But now…"

He sipped his tea.

OK, out with it. Out with it.

"Now, I have to get some things off my chest."

"All right. Go ahead."

"You understand, this must all be confidential. If I thought you'd tell other people…"

"I won't. What is it?"

He breathed deeply, then continued:

"Clifton Barrett was not an admirable man. I represented him in his various…affairs. That was my job. It did not mean I admired him."

"All right. I can understand that."

"I have no right to tell you what I'm about to say now. But someone has to say it. Someone—other than myself— needs to know it."

"Go on."

"Mr. Barrett was planning to divorce Helen Reddington."

"I know."

"You what?"

"I know. Mr. Tomlinson, Helen was my student at one time. Now I look upon her as a friend."

He nodded.

"I should have known, then. Of course she would not have kept the matter strictly confidential."

"No. She needed to talk to someone."

"There are rumors about…well, about liaisons, sexual affairs that she may or may not have been involved with."

"She wasn't."

"Photographs…"

"Fakes."

"You're certain of this?"

"I know Helen. I know her upbringing. She's a girl from Bay St. Lucy. She had the misfortune, Mr. Tomlinson, of being extremely beautiful and extremely talented. She went to the great city of New York just as one of the tourists here goes out into the great Gulf of Mexico. She wound up in the clutches of something very vile. Something that was eating her."

Tomlinson nodded, slowly.

"That may be correct. Mr. Barrett preferred...well, younger women."

"Girls such as Helen."

"I prefer to say 'younger women.' If I allowed myself to call them 'girls'..."

"You wouldn't like yourself very much."

"No."

There was a moaning, wailing sound from somewhere out at sea.

"What's that?" he asked.

"I don't know."

"A whale?"

She shook her head.

"No. Too close to shore. Sometimes we get noises like that. I'm not sure anyone who lives here knows what makes them."

They sat for a time, listening to the disappearing sound.

Tomlinson was still looking out over the water when he continued:

"There were also financial matters."

"I know about those, too."

"I had, a year or so earlier, advised Ms. Reddington to pool her resources with her husband's. His resources were somewhat less than she'd been led to believe."

"You lied to her."

"I acted on the advice of my client. I simply presented things in a particular way."

"He lost," Nina said, "most of his money. Now he was planning to use made-up scandals to divorce Helen and take all of her money. As well has her grandmother's house."

"Arrangements were to be made that would have allowed Ms. Reddington to remain in her home until..."

"…until she died or had to be put in a nursing home. I know. Good of him."

"He was, as I say, not in all respects an admirable man."

"We can probably agree on that."

"But he is dead now."

"Yes, he is."

"And, Ms. Bannister, I'm not a Shakespearean scholar as you are."

"I'm not a scholar. I'm a retired English teacher."

"You know a great deal. But I was at the performance of *Hamlet* last night. And one line does present itself to me at this moment."

"What's the line?"

"'Murder will out.' There is another phrase. 'Murder most foul'."

There was little response to that, and Nina was not much inclined to talk about Agatha Christie. Finally, she could only ask Tomlinson what she'd been avoiding asking herself all day:

"You think Clifton Barrett was murdered?"

"Don't you?"

"I have no reason to believe that."

"Really? The man had a bad back. He took a pain killer, and he took a simple medication every night so that he could sleep. Otherwise, he took no drugs. Last night he went to sleep as usual. He never woke up. Can you explain that?"

"No."

"The divorce which was to ruin his wife financially, and probably professionally, is now never to happen. All financial records are confidential, and in the hands of Mr. Bennett, who is now her personal lawyer. Mr. Barrett has no professional agent, preferring to have me—along with himself—act as his sole business representative."

"I can understand that, given the way he must have done business."

"I'll let that lie for now."

"All right."

"But you must remember that Ms. Reddington is now residing, along with her grandmother, at the residence of her old lover. She is back in the arms of Bay St. Lucy. The money that the city was to pay to Mr. Barrett is now due—a good deal of it, even after expenses for the production—to her. This lover, by the way, publicly threatened, in my presence and your presence, to kill Mr. Barrett."

"That doesn't mean he did it."

"It means he had motive. They both had motive."

"Mr. Tomlinson, are you saying Helen and John poisoned Clifton Barrett?"

He shook his head.

"No."

"Good. Because if you do that publicly…"

"I won't have to say it publicly, Ms. Bannister. The County Coroner will do that for me."

Nina stared at him.

"What are you talking about?"

"I've just been informed that there will be an autopsy."

"When?"

"Tomorrow morning at seven o'clock. I believe I know what that autopsy will show."

"Which is?"

"It will show that Clifton Barrett died of a lethal drug overdose. Now there's only one woman who could have administered such an overdose, and that is Helen Reddington."

"She's not capable of that."

"I submit that you don't know what she is or is not capable of. But I will tell you one other thing: Clifton Barrett may be gone, and I may no longer represent him legally, but I am an officer of the court, and I have an obligation to the man. Once that report comes in, I will put as much pressure on the local authorities as possible to arrest young Ms. Reddington. This thing will not be swept under the rug and labeled a 'celebrity drug overdose.' Clifton did not kill himself. And I will not stand by to watch his murder go unavenged."

"We wouldn't try to do that here. It's not like us."

Barrett pursed his lips, and poured more tea.

"We'll see."

"Mr. Tomlinson...I know nothing about these things. But let's say the autopsy says what you predict it will. Isn't it possible that Mr. Barrett did overdose, and purely by accident? These things do happen, don't they?"

He shook his head.

"Clifton Barrett had celebrated a hundred opening nights. This was not the first time he'd drunk Scotch to celebrate. He was thirty seven years old, Ms. Bannister, and whatever his lifestyle, he understood it. He was not a teenager experimenting with drugs. No. I do think he overdosed, but it was on something his wife gave him. His wife or her lover, or both."

"Mr. Tomlinson..."

"Her lover, the man who threatened Mr. Giusti, is a veterinarian, is he not?"

"Yes.'

"He understands drugs?"

"I'm sure he does."

Silence for a time.

Finally Nina asked:

"Why are you telling me all of this?"

He rose, turned his back, walked to the edge of the railing, took a deep breath, and stood facing her with his arms crossed.

"Ms. Bannister, every community has a moral leader. And in this community, that person is you."

"I'm not sure that's true."

"It is true."

"And if it is?"

"Then listen to me: I've dealt all my professional life with people who commit crimes. Some of them can live with that fact. Others can't. These two young people can't. I'm telling you, Ms. Bannister, look to them. No one deserves to die, not even a man like Clifton Barrett. And if these two young people are responsible for his death, then that fact will destroy them."

He took two steps toward the door, then turned and said:

"And it will ultimately destroy this community."

Then he left.

Nina walked along the beach until shortly before midnight.

Sophomore World Literature.

"You fixed us up. We started dating because of your class."

Oedipus Rex.

There's something unclean in your community. And the plague will remain on the community until the murderer is punished, or driven out.

The waves continued to crash in, break into foam, and dissipate into a film of water at her bare feet.

Did you do it, John?

Did you do it, Helen?

She had no idea.

But a small voice kept telling her as she walked that the world was about to find out.

And soon.

CHAPTER 16: HOPE SPRINGS

The following morning Nina drove Margot's Volkswagen up the coast to John Giusti's house.

It had been some time since she'd driven an actual automobile, let alone one that demanded a working knowledge of an actual gearshift mechanism.

But she managed it, glad in some ways that the mental effort involved in remembering German engineering (for she had driven a Volkswagen years ago, while in high school) displaced the other things—betrayal, divorce, philandering, death, murder, etc.—that would otherwise have been chasing around in her brain.

She found some consolation in the fact that there was no other traffic, and so she could wend along at a comfortable forty miles an hour.

She also took comfort in knowing the directions, and not having to ponder about this turn or that questionable road/lane/bog/ dog path.

So that, within an hour, and without too much consternation, she'd made the trip, and now found herself putt-putting up the drive.

She parked and cut off the engine.

Having unloaded part of the car, and with a suitcase grasped firmly in each hand, she began to make her way down through the dense pine foliage.

Breaking through the limbs and out over the beach, she found herself dazzled by morning sunlight wildly reflected by the clear glass Rubik's Cube of a house that stood at the end of the pier.

During her first visit, the house had been daylight by moonlight, so intensely did it reflect the night sky; now, with the sun and the early sea light to work with, it simply went insane, each sprawling panel of glass flashing a different solar flare with every step she took.

She found herself remembering the pier, how it moved, almost imperceptibly, but never without the sounds of creaking boards mixed with the grating of incoming tidal currents.

"Nina!"

Helen spotted her first and rushed out of the door, April rather than August, her face free of makeup now, her dark eyes glittering like evening jewelry worn for an early occasion.

"Nina, thank you for coming out!"

The embrace almost lifted her off the pier planking.

"It's so good of you to do this—to bring all of these things!"

"It's nothing at all, Helen. But how are you? How are you holding up? And how is your grandmother?"

"We're both as well as can be expected. John has been wonderful to us. Officer Rivard has promised us privacy until more can be learned. There have been no reporters. We've at least had a chance to get our thoughts together. Grandmamma spent yesterday afternoon walking on the beach, and she's down there now, reading."

"Nina!"

Now John bounding out of the house, barrel chested, grinning...

"Nina, it's so good that you're here! Here, let me have those suitcases!"

The three of them in a general embrace.

Now various animals joining the knot...

...there, the great Labrador retriever, sauntering his way out of the house and along the planking...

Other dogs.

And out there, on the great platform that served as a base for the house, as well as in the open windows and doors of the house itself—all the animals in the world: squirrels, rabbits, cats—probably wolves, tigers and elephants for all she knew.

...it was like she was walking toward the middle of Noah's Ark, the inhabitants of which, having just found land, were uncertain as to whether they wanted to leave their spot of brightness on the ocean.

"John, there are three other suitcases in the car."

"It's all right; I'll go back for them in a minute. Come inside, though. Come on."

Helen and John made a sandwich of her, each taking an arm, and escorted her toward The Great Kingdom of Oz, which sat glittering at the end of a yellow brick road that was a brown wooden pier.

"Isn't John's house magnificent?"

"It is, Helen. I'm not sure I'd call it a 'house.'"

"No, no, it's something different, isn't it? It's not a house at all; it's a jewel!"

They approached the jewel and she heard the appreciative and eager yowls and yelps of whatever animals were awake to welcome them; then horses of different colors—except they were small mammals mixed with the occasional iguana, the occasional wingless fowl—began to scatter before them as John reached out and opened the door.

They went outside into the house.

Things became, impossibly, brighter and breezier.

All around them was the Gulf Coast of Mississippi, laughing, luxuriating blue blue blue BLUE in a brightness it had never known, having been constrained for all its existence to show itself through human or animal eyes, and not these massive lenses created by a suicidal drunken architect.

Nina looked around her: the thing that in most houses would have passed as a living room but here could only have been called a sub-solarium, had undergone a transformation. The same pieces of furniture were still here, serving as resting places and launching platforms for the animals; but two women, having been in the space for almost a day, had tamed it and broken its spirit.

An armchair sat where it could actually have been sat in, if the dog were removed.

A white leather couch fronted a glass coffee table, which sat upon a thick—one would hope—panel of glass, beneath which sat the ocean.

Beneath which sat the bottom of the ocean.

Which one, vaguely but undeniably, from time to time but not too rarely, could actually make out.

Through fifteen feet of water.

The order of sight was:

Coffee, glass, legs and feet of guest, glass, water—and Bottom of the Sea.

In the Magic Kingdom of John Giusti!

Which was so fantastic, so transformative—that Nina almost forgot about reality.

She almost forgot the events of the last day.

Of course, that could not happen.

The great octagon of light and space drew them into it, through it, and out of it, so that within some minutes they were sitting on the same deck where, an infinite amount of time ago when the universe still made sense, John Giusti had given her shrimp.

Now they were drinking coffee.

Fifty yards or so out to sea, a school of white fish had adjourned class for recess, and the students were jumping ecstatically, each trying to outdo each other in height, all of the splashes audible above the constant grating of the waves around the deck poles.

"Nina, look back. Back on the beach!"

She turned and did so.

The beach was some distance from them, and it took some instants of Earth Sight Replacing Ocean Sight for her to realize the small pile of brightly colored rags that had washed onto the beach and was lying, motionless and straw-hatted, a few feet in front of a dense wall of forest—was Hope, reading.

Silence for a time.

Of course she was going to have to break that silence.

Dammit.

Why was she always being put in these positions?

It was the schoolteacher thing, never going away, never leaving her alone.

There they all were in the office, she having to get to the bottom of something or other, who stole whose homework, or who cheated on what test.

Except these were her best two students.

"I have to tell you both that Mr. Tomlinson visited me last night."

Helen's brow furrowed and the darkness within her eyes intensified.

"He had no right to contact you. He has no right to do anything here. He's fired."

"He knows that."

"Then what did he want from you?"

"He came to tell me—and I have to tell you—that there's to be an autopsy this morning. Actually it's probably already taken place."

A screaming patch of gulls tore over like World War II fighters, dropping on the deck and into the ocean objects that she wished might have been bombs, but that she knew were not.

John pursed his lips and said, quietly:

"That had to happen. A case like this...they couldn't just let it go."

"No, John, they couldn't. And Mr. Tomlinson thinks..."

"He thinks we committed a murder."

Nina nodded, as the words, 'Yes he does' formed in her throat, thought of going out into the room, thought better of it, and retreated into her stomach.

"Is that," whispered Helen, "what the town thinks?"

"The town, Helen, is a chicken with its head cut off. It doesn't know what to think."

"All right. Then—is that what you think?"

Nina shook her head.

"No. I told Tomlinson what I think. I know you. I know both of you. I knew your parents, and their parents. I taught you. No, I don't believe you could kill anybody."

"Thank you, Nina."

"But I have to ask you, Helen..."

"Yes?"

"That night, after the play…"

"Go on."

"There had to be a great deal of confusion. You were there in the bedroom with him. Did he ask you to give him his medication?"

"No. He never did that. He mixed a small amount of pain medication with a teaspoon of something to make him sleep. It was always the same. The only difference was, this time he seemed extremely tired, more tired than usual. He drank the medicine and then went immediately to sleep. I noticed this because…"

"Why, Helen?"

"He had drunk some Scotch after the performance."

"I know. I remember watching him give his little speech to the city."

"Often when he does that, and we go to bed…"

Silence.

John: "He becomes angry at you. And he beats you."

"Yes. Or, sometimes the other thing. You know."

"We know," said Nina, quietly.

Helen half-smiled and said, softly:

"Sometimes I'm not certain which I prefer. But night before last, nothing. He just went to sleep."

"All right. There's nothing more, then. I'm sorry I even talked to you about it."

"But Nina…"

John leaned forward.

"I have to tell you. All right, you know it, and I don't mind telling everybody, if it should come to that. I wanted the man dead. He was a monster; he had no right to live. Last night, during the play, I walked around the garden, clenching and unclenching my fists. If I'd have seen him then…"

He paused to get control of himself.

Then:

"…but I didn't see him then. I left before the play was over. I drove home and spent most of the night just lying awake. I got to Helen's just after sunup. I wanted to get the confrontation over. But the police were there, told me about Barrett's death, and also told me Helen had been taken, with her grandmother, to the hospital for observation. I was able to speak to her just before they took her inside. That was when we planned that she should come out here."

"I understand, John."

"I know it looks bad, the way I acted at the courthouse, and how we had dated. Old lover, etc. But I let Helen go once in my life and I won't do it again. Nina, if I had wanted Clifton Barrett dead, I'd have done it with my hands, not with drugs. And he would have known who was killing him. He wouldn't have died the easy way, in his sleep."

Silence for a time.

"You didn't have to tell me all of this," Nina said quietly. "I believe both of you. I know neither one of you could kill anybody."

"It's all right," said Helen. "We know we're going to have to answer these questions."

"That's not necessarily..."

The only thing that followed Nina's 'necessarily' was a symphony of barking, bellowing, yelping, screaming, and growling, all of which, she seemed to know instinctively, signified either the beginning of a Tarzan movie or the arrival of a visitor.

"Someone's out there," said John, rising.

He had crossed the kitchen and half the living room when the door swung open toward him.

Moon Rivard stood in the entranceway.

"I'm sorry to disturb you folks; Excuse me for coming in, but the door seemed to be open."

An invisible and irresistible force pulled Nina and Helen to their feet and transported them to the far edge of the living room without their being aware of it; but the effect was the same, there they all were, Moon in the doorway, John in the center of the room, and Nina and Helen backed against a bookshelf.

"It's all right, Moon," John said. "And thank you for all the help you've given us so far. We've had privacy."

"That's all right. Glad I could do it. But...well, I got to tell both of you. Things have kind of changed now."

The autopsy, Nina found herself thinking.

"How," Helen asked, "have things changed?"

"Well. Dey was an autopsy. We got the results a little more than an hour and a half ago. So I had to come out."

"What were the results?" asked Helen.

"What they found was..."

He was interrupted by a figure coming through the door, peering up and out from under everything.

"Officer Rivard! You're here!"

Moon turned and watched as Hope Reddington crept by him like the gradual movement of the sun.

"Yes, ma'am. How are you today, Ms. Hope?"

"I'm fine. I'm feeling very well. I slept wonderfully. Mr. Giusti's house is so lovely. And one can hear the ocean."

"I'm sure that's true, Ms. Hope."

"Grandmamma," said Helen, "you might want to leave us, for a moment. I think Officer Rivard has some business to discuss."

"Of course he has some business to discuss, dear. I was lying down on the beach, reading, and I saw him walking out the pier. I've been expecting him."

They all stared at her.

Finally Helen:

"Why were you expecting him, Grandmamma?"

"Because they must have had an autopsy by now; that would have been the thing to do. And after the autopsy, it would have been logical to expect to see him here, with us."

"Why?"

"Because I murdered Mister Barrett, dear. Now if you will all wait, I'll go to my room and put my things on."

So saying, she disappeared into a doorway that had heretofore been invisible, while the four of them stared at each other and neglected to breathe.

CHAPTER 17: FOUL DEEDS WILL OUT

A certain number of seconds, minutes, quarter-hours, etc., went by after Hope Reddington's announcement that she had murdered Clifton Barrett. But since the announcement was one of those events so shocking that they're able to stop time entirely, render it irrelevant, smash it and destroy it so completely that its very existence never was or could have been—those increments of chronology are irrelevant and will not be discussed here.

Time only resumed its flow after Hope, dressed now as she might have been for church, with the same immaculate white sports jacket and coral reef sequined Capri pants, the same huge-loop silver earrings the diameters of which amounted to precisely one half of her height—reentered the living room, and beamed at Nina.

"Nina, I didn't even realize that you were here! Please forgive me for not greeting you!"

"That's all right, Hope. Don't worry about it."

"You drove out with our things, didn't you?"

"Some of them."

"How thoughtful of you! But we won't be needing them now. At least I won't."

"Grandmamma…"

"Helen, you and John may want to go on staying here. That's probably for the best."

"Grandmamma, you don't need to go back into town."

For a time it was impossible to tell which was brighter, the sun or Hope's smile.

"Of course I must go back into town, dear. I must go with Officer Rivard. That's why he's come."

"Grandmamma, you're confused."

"No, I'm not. John, I've packed a small suitcase. It's in the room where I slept last night. Will you please get it for me?"

John stepped forward toward the door to the bedroom, then back toward the door to the open deck, then sideways toward the door leading outside, and then back to the spot from which he'd begun, wobbling slightly as he went through these dance steps, as though he were a large bear high on marijuana.

He did not speak.

Helen did.

"Try to think clearly, Grandmamma."

"I always try to think clearly, dear."

"This thing that you've accused yourself of...you couldn't possibly have done it."

"But I did it."

"No, no, and you must stop saying this."

"Why? Why must I? Do you wish me to deny it? That would be wrong. It would be immoral, and I'll not do it. It would be lying. And it would be unchristian. No. No, I'll none of it. Now let's get on with what must be done. I'm certain Officer Rivard has more things to do than stand around here and chat."

Moon Rivard performed the same Latinate dance step that John had attempted, only in waltz tempo rather than cut time, the alternation springing from a cross between his increased confusion and his innate Cajun blood.

He did not speak either.

Nina was not in the room at the time, or anywhere else.

So there was no possibility for anyone to speak except Helen.

She said the first thing in a great while that seemed to make sense to everyone.

"Let's go outside and sit on the deck. John, could you make some more coffee?"

The Great Coastal Bear that was John rocked back and forth in an affirmative gesture and turned back toward the kitchen, shuffling off to see if it might afford a hiding place.

It did not. There were no hiding places, and in two minutes they were sitting around the table, drinking coffee, stunned, trying to believe things were normal.

It was a splendid summer morning by the seaside.

Hope was in her element, making sure that cream was present, and sugar, but of course not sugar because now everyone used Splenda, and sugar was bad for us anyway.

"Isn't John's house beautiful?"

They all agreed that it was.

"If I lived here, John, I would never go anywhere else. I would stay in my house all day long, and probably just sit out here. Do you spend a great deal of time here?"

"Yes, Ms. Reddington, I do."

"I can understand that, dear. I really can. No, the fact is that I gave Mr. Barrett a fatal dose of Percodan."

Most of the sentence would have hung motionless above the table, not knowing what to do with itself, but the word 'Percodan' went shooting off over the ocean, twisting, jumping, squealing, and flashing in the sun as though it had become a school of flying fish.

Something very difficult not to pay attention to.

"You what?" asked Helen.

"Percodan."

"I know that's what you said, but…"

"I am nothing," said Hope, first sipping, then smiling, then earring tugging, then beginning the process again, "nothing at all, if not the dutiful pharmacist's wife. Twenty-five years of working there in the pharmacy, helping out. Nina, did you find that, after a certain number of years you felt as though you too were an attorney, just as Frank was?"

Nina attempted to say "Wadawadawada" but could not, all of her mental energies trained completely on the school of flying fish that was the word 'Percodan,' now circling gleefully in a patch of sky almost directly above them.

Hearing no answer to her question, Hope continued.

"Percodan is an effective pain killer, especially for problems with the back. But it should not be mixed with alcohol, and not with Pitocin, which I'm sure all of you know is a common sleep inducer."

There! Another flying object!

Look how it glistens in the sun!

Pitocin!

Fly, fly, little Pitocin, while we all watch you, absolutely astonished at the things one sees these days!

"Grandmamma, you could not have…"

"Please don't tell me what I could or could not have done. It does not become you, and, though I hate to seem harsh, it's…well, all right, I have to go ahead and say it. It's rude, Helen. It's actually rude of you. You should apologize."

"I'm sorry. But how could you…"

"Oh, it was quite easy. On the evening after the performance, you will remember that I came up to your bedroom to say goodnight to both of you. Mr. Barrett was…"

She was interrupted by Moon Rivard:

"Ms. Hope?"

She looked up and out from under all of the coffee accessories, and up and out from under the words 'Percodan' and 'Pitocin,' which were now buzzing like flies around the sugar bowl, and smiled at Moon Rivard:

"Yes, Officer?"

"You probably shouldn't say anymore now."

"But I…"

To which Helen interjected:

"Officer Rivard, what did they autopsy show?"

Moon Rivard pursed his lips, then said:

"The man was killed by an overdose of…well, of what Ms. Hope has just said."

"All right, then."

Helen leaned toward Nina.

"Nina, do you have the number of Jackson Bennett?"

Surprisingly, Nina found herself able to compose an answer:

"Yes."

"Please call him. We're going to need an attorney."

After that the coffee klatch dissolved into murmurs, plans, whispers, and moving arounds, while Nina found herself searching in her purse for the notebook of important numbers, and saying to herself:

"My God. She did it. She really did it."

She found the number, thought about calling it, decided that Helen should do that, then rose, and followed the others into the house.

The two words 'Percodan and Pitocin,' which now sounded like a vaudeville act, frisky as ever, brayed after her, as though they were making fun of her.

She wondered how long it would take for them to disappear.

Several hundred thousands of dollars had been poured into the new Bay St. Lucy City Administrative Center, which, in years past, would simply have been called city hall. But if the old name had been somewhat plebian, so in fact had been the structure itself. Narrow corridors, old desks whose tops were imprinted with small curves made by digging fingernails, peeling paint on muted walls of not quite yellow and a little less than blue—and everywhere the aroma of boredom and repetition.

In the new structure, people walked on marble floors, leaned against thick and solidly built walls, sat at new desks, operated new computers, spoke quietly from office to office on newly installed intercom systems, and gazed upward at new fluorescent lights which crisscrossed the ceilings and buzzed less loudly than the old ones had.

The overall effect though was exactly the same.

It was a building constructed for the purpose of making everyone want to get out of it, especially the people who worked in it, and who spent a great deal of their time whispering to themselves, "Only eighteen more years until retirement," and "Only thirteen years seven months until retirement," and...

...etc., etc., etc., until death.

This was the building in which Nina found herself, having turned down a cup of coffee—which would have been her eighth of the morning—and studying the faces of the people seated in the office of Edie Towler, County District Attorney.

Nina remembered being in the courtroom—a space just down the hall—with Edie a bit less than two weeks ago.

That appearance had involved a slap.

This one involved a murder.

Could that be?

Could this even be happening?

And why was she here?

The ostensible reason she was here was that Helen had begged her to be here, exactly why she did not know. That and the fact that she must have become a comforting presence after the Robinson case, everybody in city service somehow looking to her for answers to questions involving life or death.

She, Nina Bannister, life or death.

She who was barely able to put Furl in his cat carrier.

There were seven people in the room, all seated around a menacingly dark table once probably an entire city itself, now eroded to table size, but far too heavy ever to be moved, and filled with evil stories and maleficent spirits.

Don't touch me, the table seemed to say.

So the seven people—Edie, John Giusti, Helen Reddington, Hope Reddington, Moon Rivard, Jackson Bennett, and she, Nina—all sat deferentially spaced from it, a bit set back in their chairs, their forearms two or three inches above the deceptively smooth but actually poisonous surface.

"Hope," said Edie, in the same tone and volume as the air conditioning system, "I received a call from Jackson Bennett a little over an hour ago."

This was not a question, and so it was not answered.

It was a fact, Nina found herself musing, much like the table. No one liked or trusted it, but no one was about to mess with it, either.

"He told me some shocking things."

"They should not," said Hope, still dressed as a Mardi Gras parade, still smiling as though everyone in the room had just given birth and she was the grandmother, "be that shocking, to anyone who knew Mr. Barrett. I'm sorry, I cannot call him 'Clifton,' although he was my grandson in law."

"Hope," growled Jackson Bennett, "you must realize that the things you say are now said before witnesses. Ms. Towler is the county district attorney. If you make a statement to me, purely to me in my own office, why that's privileged information. But here—this is not a game, Hope. As your attorney, I have to warn you to be very careful about what you say."

"Is Hope," asked Edie, "your client?"

"Yes, she is. I became Helen's attorney yesterday, and just some half-hour ago I agreed to represent her grandmother."

"Excellent. Hope, I have to advise you that I'm inclined to agree with your attorney. You should probably have several meetings with him before you agree to talk to me."

"Why?"

"Because…well, because if what Mr. Bennett has told me is true, then you stand the risk of incriminating yourself."

"I mean to incriminate myself. I'm a criminal."

"Well, that's what we're here to discuss."

"I murdered Clifton Barrett."

The table breathed heavily and reeked of malice.

There was no other movement in the room and no other smell.

"How did you do this, Hope?"

"Hope, I have to tell you…"

"It's all right, Jackson."

"Grandmamma, if you'll just wait for…"

"It's all right, Helen."

"Hope, shut up," said Nina.

Hope looked at her, smiling, and said:

"No, dear."

Well, Nina thought, *so much for trying.*

The table continued to look up at them and laugh, soundlessly.

"How did you murder him?"

"I gave him an overdose of the pain killer Percodan."

"How did you do this?"

"I came up to his and Helen's room just before they were to go to bed. I pretended to say good night to them, wish them well, etc. But before I entered the room I waited until I heard Helen go into the bathroom. I went in. Clifton greeted me. I said I'd simply come to congratulate the two of them one last time before turning in. He smiled. This pleased him. Helen was in the bathroom, and she laughed. But then I told Clifton I thought I heard some drunken people down on the pier, or out in the garden. I asked him if he'd go look out the window, and try to see if anyone were there. He did so.

But while he was looking, I simply walked to the bed, where a glass was sitting with his medication on it. He always was in the habit of taking, as I'd learned in the previous days while he was a guest in my house, a small dose of Percodan for back pain and Pitocin to help him sleep. I had in the pocket of my robe a small vial of concentrated Percodan and I was able to pour that into the glass. The glass was half full, and I hoped he would not notice. He apparently did not."

"Concentrated Percodan…"

"I am, Ms. Towler, a pharmacist's wife. It's very much stronger that what I'm sure he was using. The overall effect was that he would have been drinking six times his normal dosage. With Pitocin, and after several strong drinks of Scotch…I am, I repeat, a pharmacist's wife. I know my husband's business."

"Helen…"

"Yes?"

"Do you remember this happening?"

Helen looked at Jackson, who shook his head, saying:

"I can't advise my client to say more at this time. Either of my clients."

But at that moment, Hope leaned forward, dared to put her forearms on the table, and seemed to press it six inches into the carpet, which sighed upon receiving the weight.

At that time, then, Hope Reddington was the strongest presence in the room.

"Tell the truth, dear."

It may have been the only time those words had been both said and meant in any government office.

"No," Helen replied, looking down. "No. This did not happen. Nothing at all like it ever happened. Grandmamma, why are you lying like this?"

"I'm not lying, Helen. You know I'm not lying."

"Helen..."

This from Edie Towler.

"Helen what is your version of what happened?'

"Grandmamma was never in the room. Clifton prepared his medication, then he drank it. Immediately afterwards he complained of feeling dizzy, then, within a few seconds, he was asleep."

"All right. Well. We have to decide what to do. Hope..."

"Yes, Ms. Towler?"

"Why did you do this?"

"Because the man deserved it."

"Why did he deserve it?"

"He was about to ruin the life of my granddaughter."

"You do realize that this is not a justification for murder?"

"I realize nothing of the kind. It's every justification for murder. Do I not have a right to protect my family? If the man had entered with a gun, and I had possessed another gun...would I not have had the right to shoot him?"

"But he didn't have a gun."

"No, he had a lawyer."

She looked at Jackson.

"I'm sorry, Jackson. No harm intended. Nor to the memory of your husband, Nina."

"It's all right," Nina found herself answering.

Jackson, for all the horror of the situation, seemed to be attempting not too successfully to suppress a smile.

Edie continued:

"Hope, you're well past eighty. Is it possible, just possible, that what you are telling us...well, you could have imagined it?"

"You mean, am I insane? Do I suffer from dementia? Early Alzheimer's?"

"I didn't say that."

Hope smiled, then looked at Nina and said:

"I am but mad north north west; when the wind is from the south, I know a hawk from a handsaw."

She then said:

"You are not the only one, dear Nina, who knows her Shakespeare."

Nina also found herself beginning to smile.

The smile was beginning to grow as she answered:

"No. No, I guess I'm not."

"And yes, I knew it was Polonius, all along. As I've known these long sixty five years since—as a school girl—I first read the play. I had a good teacher too, though not as good as you. "To thine own self be true," she taught us—or rather Shakespeare through her taught us—and "it shall follow as the night the day, thou canst not then be false to any man.' Can you, Nina?"

"No, Hope."

My God, Nina realized.

I'm crying.

"No, you can't, Hope. No, you can't."

The meeting broke up.

Then Nina broke up, sitting there for a time, hands pressed against her face, sobbing.

By noon, downtown Bay St. Lucy had begun to empty. In the winter it would have been completely deserted, because downtown businesses—government offices, insurance offices, and law firms—were frequented by true beach dwellers only in three distinct time periods: 1) mornings (grudgingly), 2) afternoons (belligerently and with great resentment), 3) during lunch hour (in a state of unconsciousness, with death near). Still, during the warm summer days tourists wandered the streets unaware that boredom and bureaucracy existed in this paradise just as it did in their own home towns of Omaha and Little Rock, and always hoping to find something new, something to take another picture of. Accordingly, hastily-built ramshackle ice cream parlors and soda shops did a land office business at such unheard of times as 12:15 and 12:45, and curiosity shops—especially those catering to ten year olds and under—continued to sell plastic models of fish and sea turtles at a time when most seamen, painters, or pot-throwers would have been beginning a three hour nap.

Nina could not come downtown without feeling some nostalgia, nor could she look up and see the light burning in what had been Frank's old law office without imagining that he himself was up there, "burning the midnight oil through lunch time," as he had put it so many times.

As she stood before the front door, her Vespa chained and locked in precisely the same way she'd always done it, and secured to the same metal bicycle rack, she half expected to see him appear at the window, his face breaking into a smile as he gestured enthusiastically, mouthing the words: 'Come on up, the door's open!'

No face at the window now.

Jackson was, she knew, sitting in the office, burning Frank's midnight oil at lunch time, toiling away not at this divorce agreement or that land settlement, but at the shocking case he'd just been handed.

He was expecting her of course, for she was here at his request; but still he might not hear her knock, or ring if the door were locked.

She pushed it.

It was not locked.

She made her way up the narrow and still ill-lighted stairs, wondering why neither Frank nor Jackson had ever heeded their wives' advice to cover the slate gray walls with pictures, testimonials, shots of the two of them embracing governors or senators or presidents or babies or big, happy dogs.

It was simply not in the character of either man to do so, though, and so the narrow staircase remained bare as it always had, creaking underfoot, and leading to a nondescript door which pronounced merely "Law Offices" and let it go at that.

She stepped forward and knocked on the door.

She could hear someone rustling about inside.

There was the sound of soft music, soothing music.

It disappeared, replaced by the creak of Jackson's chair and the heavy sound of his footsteps coming across the office.

The door opened and revealed his bulk, somewhat gone to seed now but still so imposing as to be almost frightening, had its effect not been dampened by the ever-present smile, which illuminated the upper part of the staircase, the few light fixtures having been attached for that purpose clearly not being sufficient.

"Nina. Come on in."

She did so, following him through the reception area, and into his office.

It glowed green, golden, mahogany and leather, just as it had in Frank's day, just as any good law office, she had always told herself, should glow.

"Sit down."

She did so.

They sat for a time, before he finally shook his head and said, more to his desk than to her:

"What a mess."

"Yeah."

"Thanks for coming up."

"No problem."

"The Reddingtons, Helen especially but Hope, too, insist on you being kept in the loop. You're kind of like family."

"I guess that's true."

"So I'll tell you where we are, at least as far as I know it now."

"All right."

"I've been on the phone since I got back to the office about 10:30. I'm trying to learn what I can about this."

"So what have you learned?"

"To begin with, the Reddingtons are at home. There were still some people from the crime lab going over…well, the room, and the bathroom, all of that."

"Of course."

"But there's no place else for them to go. They can't go back out to Giusti's."

"No."

"And, Nina, Hope is eighty years old. They're not just going to throw her into a holding tank like they might a drunk college student."

"So what happens now? Is Helen still denying everything her grandmother said?"

"Every word of it. But of course Helen might be lying to protect her grandmother."

"So what do we do?"

He shrugged.

"Hope has to be arraigned. She has to give a formal statement."

"What can happen to her?"

"She committed murder, or at least she says she did. Not only that, but she committed first degree murder. She planned it out to the last detail."

"So what can happen to her?"

"I...I just don't know. We have a couple of choices."

"What are they?"

"Well, we can plead insanity and cite mental instability. But Hope insists on quoting Shakespeare fifteen verses at a time, and sounding like the most rational woman I've ever heard in my life."

"Which she may well be. So what's the second choice?"

"We make public all the financial records—and other things—that Tomlinson had been forced to hand over to me, and which I had consigned to the strongest safe in the city."

"Oh, no."

"Oh, yes. We have to show now that this man was about to ruin the Reddingtons. Every slimy little detail about money. And every slimy little detail about the affairs Helen may or may not have had. That all goes to motive. Every mother—and grandmother—in the courtroom, will be on Hope's side. We won't actually be saying she's insane. But we will be trying to lay the basis of a justifiable homicide defense. She felt, literally, as though her granddaughter's life was on the line."

"Can you make a jury buy that?"

"I can do my best. I read the stuff Tomlinson gave me. The man was a crook and a child molester. Mississippi jurors don't like those things."

"No."

"But the downside…the huge downside…is that it has to start now."

"What do you mean?"

"We have to arraign Hope Reddington, charge her, and begin her defense now, right now."

"Why?"

He leaned forward:

"Nina, the same scandal reporters we've been so worried about have got to be seen now as our biggest allies. I'm not sure we can blow up the sex scandal stories, but the money stuff is right there."

"You'd leak it."

"In a New York minute. Excuse the reference. Every group in the country that cares about the welfare of women—and every other group that has a dime's worth of self-respect—is going to be camped out here, advocating the cause of Helen and Hope."

"But?…"

"Helen's private life is over. And John's. She's a tabloid queen. It's the one thing Helen didn't want."

"I can't believe this is happening."

"I can't either. We do have one thing in our favor, though."

"What's that?"

"Hope's story is so detailed, I'm inclined to believe her."

"And that's good?"

"What's good is knowing the truth. If she did it, she did it. Now we can set about preparing a defense. We just don't need any more surprises."

The phone rang.

"Hold on a second, let me get that."

"Sure."

He lifted the receiver and growled into it.

"Yeah."

Silence. A crackle of static from the other end.

Another growl.

"Yeah, I got it."

He hung up, then rose, ponderously, gesturing to Nina that she should do the same.

"Come on."

"Where?"

"The Reddingtons. Helen Reddington just confessed to murdering her husband."

CHAPTER 18: FAMILY SQUABBLES

By two o'clock in the afternoon, a film of heat shimmered over Bay St. Lucy. The town appeared behind a scrim, as though all buildings and trees in it were the face of a fading movie actress a year or so too old to face the harsh camera. The outlines of everything—cars, roofs, trees, Spanish moss, truth—especially truth—had begun to blur and waver, somewhat picturesque but completely impossible to pin down.

Several vehicles had already parked in the Reddington driveway, and there was a small group of people gathered in the front yard, around a goldfish pond that Nina had completely forgotten existed.

She and Jackson Bennett walked across the lawn, shoes squishing in sod still moist from the storm of two days earlier.

The fish pond viewers rose as they approached.

Then everyone sat down, so that, for a few seconds, all present—Edie Towler, Helen, and a young police woman Nina had never seen but who appeared quite striking in her "Bay St. Lucy" navy blue uniform and her raven black Bay St. Lucy hair—simply stared at the foot long golden carp that made their way leisurely about their appointed duties, cruising the perimeter of the six foot diameter pool, making sure nothing was wrong with the brown stones that surrounded it or the alabaster surface that floored it.

Finally Edie looked at Helen and said:

"Please tell Mr. Bennett what you've told me."

Helen looked at Mr. Bennett and did so.

"I killed my husband."

The fish continued to do what they were paid to do.

Jackson leaned forward in his chair, which was a gaudy apparatus made of chrome piping, alternate blue and white cloth bands, and invisible baling wire.

Nina gave it perhaps a half-minute before collapse.

He appeared to think for a while.

Then he put his head in his hands, pressed his fingertips against his forehead, breathed, exhaled, breathed again, waited while the flow of blood to his scalp ceased entirely, and finally said, thoughtfully:

"What?"

"I killed my husband."

Overhead an airplane droned. Nina looked up at it, grateful to have something to do that she understood. It was the same vintage World War II airplane that she'd seen ten days or so earlier, in the statuary garden, when Helen was divulging to her what she at that time thought were interesting and disturbing things, but which in the light of present events now seemed to have been no more than fanciful musings.

The same banner trailed behind the airplane.

It read:

"Hot sausage!"

How strange! Nine found herself thinking. Again.

Edie rose, and gestured to the other officer to do likewise, which she did.

Then Edie spoke directly to Jackson, ignoring Helen entirely.

"Now. Let me tell you what the situation is. I have in my office the final autopsy report, which states conclusively that Mr. Barrett died of a severe overdose of the drug Percodan. I have outside of my office the attorney Tomlinson, who, although he retains no legal status as the Barretts' attorney, has in fact retained his equally significant status as Royal Pain in the Neck. I have surrounding him several thousand reporters—the last batch just flew in from The Maringue Islands, which I do not know even where they are—all clamoring that I release the results of said report."

She paused.

No one looked at the airplane except Nina, who did so subtly, as though she were craning her neck in order to shade her eyes.

"Now, going on: I've scheduled a press conference for nine o'clock this evening. Many television cameras will be present. Holding it that late is going to outrage all of the reporters and media hounds in town, but I don't care. I'm going to barricade myself in the office and play one-person scrabble. It's a game I've invented. Jackson, I'm sick of this. I will not be made a fool of. I want the truth, and I want it damned soon. It may be that your clients, having read one dime-store mystery too many, may think that be confessing to the same crime, they can somehow get off scott free. Unable to judge who the real killer is, the jury just lets everybody go. Well, that will not happen. I was, until an hour or so ago, quite willing to be as lenient as possible with Hope Reddington, simply because of her age. I was not going to let her be jailed, and I was going to do everything I could to help you in your defense of her, which I would have assumed took her age and health into account."

"It would have."

"But I no longer care. I'm leaving now. You stay here and talk to your clients. Tell them I want the truth. I don't care what it is, but I want to know it, and I want to know it soon. Listen to me, Jackson: if both of these women continue to insist that they did the crime, then I'll take them at their word and charge them both. We can sort out the details at trial, but I promise you, they will both be in jail tonight. Do you understand this?"

"Yes, Edie."

"I hope you do."

And, so saying, she left.

After a time, her car had pulled away.

Nina, needing to do something if only to verify her own continued existence, looked at Helen and asked:

"Where is John?"

"His clinic. He had to be there. I'm sure he'll be back soon."

"Does he know you've made this confession?"

"No."

She avoided the real question, which was, 'Did you do it?,' but Jackson did not.

"Did you do it?"

"Yes."

"Why did you let your grandmother confess?"

"I didn't think you would believe her."

Silence for a time. One of the carp flopped over on its massive sickly yellow side and decided to float that way for a few seconds, finally having second thoughts and whacked the water like a board as it returned to its perimeter watch.

"I thought she'd simply be regarded as a senile old woman. But I was wrong. She isn't senile."

"No. No, she isn't. So how did you do this thing?"

"Much as she herself described having done it."

"She wasn't there at all?"

"No. She made that all up."

"She didn't come up to say good night?"

"No, she was too tired, and simply went to bed."

"Where did you get the Percodan?"

"I used Clifton's. He had a large bottle of it. He went to the window to look at something or other. I went to the bathroom, poured out the mixture he'd prepared, and…well, made a new one of my own. He drank it, complained of feeling dizzy, went to bed, and went to sleep."

"I see."

"I knew that there would be an autopsy, of course. I knew that Percodan—in a fatal dosage—would be detected. But I'm not naïve. I also know that in many such cases, especially those involving celebrities, it's impossible to prove that the overdose has not been the result of carelessness on the part of the victim. I hoped this would be the case. How, in final analysis, could anyone prove that Clifton had not simply made a mistake, and taken too much?"

"You hoped the final verdict would be accidental death?"

"Yes. And I'm convinced it would have been."

"Except for…"

"Except for Grandmamma. And her startlingly real narrative. She is, as she said, a pharmacist's wife. She was quite aware of what drugs Clifton was taking, but I do give her credit for the detail of her story. She was quite accurate, without even having heard the results of the autopsy. No, Mr. Bennett, I'm convinced that my grandmother would cheerfully spend the rest of her life in jail, just to give me a...well, a second chance. A chance with John. But I'm not going to allow that."

"All right. Now. I'm going to be very frank with you."

"Please do."

"As far as I can tell, we have two versions of this crime. Both are completely believable."

"I understand that."

"But it's not going to go on that way. Edie Towler is a damn fine district attorney. And I'm no beginner at my job. I will not be lied to, though, and one of you is lying. Where is your grandmother now, Helen?"

"She's lying down inside, resting."

"OK, Nina?"

Nina felt as though she'd been shot.

This was a movie she was watching, wasn't it?

Now someone was reaching through the screen and grabbing at her.

"Yes?" she said, wondering what had happened to the popcorn.

"Nina, you know the house, don't you?"

"Like my own."

"Would you go and get Hope, and bring her out here?"

"Mr. Bennett, Grandmamma is..."

"Your grandmamma is coming out here, right now, and we are going to get to the bottom of this thing. Nina, please go and get Hope."

"All right."

Nina rose, as Helen said: "She's lying on the day bed in the study downstairs."

Nina entered the house.

There they all were again, dead people.

Astonishing, she thought, that they still seemed content.

Waiting.

The musty smell of the rooms was not really that; it was, she decided, not a musty smell at all; it was a musty memory.

She crossed the main living room, carpet sinking beneath her feet, clocks ticking, and the sound of an overhead ceiling fan that growled as though it were a retired airplane propeller.

Hope was in fact lying on the small single bed in what had been her husband's study.

She rose on an elbow as Nina entered.

"Nina!"

"Hello, Hope."

"You've come for a visit!"

"Not…not really."

"There's cucumber salad!"

"I can't have any right now," she said, feeling thankful that there was a murder and because of it she did not have to.

"Oh, just a bit? It must be nearly dinner time!"

"Maybe a little later."

"Then you can stay?"

"For a while. Hope, Jackson is outside with Helen."

"Jackson Bennett?"

"Yes."

"Oh my, a party has begun!"

"Not really, Hope. It's just…there are some questions about what happened."

"What happened when?"

"Last night."

My God, Nina found herself thinking. *Was it only last night?*

"Some questions about what happened last night."

"I thought that I'd answered all of those things."

"You did, Hope, but…"

"Was I not clear?"

"You were. But maybe you should come outside with me."

"All right."

Hope rose, looked around the room, and said:

"You must forgive my appearance. This old sweatshirt, and these baggy pants…"

"Doesn't matter."

"Has Helen offered either of you something to drink? Tea perhaps?"

"I don't think we need anything, Hope."

"All right. Well, I shall ask, all the same."

The two of them made their way back through Reddington Mausoleum and out into the yard, above which the sky seemed to be exploding, small fragments of Blue Sky falling on everything in sight.

"Jackson! So good of you to come!"

"Thank you, Hope."

"Helen, you should have taken them into the back. It's so much cooler by the bayou."

"Sorry, Grandmamma."

"And you've offered them nothing to drink or eat!"

"Grandmamma…"

"We really can't," said Jackson. "Mrs. Reddington, will you please sit down?"

Hope did so, shaking her head and muttering:

"I'm so sorry that the two of us have turned to bad hostessing."

"It's all right."

"Its' just that with all of the confusion…"

"Grandmamma," said Helen, leaning forward: "I've told them the truth. I've told them that I gave Clifton the overdose."

"What?"

"You must take back your story."

"What story?"

"The one about your coming up to our room, and pouring concentrated Percodan into Clifton's glass."

"But I did that!"

"No, you did not, Grandmamma!"

"Don't tell me what I did or did not do! Do you think I'm addled?"

"Of course not; I think you're trying to protect me!"

"Protect you from what, child?"

Jackson Bennett leaned forward in the mangled parachute apparatus that had once resembled a lawn chair and said:

"Hope, Helen has confessed to the murder of Mr. Barrett."

The transformer that been supplying electrical energy to several million of Hope's brain cell apartments exploded, leaving her mental city completely dark.

"What?"

"It's true, Grandmamma. I killed him."

"You did no such thing! I killed him!"

Again, Jackson Bennett:

"Both of you. You have to stop this. We've got to know the truth, and we must know it now, or you're both going to be prosecuted. I can get you off from this, whichever one did it, by showing cause. But I can't represent you if I don't know the truth.

Hope, though, was still staring at her granddaughter.

"I will not allow you to confess to this, young lady. I will not tolerate it."

"Grandmamma, I'm not going to allow you to go to prison for something I've done."

"I will go wherever I wish!"

"But you didn't do this thing. You couldn't have."

"And what is that supposed to mean?"

"It means you're not capable of murdering anybody!"

"And why not?"

"I don't...I just..."

Hope leaned forward, the shifting of her twenty-six or so pounds of weight having absolutely no effect at all on the chair, an inch or so above which she seemed to be floating.

"You don't think I'm smart enough to commit murder, do you?"

"Of course you are. It's just..."

"Just what? That I'm too old?"

"No! It's just..."

"Old people can do things too, you know!"

"I know that, Grandmamma, but..."

Hope rose, stared at Nina, stared at Jackson, and finally stared at Helen, hissing:

"You're *just like your mother!*"

Then she turned and stomped back into the house.

Jackson stared at the place where she'd been only a few second before, shook his head, and said:

"Shit."

Then he got up and walked away.

CHAPTER 19: A FEW THOUGHTS CONCERNING DRUGS, THEIR PROPER USAGE, AND THEIR LIKELY EFFECTS

There was something about Margot's shop that attracted Nina.

Even now, in mid afternoon, empty and locked as it was, it seemed a kind of haven.

She parked the Vespa, took the shop key from the Bannister Canister, walked inside, and simply breathed.

Art and nature, art and nature.

Beautiful paintings, lush and verdant ferns. Plants everywhere, water tinkling from the garden fountain.

She sat at the table where she and Margot spent most of their time gossiping, and she luxuriated in the various colors of light making their way through the glass paneled ceiling.

What could she do?

How could she help Helen? Or Hope? Or John?

This was simply a mess. One of her two favorite people in the world was a murderess, each denying it was the other.

Helen was not going to let her grandmother go to jail; Hope was not going to let her granddaughter go to jail.

The bottom line was, they were probably both going to jail.

She winced as she thought of what the newspapers would say.

When?

Starting tonight. Press conference; nine o'clock.

She found herself wondering if Hope and Helen were being arrested even now, but decided that was improbable, given the fact that the city jail was probably surrounded by reporters.

No, Edie would be as good as her word.

She would give Jackson Bennett a few more hours to get at the truth.

Then, should he fail, she'd have no choice.

She'd have both women picked up, brought to jail, and incarcerated, announcing that one or both of them had been responsible for administering a fatal dose of Percodan to one of New York City's most famous stage stars.

Then all hell would break loose.

Poor Alana: The Bay St. Lucy Summer Festival now something between a bad joke and a house of horrors.

Poor Bay St. Lucy. Tabloid reporters for months to come.

Not the fate that Eve Ivory would have had determined for the town.

But almost as bad.

Worse, in some ways.

And of course poor Hope, John, and Helen.

It would have been better if they'd let the man fly back to New York and do his worst.

At least the three of them would have been here, together, and at least they would have had the community to support them.

But now…

She thought for a while, and then came to a decision.

She would take the Vespa, in a few minutes, back over to the Reddingtons' house.

Jackson might be there, certainly, but he'd left in the kind of humor that made that seem improbable.

He was probably back in his office, preferring the study of present legal options to the hearing of loud stubborn women.

No, it was her place to go back.

She was a calming effect, and both Hope and Helen respected her.

She'd be able to talk to one of them at a time.

One was going to have to admit to this murder; but the other, the one who'd no part in it, had to affirm that fact.

Surely she could make them see that.

And so, yes, she'd wait half an hour, and then go back.

This was not going to be like last Christmas. She was not going to save the day, unmask a completely unsuspected murderer, and watch the town celebrate its salvation.

That was the kind of thing that happened in cozy mysteries.

But she did not have to be useless, either.

She could at least help make the situation better.

Yes, she could.

So that's what she would do.

These reveries were interrupted by the jangle of the door opening, and Margot, dressed in a blend of German expressionism and The Wizard of Oz, taking off her great straw hat and laying it down carefully so that it covered the northern half of the shop.

"Hi."

"Hello, Margot."

"Just get here?"

"Yeah."

Margot joined her, staring intensely across the table.

"Do you know anything?"

Nina shook her head, then nodded.

"Yes. No. No. Yes."

"So you do know something. How is it that you always know something, when none of the rest of us do and don't realize it?"

"I don't know."

"Well. I've just come from the Auberge des Arts."

"Doing what?"

"The Community Theater Group is helping Alana and some of the other Arts Council people. The place is a disaster from last night. They haven't even begun to clean the kitchen yet and glasses are everywhere."

"Well. When the news got out about Barrett..."

"Yes. It was like a fairy tale but bad. Everything froze. Most of the actors have spent the afternoon over there, getting their stuff together. A lot are flying out tonight for Memphis."

"How are they taking it?"

"Shock. Soft talking. Head shaking, that kind of thing. The truth is, I think, they all hated him. But of course they can't admit that."

"No."

"So what do you know?"

"Things I can't tell you."

"Why is that always the case? Well, anyway, the gossip around town is that it's a drug overdose. Reporters are going crazy, digging around like rabid dogs. A rumor has it that there's going to be another press conference tonight. Anything to that?"

"Maybe."

Actually, Margot, there's quite a bit to that. There probably will be a press conference, and it will be called by Edie Towler, and it will be at nine o'clock, and it will be for the purpose of telling Bay St. Lucy that it's most honored and respected citizen, Hope Reddington, and her granddaughter, Helen, are murderers. That they—one of them, God knows which—had put Percodan in Clifton Barrett's medication, that he had drunk it, had gone to bed feeling dizzy, and had never waked up.

"Maybe."

"Just can't shut you up, can I?"

"No, you just can't…"

Silence for a time.

And there they were again, those two flying fish words, jumping out of the water and glistening in the sun and sporting themselves like truant children on the First Grand Day of May.

Yes, there they were.

Percodan and Pitocin.

The vaudeville act.

What great dancers they both were, old Percodan and Pitocin.

Helen, saying, so definitively:

"He took his medication; then he complained of feeling dizzy. Then he went to bed and fell immediately asleep."

Then Nina: "Margot?"

"Yes?"

"I want to ask you about something."

"Go ahead."

"Do you know anything about drugs?"

Some minutes later, when Margot had finished laughing, Nina was able to pose the question again:

"Do you know anything about drugs?"

"Of course I do, Nina."

"Well. I've just spent some time with a pharmacist's wife."

"I," Margot answered, "have spent a good deal of my time as a pharmacist's livelihood."

"You know about Percodan?"

"Of course. It's a pain killer."

"Pitocin?"

"Sleeping pill."

"You ever take them?"

"You mean together?"

"Yes."

"Let me see, when might I have taken Percodan and Pitocin together? Oh. Summer of 73 in Colorado. Four times I think. But I moved on. High school was waiting for me."

"Could taking those things together kill you?"

"Of course. Why else would one take them?"

"Didn't kill you though."

"I would have to check."

"What's it like?"

"Mixing them?"

"Right. Also, add four or five shots of Scotch."

"Well, that goes without saying."

"What's it like?"

"Oh, I'm trying to remember. Ahhh, nothing for a while then happy then amorous then dizzy then unconscious and then dead or dreadfully hung over, depending on the dosage."

"Nothing for a while."

"No. Then…"

"Nothing for a while."

"No."

"Okay."

She sat for a time, thinking.

Then she asked:

"What if neither one of them did it?"

"Did what?"

"It."

"I don't know what you could be talking about."

"Maybe neither of them does, either."

"Nina, have you taken these drugs, Percodan and Pitocin? Is that why you're asking me about them? Because if you have, we need to get you to a doctor."

"How long do we have?"

"Nina!"

"How long do we have?"

"Half an hour, but not much more!"

"Half an hour. Half an hour."

"You're scaring me! Nina, do we really need to go to the hospital?"

Nina shook her head.

"No, Margot. We need to go to the Auberge des Arts."

"Why?"

"Maybe to catch a killer, Margot."

"What are you talking about?"

"Come on. The play's the thing, wherewith we'll catch the conscience of the king. And who knows? Maybe life is a cozy mystery after all."

They left the shop together.

CHAPTER 20: THE PLAY'S THE THING…

Within ten minutes, they were driving through the grounds of the Auberge des Arts, which now resembled Galveston after the Great Hurricane of 1901. Trash was everywhere, and, as far as the eye could see, nothing existed but stark reminders of the power of nature over once great civilizations.

Tables were overturned.

Dogs wandered aimlessly, too exhausted to bark.

Young men in white coats followed the dogs around, trying to avoid strange twisted metallic objects that had either been chairs or small helicopters.

Clothes lay discarded on motorcycles.

"It was really," Margot remarked, parking the Volkswagen and killing the engine, "a good party after the play was over."

"You enjoyed it, did you?"

"I don't remember it. That's always a good sign."

They got out, ducked out of the principle of general fear, and began to make their way toward the entranceway, trying to avoid stepping in anything that looked liquid.

"You can see a lot of the actors wandering around," said Margot. "There's Laertes. Really hot, is Laertes."

"Did you proposition him last night?"

"I tried, but the best offer I got was from Polonius, and he collapsed just after making it."

"So you said no."

"Actually I said, yes, but…"

"I don't want to know. Here. We go in here."

They made their way through the vestibule, the entrance hallway, the black box theater space, the children's writing area, the retired person's archery range, the beanbag storytelling area, the weight room, the small dining hall, the larger dining hall, the cinema, the bowling alley, and finally, the theater itself, where Alana DelaFosse spotted them and rushed to Nina.

"Are you all right, dear?"

"I'm all right."

"Are you aware of what's been happening? One horror after another."

"I'm aware of a few things."

"Come then. I'll fill you in."

Alana was dressed as Margot was dressed except with food stains, and what appeared to be a few splotches of blood.

She took Nina and Margot to a small table that had been set up just in front of the stage, and, as chaos reigned all around them, Alana explained the situation, as she now understood it, on the basis of listening to a day's gossip.

"Hope is in New York, apparently in intensive care."

"All right," Nina said quietly, realizing the utter stupidity of contradicting utter stupidity.

"Helen has left the country. For what destination, no one knows."

"Check."

"There was an autopsy this morning. The results are not yet official, but word has it that Clifton Barrett was actually strangled by one of his own shoelaces."

"Amazing."

"This is all I know up to now. But news is coming in all of the time."

"I'm sure it is."

"This is one of the advantages one gets from associating with truly artistic people."

"I'm sorry," said Nina, "that I've missed out on it."

"It's never too late to begin, My Dear."

"I hope it is, for me. How is the cleaning going?"

"We won't even start on it until tomorrow."

"Good."

"Pardon?"

"Nothing. Alana, I have a big favor to ask."

"Ask anything, Darling Nina."

"There's a tape of last night's play, isn't there?"

"Of course. Actually there are several. The master tape that will be broadcast nationally has already been sent to New York."

"Could I see it?"

"You want to watch *Hamlet*? Now? Nina, how can you even think of doing that, knowing what has happened to Clifton Barrett?"

"You have to humor me. Is there a place where I can watch it?"

"I suppose it could be set up in the cinema area. But I still don't understand…"

"Please do it, Alana. And hurry. There may not be much time."

Alana looked at Margot, saying:

"Do you know what she's talking about?"

Margot shook her head.

"I never know what she's talking about."

Within a few minutes she and Margot were seated in what seemed a small movie theater, Alana holding out a tape.

"Here's one of our copies, Nina. There are several others."

"Can you take it back to the projection room, put it in and play it?"

"Of course not."

"Margot, can you?"

"Of course not."

"Alana, is there anybody here who can?"

"There are technicians from The Public Broadcasting Company."

"I need six."

"I'll try to find them at once."

She left.

"Nina," said Margot, "you've got to tell me what this is all about."

"I think," said Nina, quietly, "it's about the night you slapped Clifton Barrett."

"Yes, that was one of my finer hours, wasn't it?"

"Certainly was."

"I'll never forgive myself for apologizing."

"I'll never forgive myself for being so blind."

"What do you mean? You saw me slap him, didn't you?"

"Yes. But that was all I saw. That was the only part of the play I focused on. The rest of it, the most important part, went flying right over my head. There it was in front of us, the whole answer. And we didn't even see it."

"Nina, sometimes I simply…"

"Ladies?"

They were interrupted by a young straw haired man in an orange jump suit. He looked like a prisoner on the county road crew, except for the letters PBC stitched neatly in blue on his left shirt pocket.

"I'm told you need some technical assistance."

"There is," said Nina, sullenly, "only one of you."

"Well," he said, smiling, "I'm head of technical services for the Mississippi branch of the Public Broadcasting Company."

"Don't' you need an assistant?"

"A lot of things I can do myself. What is it that you need done?"

Nina held out the tape, which was larger than those that she'd never been able to play as a classroom teacher, but just as forbidding.

"I need you to play this tape."

He took it, still smiling.

"That's all?"

"No. It's more complicated than that."

"Tell me. Do you need a remix or an editing job or…"

"I need you to make it go faster at times."

"Fast forward?"

"Whatever it's called. Is it possible, technically?'

"It may be. I know I've seen it done. We studied about it at MIT."

"Nina," whispered Margot, "He's being sarcastic."

"That isn't true," said the young man, taking the tape. "I'm a tech guy. We don't understand sarcasm. But let me see what I can do with this."

He disappeared into the back of the room, and, in a minute or so, could be seen in the dimly lighted projection room.

The screen before them burst into bright blue light; regal music surrounded them, and there, marching along above what were either the misty fiords of Denmark or the back fifty acres of Mississippi State University, were the names of the cast and crew that had produced this *Hamlet.*

Then Bernardo and Francisco, on the parapets of the Old Robinson Mansion that had become the new Auberge des Arts that had become the timeless Elsinore.

"Who's there?"

"Nay, answer me. Stand and unfold yourself!"

"Yes," Nina whispered. "Unfold yourself."

"What did you say?"

"I said, Margot, that the play's the thing, wherewith we'll catch the conscience of the king. But it's not the king, I think. Not this time."

"Nina, this is just the same play we all saw last night."

"No. It's the play we didn't see last night?"

"What are you talking about?"

"The mousetrap. We missed the mousetrap."

"Are you sure you haven't mixed Percodan and Pitocin? If you have, we're about out of time."

But Nina was standing now, shouting to the man from MIT who understood time travel:

"Make it go forward."

There was the crackle of an amplification system, and a metallic disembodied voice asked:

"To where?"

"Act III: scene 4."

"Act III: scene 4 it is."

And it was. And there was Hamlet, lunging at the tapestry, shouting, "Dead for a Ducat!" and there was Hope, leaping to her feet and shouting, "It's Polonius!"

"Dear Hope," whispered Margot. "Poor thing."

Nina sat down, shaking her head, replying:

"That's what we were all watching, wasn't it? Hamlet. And Polonius. And Hope. So we missed the play."

"I still can't…"

"Listen. Listen to Gertrude. Listen to the queen, talking to Hamlet."

"What have I done, that thou darest wag thy tongue in noise so rude against me?"

"You didn't do anything," said Nina. "Nothing at all."

"Who are you talking to?"

"Listen, Margot. Listen to the queen."

"Oh, Hamlet, speak no more: Thou turnst mine eyes into my very soul; and there I see such black and grained spots, as will not leave their tinct. Speak to me no more, these words, like daggers, enter in mine ears."

"Remember, Margot. Remember how the old king died. "And in the porches of mine ears didst pour the leprous distilment." Now listen, listen to Gertrude:

"Ah, Hamlet, thou hast cleft my heart in twain."

"That's it," whispered Nina. "That's it. That's the line. All right! Stop it. Now I need one thing more!"

Lights went up in the room.

She looked back and up, able to see the engineer's smiling face and hear his electrified voice:

"You see? It worked. Forward. Backward. Eight years of higher education, but it's worth it!"

"Yes, it is. Now I want one more thing."

"Just name it."

"I'm going to try to find another tape. Can you meet me here in ten minutes or so and play it?"

"I'm your man."

"Wonderful. Now, come on, Margot."

They left the cinema and made their way back to the main stage where Hamlet had been performed.

Alana was just as she had been, running back and forth, yelling at the walls, and apologizing to people who thought she was yelling at them.

"Alana!"

"Oh Nina, I'm glad you're back! Did you see the play again?"

"No. I saw it for the first time."

Alana frowned, then looked at Margot while gesturing toward Nina and asked:

"How long has poor Ophelia been thus?"

"Will you two," Margot shouted, "stop quoting Shakespeare?"

"Alana," said Nina, ignoring Margot. "I need two big favors from you now."

"Name them."

"First, lock the kitchen."

"What?"

"You said nothing was going to be cleaned in there until tomorrow?"

"That's right."

"Then lock it. Just don't let anybody go in there."

"But I don't…"

"Please, Alana."

"All right. Probably no one was going in there anyway."

"Good. Now the second thing, and this is most important. I need another tape."

"Of *Hamlet*?"

"No. I need a tape of the real play."

"What are you talking about?"

"Do you remember the gathering after the play was over? When Clifton Barrett made his speech to Bay St. Lucy?"

"Yes, of course. I was taping it myself. So were all the reporters there, all ten thousand or so of them."

"You're an angel!"

"I know, dear, but what does Mr. Barrett's speech have to do with it?"

"The man who showed the tape of *Hamlet*…"

"From the PBC you mean?"

"Yes. He's supposed to be meeting us back at the cinema. Can you get your tape, and let him have it, so he can play it?"

"Of course."

And she did.

And he did.

And there, standing on a sodden post-deluge platform, dressed in black, with Ophelia standing beside him and a crowd of adoring people in front of him, was Clifton Barrett again, beaming, orating, gesturing, thanking—and drinking Scotch.

Now putting the glass down.

And now orating again.

And now...

"Look, Margot."

"At what? He's just making that speech again."

"No. He's drinking Scotch."

"So what?"

"So where is he getting it from, Margot? Where is he getting it from?"

"I don't...I don't.."

"Into the porches of mine ear."

"What are you talking about?"

"The mousetrap. There is the mousetrap. Look. He's reaching back, and sticking his hand right into it."

"You're insane."

"Just North by Northwest, Margot."

She rose, stepped into the aisle, and gestured for her friend to follow:

"But it's the Gulf, remember? And tonight the wind is from the south. Now I've got to go and catch a killer. And by the way—I may need your autograph book."

So saying, she walked out of the room.

CHAPTER 21: THE MOUSETRAP

There are a great many things that one can do at sunset on the Mississippi Gulf Coast.

One can dine. One can frolic in the surf. One can prepare for an evening in the theater or cinema. One can fish.

Or one can simply sit anywhere a chair happens to be handy and watch, awe struck, as the near inevitable thunderstorm begins to form some forty miles distant—whether offshore or inland matters little—and goes on to do its own particular cloud thing, billowing, glowing golden, shading itself an evil purple, flattening out anvil-like on top, lacing itself with streak lightning, belching out a thundermoan now and then, and foaming like aerial cotton candy as the sun gradually sets, leaving it to go where thunderstorms go when not wanted any more, to vegetate in a Storm Retirement Village and muse about old glories and past magnificence.

Such a storm was billowing up to the East when Moon Rivard's squad car, Nina sitting ensconced in the back seat, made its way into Bay St. Lucy's airport parking lot.

The air was deathly hot, making creosote underfoot tend to liquefy and emit an odor redolent of licorice and paint thinner.

"There. That's the plane."

They were both walking toward the main airport terminal.

"That may be the plane, Miss. But they ain't on it yet."

And they were not.

They, meaning those cast members scheduled to fly to Memphis on the 7:30 puddle-jumper that held perhaps twenty people and also allowed all of them to take part in flying the airplane, so close were they to the cockpit controls—they were spread out in the waiting area, talking in small groups, or perhaps giving one last interview to the representatives of tabloid journalism, an interview marked by low tones, sad whispers, and completely hypocritical eulogies to a dead reprobate.

As she entered the terminal and glanced at the requisite flight insurance kiosks, car rental booths, and arrival/departure screens, Nina could not help flash back a month—no, it had not been quite that long—well, however long it had been, to that night in early July when Hope Reddington had stepped off the plane and plunged into a world of adoration.

And now...

And now...

She stepped onto the escalator, watching as the lower floor and baggage claim disappeared, then peering upward at the great glass windows of the airport, through which the thunderstorm, now seemingly twice as large, could now be seen exercising its quiet and awful grandeur.

"There. There they are."

"Yes, Ma'am. Do you want me to..."

Nina simply shook her head.

"I don't think you're going to need to do anything, Moon. Is someone else on the way?"

"Yes. Another patrol car coming. Are you sure you right about this?"

"I'm as sure as I can get, Moon. It's the only thing that makes any sense."

"All right. Then you do what you have to do."

And Nina did.

In the far corner of the upper floor of the Bay St. Lucy Airport, a small press conference was being held. The conference involved three reporters, who were quietly asking questions, and the woman who was the subject of their interview.

The woman, an elegant fur boa around her neck despite the heat outside, a diamond tiara glistening in the harsh airport lighting...

...the woman dressed like a Christmas tree, just as she had been the first night Nina had ever seen her at Hope's garden party, and as she had been the night Margot had slapped Barrett...

...the woman whom everyone had forgotten about.

The woman whose name Nina had not even bothered to learn...just as she had not learned the name of the actor who played Polonius, or Laertes, or Fortinbras...

...this woman, who, channeling Queen Gertrude, had said only two nights ago, "Oh, Hamlet, thou hast cleft my heart in twain!"

...this woman, Constance Briarworth, looked up as Nina approached the group.

And she smiled, the kind of a smile only a Christmas tree can emit.

"Can I," she asked huskily, "help you?"

"I'd like," Nina said, quietly as the three reporters stepped back, "an autograph."

"Certainly. Do you have something for me to sign?"

Nina nodded and pulled from the back pocket of her blue jeans a small notebook, not much larger than a deck of cards.

She flipped it open, took a ball point pen from the pocket of her blouse, and wrote on it:

WE KNOW YOU DID IT.

Then she handed it to Constance Briarworth.

There was no change of expression at all.

Finally the woman lifted her head and stared hard at Nina, who merely gestured subtly toward Moon.

Moon had now been joined by another young officer.

They stood at a respectful distance, just beside the escalators.

Then Constance Briarworth wrote something on the small tablet, which she handing back to Nina.

On it were the words:

THE REST IS SILENCE.

Then, after more smiles all around, to the young reporters:

"Well. If that will be all, I believe I have another small meeting to attend before the flight leaves."

"Yes, ma'am."

"Yes, ma'am."

"Yes, ma'am."

And they left, disappearing into the milling flow of passengers coming and going.

"So…"

Queen Gertrude stood waiting.

"Over there," said Nina.

"All right, dear. Let's go."

She strode off.

And Nina followed.

CHAPTER 22: ANSWERS

At 8:30 p.m. Nina arrived on her Vespa at the entranceway to the Reddington home.

The entire area was deserted.

Lights glowed in the living room of the house, but there were no police cars, no news vans, and no panhandlers selling posters of Clifton Barrett.

"Everything," she whispered as she dismounted and toed the kickstand, "is going on downtown."

And that was the case. Constance Briarworth having confessed in a tearful but brief interview…to which Nina had been privy…that she'd given Clifton Barrett an overdose of Percodan, pouring it into several glasses of Scotch—the world had begun to follow her, to the exclusion of everyone else.

No one knew where she was at this time, but word somehow leaked out that the nine o'clock press conference would feature a 'new development to the case.'

Nothing so baited, so tantalized, the wild dogs of journalism as the words 'new development.'

And so it came to pass that the placid, moss-overgrown and gas-lamped yard of Hope Reddington had returned to its former times, its summer night card party innocence, when merely the sound of crickets mixed with the quiet burble of Plaquemine Bayou flowing by in the back.

John Giusti stepped out of the house just as she approached it.

"John!"

"Come on through, Nina. They're out in the back, sitting on the pier."

"Have you heard, John?"

He opened the door for her, and asked quietly as she entered the house:

"Heard what?"

"No one has called you?"

He shook his head:

"The phone's been ringing, but we haven't answered. A couple of hours earlier Jackson Bennett came by. He tried to talk to both Hope and Helen again, but they won't say anything. Then he left, kind of put out, and said not to answer the phone. So we haven't."

"The police haven't been here?"

"According to Jackson, they're probably going to show up in a few minutes. There's going to be press conference, I guess. But both Hope and Helen are ready to…well, to be taken away."

"And no one has told you what's happened?"

"What do you mean?"

"Let's go out to the pier."

He led the way, Nina all the while wondering why had no one come to inform the Reddingtons that they were free now, and would have to go nowhere.

Of course, she asked herself, *who would this informer have been?*

Certainly no one from the police force, which, in the first place, had its hands busy with events happening downtown; and not Jackson, who had not been informed himself.

Who would have informed him?

He was not Constance Briarworth's attorney.

So that was the case as she followed John through the kitchen and out onto the pier.

Helen Reddington sat at a metal table, situated on the rocking pier almost directly beneath her window.

Some six feet away sat her grandmother, staring out across the bayou.

Helen was smoking a cigarette, which smoldered in the ashtray before her.

Hope, hearing the kitchen door close, turned, looked at Nina, and then at her granddaughter.

"She's taken up," she said, icily, "smoking."

Helen said nothing, but merely drew hard on the cigarette and set it in the ashtray, causing Hope to say:

"Filthy habit."

"Grandmamma…"

John placed himself between the two women, looked down first at one, then at the other, and said, softly:

"Both of you. You've got to give this up."

Neither woman spoke.

"The police will be coming soon. There's going to be a press conference. If one of you did this thing, then that's all right. The whole community is on your side. The man was a monster. There will be money to defend whoever did it. We've just got to know."

"As far as I'm concerned," said Hope, her head swiveling like that of a bird so that she found herself peering again across the water, "we know now. I gave the man an overdose. He was, like Polonius, a rash intruding fool. And he got what he deserved. I murdered him."

"Grandmamma," said Helen, darkly, "you did no such thing."

"I did!"

"*You* didn't! *I* did!"

"You did not! And I'm so disappointed in you for lying in this way. Your parents brought you up to know better."

Hope looked at Nina then and said:

"Nina. You tell me. What has happened to values in this country?"

"Hope, I…"

"What are we teaching our children, anyway? If I had gone to my mother, or my grandmother, and told either of them that I was a murderess, I'd have been believed. But now…perhaps it's the drugs. Or television."

"Grandmamma, I just will not…"

"Neither of you did it."

A turtle, close by on the bank, plopped into the water.

Fireflies were swarming on one of the bushes that had covered the far pier post.

A meteor lined its way directly overhead, somewhere between Antares and Vega, and Nina thought she could hear its soft hissing as it made its way toward the Milky Way.

Because of these great noises there could not have been said to be silence; but what there was was close enough, so that John Giusti's words rang across the bayou like shots from a small rifle when he said:

"What did you say?"

"Neither of them did it."

Both women were looking at her now.

"What?" asked one of them, the specific identity unimportant since they were, genetically, except for the matter of a few decades, the same woman.

"What?"

Same thing, same unimportant identity.

Helen picked up her cigarette, hurled it into the bayou, and took two steps closer.

Hope watched the cigarette disappear into the dark water, chastised the dying cigarette, its smoker, and its manufacturer—and also took two steps closer.

They were all standing now.

"What?"

The word had become like an opera chorus now, repeated with increasing degrees of intensity, first given by the soprano—Hope, the alto—Helen, and the base—John.

"What. What? WHAT?"

Nina to the two women singers:

"Neither of you did it."

Nina to John:

"Neither of them did it."

A nameless creature came up out of the bayou, stuck its head over the planking of the pier, and asked:

"Then who did do it?"

To which Nina answered:

"Constance Briarworth."

Silence.

John stepped forward and asked:

"Who the hell is Constance Briarworth?"

And then the police arrived.

If the previous moment had featured a small chorus involving three voices, the next half hour turned into *The*

Pirates of Penzance, with everybody arriving at once: Moon Rivard, Jackson Bennett, representatives from Edie Towler's office, and a number of people carrying around cell phones, some of which were actually cameras, some of which were miniature television sets, some of which were computers, and some of which were just little video games.

The long and short of this was that Nina, at precisely 9 p.m., had the choice of watching Edie Towler on at least three screens, one huge one that had been set up in the now-magical-again backyard, one medium-sized which had been set up on one of the pier tables, and one secretive and tiny, which radiated like a silver dollar or a tumor in the palm of the man standing beside her.

"I can now tell you that we've identified a person of interest connected with the death of Mr. Clifton Barrett."

"Can you tell us…"

"That is all I can tell you at this time. This ends the press conference."

Then all of the screens in the garden showed cans of dog food.

Then they went blank.

After which there followed a period of mass confusion, with Helen hugging John, and John hugging Nina, and Hope hugging Nina, and all of the cats in the neighborhood going out on the pier and pooping.

Finally Nina found herself in a good place, which was within the encirclement of Jackson Bennett's arms, being led into the house.

It took some minutes but the reporters were ejected, and the Reddingtons seated, Nina in the middle, Jackson looking cautiously out of all windows at once.

"All right," he said. "This is a much better meeting than I thought we would be having. As I think Nina must have told you by now, Constance Briarworth has been arrested for giving Clifton Barrett a fatal overdose of Percodan."

John stated what had now become his theme:

"Who the hell is Constance Briarworth?"

But Helen interrupted.

"Constance? Constance was Clifton's Gertrude. She was his first Gertrude, actually. In fact, she discovered him."

"Yes," Jackson countered. "But, as I learned on the police tape I just got from Moon Rivard—the tape of the confession, made out at the airport—that was the problem. She did discover him when he was quite young. Actually she did more than that. She married him."

"Married him?" gasped Helen.

"Yes. But that did not turn out too well for Miss Briarworth."

"She didn't know," Helen whispered, "who she was getting involved with."

"No," Jackson continued. "He exploited her. He used her contacts to further his career. And then his interests became obvious."

"Younger women," hissed Helen.

"And so he divorced Constance Briarworth, much in the same way he was planning to divorce you, Helen. He ruined her career and took her money."

"So why did she agree to come here?" asked John.

Jackson nodded:

"We got all of this from her confession. It turns out that she never actually revealed to Clifton Barrett the depth of her bitterness. She continued to call him from time to time, and act as though she was still an 'old friend.' But she kept up with his exploits, keeping a mental list of the younger women."

"And biding," said Helen, quietly, "her time."

"Yes. Until now. She learned there was to be a *Hamlet;* she approached him in some manner, I'm not quite sure how; and she volunteered to do Gertrude one last time, "for old times.""

"For old times," Nina found herself echoing.

"Of course," Jackson continued, "she knew what drugs he took. And then..well, we should let Nina take it from there."

Nina did.

"I'm not that knowledgeable about drugs. But one thing didn't make sense, Hope, in either your story or Helen's. In both of your accounts Clifton Barrett drank the medication, immediately felt dizzy, and passed out in bed. But that couldn't have happened. It would have taken some time—at least a half an hour according to my encyclopedia of dangerous drugs (She smiled inwardly, wondering how Margot would react to this new title) for the overdose to make him feel anything at all, other than amorous. That he was certainly feeling while he gave his farewell speech. Everybody was aware of it."

"Yes," said Helen, demurely, "his hands were quite—active."

"The cad," muttered Hope.

John muttered something else.

"And that's what we were all watching. But we didn't see the mouse trap that he was reaching back into, and from which he was taking his Scotch. First one glass, then another, then another."

"I didn't notice it myself," said Helen.

"No, because you were dealing with his hands. But only one hand at a time. Behind him, almost but not quite out of the sight of the video cameras, someone—Constance—was pouring 'juice of cursed hebenon into the porches of his ears.' Except not ears in this case but mouth. And the cursed hebenon was Percodan. She put a huge dose in every glass of Scotch. Thank heaven nobody bothered to clean the kitchen today, and Alana has promised me to lock it That glass is surely there, with the Percodan traces left in it. Even if Constance Briarworth recants her story—which I doubt she will do—the proof is there. At any rate, Barrett was feeling the drug when he got home. He did in fact take his normal amount of Pitocin…not a spiked amount, because neither you, Helen, nor you, Hope, ever spiked the medication at all…but when that amount of Pitocin reacted with the giant amount of Percodan he had already ingested…well, the end was near. He had only an hour or so to live."

Jackson Bennett interrupted at this point. He looked at Helen, then at Hope and asked:

"So let me get this straight, you two: Hope, you actually thought your daughter had given Barrett the overdose?"

Hope shrugged:

"I didn't see any other possibility. Helen had told me the truth about her husband, and what he was about to do to both of us. I'd seen him strike her—something I shall never forget. I'm, as I have said, a pharmacist's wife. I've seen many users of drugs. Barrett did not seem to me the kind of man who would accidently overdose. Once I learned that he was dead, I had no choice but to believe that Helen had done it...and that she would be arrested for it. I could not let that happen."

"But Helen...you knew your grandmother hadn't done it."

"Of course I did. She never came into the room, and I was certain of that. Once I realized that morning that Clifton was dead, I honestly assumed that he'd overdosed, and that the autopsy would prove that. But when Grandmamma stepped in and made her confession...such a strikingly detailed confession—I simply had no choice. I had to make up the story that I had done it."

"Would both of you have gone to jail?"

There was silence for a time.

Finally Hope began to form the thing that was, after several hours of reintensification, to become her smile.

"I'm a very stubborn lady."

"Yes, you are," said Helen.

"And I still resent your implication that I could not have killed the man. I was just as capable of doing so as you."

"Neither one of you could kill anybody," said Nina. "And you know it."

"Well..."

"Well..."

"Jackson," asked Nina, "where is Constance Briarworth now?"

"On a plane to New York."

"New York? Why?"

"Because that's where everybody involved wants this trial to take place. We've already granted extradition. That's also why Edie said so little at the press conference."

"I don't understand, Jackson."

He shook his head:

"Let me put it this way. Let's say a married couple from Bay St. Lucy took a trip to New York City, and stayed in a hotel room. One got mad at the other and committed murder."

"We would want the trial to take place here."

"Of course. They're Bay St. Lucy people. It would be our affair, not the city of New York's. And that's the way it is here. If there's going to be a media circus, it belongs in New York. Clifton Barrett brought his own evil here, and it devoured him. But it was an evil that had been building up for a long time. Now it's gone back to where it originated."

"So the press conference announcing the real murder, and revealing the murderess…"

"Will be tomorrow morning. In New York. Where it belongs."

Another period of silence, after which John said:

"Nina. You did it again."

She shook her head.

"I knew these two couldn't kill anybody. They're Bay St. Lucyans. We don't do things that way. And when you think about it, we're not really *Hamlet* kind of people, anyway."

Jackson, smiling, asked:

"What kind of people are we?"

Nina rose.

"Just walk down the street, Jackson. You can't help hearing it. Summer mornings in front of The Stink Shak, or every afternoon when the tinkly little bell rings at Margot's shop. Or when the high school band has a concert in city park or the ice cream truck passes in front of the library. Or the ocean just makes the noise it always makes, and the sea breeze blows through the wind chimes. No, Jackson, to quote T. S. Eliot, 'We are not Prince Hamlet, nor were we meant to be'."

She took a step toward the door.

"Our little hills are alive with the Sound of Music. Now—I've had a very full day for an old retired school teacher…I'm going home."

And she did so.

CHAPTER 23: EPILOGUE

The real summer highlight in the village of Bay St. Lucy, Mississippi, occurred seven days before the first day of autumn, on September fifteenth, Saturday morning, at 10 a.m.

It occurred when John Giusti married Helen Reddington in the Second Methodist Church, with Nina giving Helen away, Jackson serving as John's best man, and Hope's face serving as an electric light bulb radiating white luminosity from the front pew.

The couple were, immediately after the ceremony, to be whisked away for a week's exotic honeymoon in Hattiesburg, Mississippi, where they would do heaven only knew what.

But now there were other matters to attend to.

Nina, standing some ten feet behind Helen, could only behold children from the congregation picking at the immense bridal train, grabbing for this imaginary leaf or that minute bit of dust that might somehow dim the impossible radiance of the gown, which could only be compared to The Continent of Antarctica but starched.

Nina picked her way around it, slowly, carefully, don't step in a crevasse, watch for polar bears…

Finally she reached the gown's headquarters, which was Helen herself.

"Ready?" she asked.

Helen turned to look at her.

This movement, small though it was, set off several minor tremors in the gown, causing the children to panic and start grabbing for a new assortment of things drifting down through the atmosphere and landing on the pure and driven snow that trailed The Bride.

"I think so."

"This is your big number."

"I know."

"Nervous?"

"As a cat."

"Well, you don't know much about theater."

"You know, you're right, Nina. I have a feeling this is my premiere."

"You'll be fine. Just hope that John doesn't drop the ring."

"He won't. He's amazing. He's the real performer in the family now."

"All right, but remember…"

"Be quiet, you two!" hissed someone who'd also crowded into the church's vestibule. "I think the organ is beginning to play!"

"All right, then," said Helen. "Five, four, three two one…"

NOW!

And the doors of the church itself blew open, revealing nothing stretching between the bridal party and the stage itself but pew after pew after pew, all filled with smiling people. They stood as one now and began applauding while the organ roared Mendelsohn's *Wedding March*.

Nina stood on tiptoe, so that she could see past the children carrying the train, and past Helen, walking slowly, a halo of radiance emitting from the smile that she now must be training on the stage itself.

Where stood John Giusti, trusty John Giusti, his tuxedo as elegant as the captain's outfit he had worn in *The Sound of Music*, his cuff links gold-glowing in what seemed celestial light flooding down from the choir loft.

And so she arrived onstage, her grandmother leaping from the front pew to stand beside her.

And so he said, 'I do,' and so she said 'I do,' and so the community looked on and approved.

And Nina found herself thinking that things—all things connected with this couple—and with the Bay St. Lucy that had raised them—were going to be all right.

And in thinking all of these things...she was exactly right.

THE END

ABOUT THE AUTHORS

Pam Britton (T'Gracie) Reese is an Assistant Professor in the Communication Science and Disorders Department at Indiana/Purdue University at Fort Wayne. Previously, she worked as a speech pathologist in schools in private practice. She was also a supervisor in communication disorders at Ohio University. She likes nothing better, professionally, than helping small, silent two year old boys start talking. She has also published books about autism with LinguiSystems for the last 15 years. *The Circle of Autism* was previously published on-line at ken*again e-magazine

Joe Reese is a novelist, playwright, storyteller, and college teacher. He has published four novels, several plays, and a number of stories and articles. When he is not teaching (English and German), he enjoys visiting elementary schools, where he tells stories from his Katie Dee novels and talks to students about writing. He and his wife Pam have three children: Kate, Matthew, and Sam.

www.ingramcontent.com/pod-product-compliance
Lightning Source LLC
Chambersburg PA
CBHW050413260626

47156CB00003B/988